THE
STINGING
FLY

GU00801776

'… God has specially appointed me to
this city, so as though it were a large
thouroughbred horse which because of its
great size is inclined to be lazy and needs
the stimulation of some stinging fly…'

—Plato, *The Last Days of Socrates*

Issue 38 • Volume Two • Summer 2018

The Stinging Fly
new writers, new writing
PO Box 6016, Dublin 1
info@stingingfly.org

Editor: Sally Rooney

Publisher
Declan Meade

Poetry Editor
Eabhan Ní Shúileabháin

Design & Layout
Fergal Condon

Assistant Editor
Sara O'Rourke

Eagarthóir Filíochta:
Aifric MacAodha

Website
Ian Maleney

Contributing Editors
Gavin Corbett, Mia Gallagher, Dave Lordan, Thomas Morris
Lisa McInerney & Sean O'Reilly

Printed by Walsh Colour Print, County Kerry

ISBN 978-1-906539-70-2   ISSN 1393-5690

The Stinging Fly gratefully acknowledges the support of The Arts Council /
An Chomhairle Ealaíon.

ESSAYS

COVER ILLUSTRATION & DESIGN

Tom Godfrey

The Stinging Fly was established in 1997 to publish and promote
the best new Irish and international writing.

Published twice a year, we welcome submissions on a regular basis.

The next open submission window is from June 1st to July 12th 2018.

Please read the submission guidelines on our website.

Keep in touch: sign up to our e-mail newsletter, become a fan on Facebook, or follow
us on Twitter for regular updates about our publications, workshops and events.

stingingfly.org | facebook.com/StingingFly | @stingingfly

Editorial

What connects the stories, poems and essays in this issue of *The Stinging Fly*? Geographically they span continents, from the 'bright prodigal river' of Belfast in the work of our Featured Poet Conor Cleary, to Naoise Dolan's story of an English teacher in Hong Kong, to the Canadian psychiatric ward in Jill Talbot's poem 'The Good News'. Youth and immaturity are here, as in Fiona O'Connor's masterly story of a child and his mother, but so too is adulthood in all its complexities, pleasures and disappointments. There are accounts of work—fast-food delivery drivers, student bartenders, professional footballers nearing retirement—and accounts of unemployment, as in Brian Davey's thoughtful and probing essay 'Dromomania'.

Maybe the connecting philosophy of this issue is just the idea of connection itself. The short story is often seen as a form concerned with isolation and loneliness—Frank O'Connor's 1962 study *The Lonely Voice* may have something to do with the dominance of that theory—but as human beings we are caught up in the net of social and economic relations whether we know it or not. One might even say there is no such thing as an individual: there is only society. Without farm labourers and factory workers and midwives there would certainly be no literary magazines. A character in Ridwan Tijani's story 'Scenes from a Private Life' remarks that 'the globe is a tennis ball of interconnected lines': patterns of migration and movement, trade and distribution routes, borders drawn and redrawn.

But if connection is inescapable, then why seek it out? Everywhere in this issue you'll notice people, real and imaginary, pursuing human contact. In John Harris's story 'Looking for Business', the protagonist becomes fascinated by a young woman, probably a sex worker, who propositions him on the street. In Tijani's story, set in Lagos, a character recounts browsing pornography websites to find Nigerian videos, searching for 'connection' through a sense of closeness and familiarity. Sophie Mackintosh's 'Revivalists', a futuristic tale of life and afterlife, sees its characters recognising the reincarnations of their dead loved ones in television presenters, babies and small birds. These characters yearn for a form of relationship that is more than transactional, more than economic: personal intimacy, authentic communication, love.

As editor, I tried to organise this issue with the idea of connection in mind. Thus Christine Valters Paintner's poem 'St. Dearbhla's Eyes', about the sixth-century Irish saint, sits alongside Serena Lawless's essay 'Kaleidoscope Eye', a memoir of multiple failed eye surgeries; concepts of vision, injury, suffering and acceptance link the two. M.W. Bewick's 'Caution Please' introduces Roisin Kiberd's timely and unsettling essay on new forms of connectivity, embodied in Facebook CEO Mark Zuckerberg. And in honour of this magazine's central commitment to short fiction, the issue begins with Rebecca Ivory's arresting and inventive story 'Made in China' and finishes with John Patrick McHugh's 'The First Real Time'.

Speaking of first times: this is in fact my first issue as editor of *The Stinging Fly*. Over seven hundred stories were submitted this time around, and I read every one of them between January and March of this year. I believe that I emerged with a better understanding of the short story, and of fiction, and of what I like to read; or at least, I hope so. I do know that I read a lot of insightful, affecting and beautiful writing, the very best of which is published here. As I write these lines, Ireland is preparing for a historic referendum on reproductive rights; by the time you read this, that event has likely become history already. If so, you know more than I know. I just hope you are reading this with a sense of optimism, in a place where change seems possible, where new ways of thinking and living may be just within reach.

Sally Rooney
Dublin, May 2018

Made in China
Rebecca Ivory

I dreamt last night that it was Christmas Day and that my mother died in a car accident on her way home from the post office, though she hasn't worked there since I was a child. In my dream the day grew hotter until the edges of it seemed to catch flames. There was some glitch in that dream's design. My mind was given the image of a white sun but could only provide the sense of heat for it, couldn't reconcile it with winter's frost. Well, she's probably as well off, said my father when I told him that she had died. He shrugged and smiled with his chin in his hand, talking through his fingers, self-conscious about his toothless mouth. Good of her to pick today. What else would you be doing on Christmas, anyway? It's a very long day, isn't it? You only end up sitting around doing nothing and eating too much just for the sake of it, he said. The death and the weather and his response were surreal, but in a way it would actually be typical of him to think that no one does anything on Christmas Day and that all the arrangements happen of their own accord. In reality, no one in our family died on Christmas Day but we sat around talking about the celebrities who had. There were music videos on the television and if it were quiet one of us would go, God, yeah, he's dead now, to guide us safely out of the silence. My mother would try to answer when someone asked who they had been married to and my father would say no, no that's not who it was. Aoife, go on and look it up there. And in fairness to her, she would actually be right most of the time but that wouldn't matter to him.

At breakfast he was sat there smoking and talking about getting redundancy and going on a cruise even though he barely had the money to tax the car because wasn't Mam out on unpaid leave for so long during her stint on the ward in St Pat's. Then his head shot up because there was something stinking and burning in the old and broken toaster and he was cursing it. Smoke from the bread and his cigarette swirled about his face and he squinted against it. Fuck it, no rest for the wicked. We'll have to replace this thing too. Does it ever end, at all? And he threw what couldn't be salvaged with the scrape of a knife at Sam the dog. Yeah, there you are now pet, Happy Christmas.

On St. Stephen's Day, I went for dinner with my friend Michael and his family in town for his mother's birthday. Michael's sister Anna had booked the restaurant for the wrong day and she nearly had her husband killed looking for another place to eat. The poor man was white and damp with sweat by the time he met us back in the pub where we were waiting, everyone drinking and pretending to think of an alternative. A fat tear escaped from Anna's eye and her head snapped indignantly toward Michael, who had been teasing her. I couldn't hear her retaliation but it came through gritted teeth. Michael's father warned him to not say another thing to her but was then distracted by the shortage of seats. Michael's brother and Anna's husband pretended not to notice the last stool because neither of them wanted to take it and look rude. Michael's father was puzzled by this pointless civility and asked them did they not see the seat before them and they both looked at it as if they hadn't a clue what it was for. Oh, here, said Michael and he sacrificed his own like he was the only one in the whole place with any sense. He threw his skinny legs over my stool because we're both the same size and I felt happy to have him wedged so tightly against me. We were content enough with what was on offer in that pub and more drinks were ordered, all of us quietly hoping that no one would suggest persevering in the search for a restaurant. I had been meant to get home to my own parents ages ago. But I was delighted with myself sitting there, being able to enjoy another person's family, which seems to be the only category of family most people can tolerate at Christmas. Michael's mother is Irish and his father is Chinese. He went from Shanghai to Liverpool to work in chip vans, then on to Dublin at twenty. When he met his wife Margaret, her mother decided that his name wasn't Kun-Yin anymore, it was Eamon. He is as affable a man as you'll ever meet. He's been walking around introducing himself as A-men for the last thirty-five years, smiling as if it were a very amusing detail and of no relevance or consequence anyway. He always looks like he's fallen from the sky. I wonder is there anyone in Shanghai looking for him.

That night, Margaret talked to me across Eamon's lap and his ochre-coloured fingers tapped the veins on her hand, like Morse code. She said she worried that

Eamon's English was deteriorating. As Michael and his siblings have grown and left, Eamon has had less reason to interact with neighbours and teachers. I felt uncomfortable being told this in his presence, not wanting to be complicit in embarassing him. But he wasn't listening. Instead, he had sat back to create the space Margaret needed to lean closer to me. He moved his head from left to right, watching the multiple conversations happening around him, looking like the least self-conscious person in the room.

Margaret told me Eamon watches Chinese television and reads Chinese newspapers, exclusively. He once asked Michael why he has friends. He has retreated further into his garden where only Margaret can meet him. I think he exhausts all his English with her, there's none left for anyone else. Everything they say is funny to each other. They laugh and call each other old and fat and speak over one another. I hear what she says but he's always too late to add anything, he can't beat her to it. He says, Ahh, ahh, ahh, never getting to continue because she does it for him.

Margaret's face turned from mine then to speak to her sister. Eamon stayed facing me but his hand was still resting on Margaret's. Her unexpected absence created a sudden vacuum between us, the two outsiders of the family. I was only Michael's housemate and nobody was entirely sure of where Eamon came from. This is nice, he said, to fill the silence. I prefer this. He waved his hand before him, meaning the pub food and the cramped seating. This was the closest we had ever come to having a conversation that wasn't navigated by Margaret. I felt suddenly that I needed to say something and resented the strange intimacy. He leaned behind me to shake Michael's shoulder. Ahh, my boy, a good boy. He called Michael gorgeous, a word provided to him by Margaret, used to convey his own pleasure, and I felt touched. I know, Eamon, isn't he just? I said, because I did know what he was getting at, and he likes me to join in on the act. But he's cuter than you'd think because he knows as well as anyone that it wouldn't matter how stuck for the ride I was, Michael only does that with men.

But Michael is so beautiful that I wouldn't mind his hand stroking the length of my side, his fingers drawing spirals across my belly before bearing down between my legs. I like to lean on his back and wrap my arms around his shoulders while he sits at our kitchen table. I smell his neck and feel an unbidden urge to bite into him. He's a real performer, whether you're able for it or not. One night I opened the door to our long and cramped hallway in Fairview to see him lying on his back at the bottom of the stairs with a wooden spear jammed into his heart. His legs were propped up on the bottom few steps.

Once I scrambled past the bikes and bags choking my path, I saw it was just a broom handle that he was holding rigid in his armpit. There wasn't a lunatic on the landing waiting to prise the spear from Michael's chest and plunge it in mine but the reptilian part of my brain had already reacted, flooding my body with adrenaline. My horror was too much for Michael. He rolled over to his side, cackling. The broom handle fell away and I ran past him, with my hands covering my cheeks, into the kitchen. I ran out of ground when I reached the sink and turned to face him. I was laughing too but my eyes hadn't copped on yet and there were tears on my face. He hugged me and rocked me and kept laughing and saying: Sorry, sorry, sorry. That was lousy, here, here, I am sorry. My hand was trapped between my mouth and his shoulder. You bastard, you absolute bastard, how long were you lying there? You fucking psychopath. But I was hugging him too and the pair of us were swaying side to side, together in the dim and dirty kitchen.

He's a right contortionist. Our bedrooms aren't close enough. I like to lie across the dusty carpet on our landing and watch him dart around his room, the open door like a frame for him. The glass corrupts the sunshine to make it warmer and brighter and the light of it is so white it does away with the floor beneath him altogether and he looks like he's levitating. I think he's magical. So I believed him when he sat on the stairs and presented me with the small jade stone he keeps beside his bed and told me it was ancient and charmed, that old Kun-Yin won it in China. I was on my back in my pyjamas, open mouthed and completely enchanted by this green veiny orb and the link I imagined it offered Michael to his heritage. I fantasised about a trip to China, where I would facilitate a meeting between him and his paternal grandparents who would offer him a calm but warm greeting in Chinese, as if they had known this day would come all along. Whenever Eamon speaks to Michael in Chinese, they end up looking at each other in complete despair. But Michael would instinctively know what to say to his simple and decent mountain-dwelling grandparents, probably because he can access the power of this authentic relic, luminous with mysticism.

This went on and on until he became outraged with incredulity that I would believe him. He even accused me of veiled and unintentional racism. You might not know it or mean it, he said, but you're a racist. Do you honestly believe my Dad had to kill a mountain lion to get this stone, as part of some oriental village tradition? Fucking hell, he's from Shanghai. But don't let that get in the way of your devotion to Eastern sorcery, whatever you do. He was holding the thing above my face. I went to swipe it from him but he yanked it away. You think my Dad is this wise and refined being just because he's elderly and Asian. Poor old A-men, he's only quiet because he's tired and doesn't speak English. He put the stone between us. Against the faded and flattened carpet, it had lost the lustrous glow and become an inert lump. It's a paperweight, you idiot. My Dad got it in one of those pokey little market shops in Spain. You know them, the ones that keep dirty videos next to children's toys and incense. By then I was helpless with unrelenting laughter. It eased to breathlessness before erupting again when he said: I mean, for God's sake, there's a Made in China sticker on the bottom, Aoife. You're having me on. Did you actually think it was real?

But I always believe in the wrong things anyway. Pliable and easily led, I never trust or know what's right and what's real. I had only been going out with David for few months so I was delighted when he bought me tickets to the stage version of my favourite book. At the time it was important to me, because in the book the protagonist's wife was constantly upset and puzzled by her husband's cold and indifferent behaviour. But in the end you got to see he adored her, really and truly. He was just a troubled introvert, unable to express warmth, no culpability required or demanded. Not from me or from her. It simplified my relationship with David, giving me permission to tolerate and forgive any distance or withdrawal. A stupid little part of me thought that was why he gave me the book, to let it communicate to me what he could not. He had never even read it, it didn't mean a thing to him. That didn't strike me as important at the time though.

On the night I was unsettled by the actor. He wasn't what my mind had invented. The coldness his wife endured wasn't tempered by any hidden tenderness. There was nothing throughout that led you to expect an explanation, nothing that belied the cruelty. This wasn't the story I had read, the actor on stage wasn't the man in the book nor was he the man I was sleeping with. But given David was sat beside me clutching my folded knee, that wouldn't have been possible. Not that I hadn't accused him of duplicity in the past, before backtracking on myself, doubting my own perception. Sure, I always nursed a fear that he was just pacing his own stage when we were together.

He didn't do the book a bit of justice, I said to David and he laughed at me for believing everyone should live up to my expectations. It's your world, we're all just living in it, he said. But isn't that the biggest problem with relationships? We all decide what we know about a person. We love them enough, too much, so we don't demand or need reassurance. And never you mind the worry that burgeons within your coiled gut; it only offers a sense that you may be owed it. And what use is that?

Any honesty and confidence between us was only found when we were shrouded in the privacy of darkness and the duvet. But that night I didn't speak so neither did he. I fell asleep to the unintelligible whisper of his legs shifting and rustling restlessly against the old and stiff sheets. I woke up in the middle of the night, feeling his hardness sawing up and down my back. I peered at him over my shoulder and he kissed my cheek before turning me on my stomach. His palm flattened against my back, pressing hard. There was pain and resistance and I counted one, two, three and more to myself rather than doing anything else. My ear was turned into the pillow and I could hear the sea. The rise and roar of it continued until I heard a short cry from him as he pulled away to spill himself on my thighs and back. Then there was only the sound of breath and blood pumping and he reached across to the radiator and grabbed a towel to dry me. He kissed my cheek again and silence was restored.

I was nervous and excited because his mother was coming to Dublin the next morning. We had been to the Phoenix Park the day before and I had paid stupid money for a bag of fudge from the market because he told me once she was mad about the stuff. If he guessed why I was buying it he never said. We left to meet her at Busáras where she had gotten the coach to from Derry. At a set of traffic lights his hand landed on my leg. That was some going last night, he said, biting his lip and smiling at the car in front of us. Jesus, you were well able for it. He turned to me then, still grinning and I was ashamed of myself for returning the smile, for wanting him to be so pleased with me. I don't know what's wrong with me, to have felt that way, but there must be something. It didn't occur to me until later that he might have wanted to hurt me, just a little bit, but then I wasn't sure why.

We reached the junction at Christ Church before carrying on across to the quays. Where's handiest to leave you off? He looked at me, then back at the road. I was going to say that we didn't need to decide that now, that it could wait until after we collected his mother but I realised my mistake before the words left my mouth. Sure I can leave you on Eden Quay, you can jump on a 27 from there, am I right? he suggested before I answered. I made a noise that resembled agreement. Mammy's very awkward, he said, which was sad because I knew then he understood I had expected to meet her. I felt retrospectively foolish because he must have been anxious about dealing with it since we left the house and there I was without a clue. He was squinting against the glare, weaving the car closer to the path to leave me off. I felt childish and embarrassed for causing him the hassle because I didn't own a car and anyway I couldn't even drive. He got lucky at a red light and I was scrambling to gather my bags and my coat before he had to drive off. I nearly had the door closed when he said, Oh, don't forget your wee bag of sweets. The woman is wild for those, she'll have them gone from you. He tossed the brown bag at me and I bolted, not wanting to hold him up. But I needn't have bothered rushing because he was ages sat in traffic beside the bus stop. I ducked into a newsagent's to save us having to avoid eye contact.

Whatever Michael says, he believes in what suits him, too. The big trick in life is that it's very difficult to apply the wisdom you've acquired to yourself. He's no different to anyone else. On his nineteenth birthday, we were both twisted on wine that tasted less like hairspray the more you drank of it. I brought him home to my single bed in my student house where I didn't have any friends because I hardly made the effort to find them. We lay facing one another. My hands were tucked under my chin between us. He had been subdued that first year in college. In school we'd had high expectations for living independently of our parents. It was disappointing how little we'd seemed to change as individuals once this came to pass. I felt overwhelmed and self-conscious. I assumed he was having a similar experience but we rarely spoke about these kinds of anxieties with each other, they were too vague to vocalise. That night, I went to kiss him but his face was wet. I felt a tear burst on my hand. I didn't turn on the lamp or move to hug him. Is it because you're gay, Michael? I asked, stupidly. He gave a weary sigh so I knew it was the wrong question. I lay still and mute, afraid to disturb him, as if he were talking in his sleep. Michael's neighbour had only been a teenager herself at the time. Michael was still a boy but his parents saw no harm in this friendship, and they were right because none existed, she doted on him. The two might have naturally parted ways had they only ever slept in Michael's house. One night, Michael lay prone in his friend's bed and woke to see the father of the girl sat over his daughter, his body coiled tightly so not to draw noise from the mattress or floorboards. The flux of fear was heightened by Michael's lingering, childish belief in spectres. He knew this man was his friend's father but some nocturnal metamorphosis had rendered him sinister and unrecognisable.

I thought of Michael as a ten-year-old, whose understanding of the world was still defined by the supernatural, good and bad, of how this understanding had been ruptured. I was crying harder than he was then. He didn't even bother closing the bedroom door, he said, he knew I wasn't going to say a thing, that I wouldn't be able to push him away. Michael laughed suddenly at the idea, thinking it was maybe ridiculous. He probably knew I wouldn't even try.

I've never felt as small and as wretched as I did the next morning. I pretended to sleep while Michael gathered his clothes to leave. On his way out, he shut the door quietly and completely. My best friend, imagine that. It was months before I spoke to him about it again and by then he must have been hurting worse than anything. We were in my bed again and there had been a lot of drink. He had fallen asleep but I couldn't. I shook him awake, selfish person that I am, seeking forgiveness. I asked him about it with the kind of temerity that only a lot of drink allows for. The only time in my life I've ever shown any courage, wasted because I could barely put one word before the other in a tactful manner. I was met with sleepy confusion and then a belligerent denial. I sought his hand beneath the sheet and worried the knuckle of his thumb between my fingers like a rosary bead. I tried offering the kindest words and reassurances I could summon. Michael, please pet, I'm sorry. Please, I am so sorry. His own response was a plea too but a watery one so I closed the space between us and cast it from my mind, out of compassion, out of shame. And he was glad of it too, I think. He had revealed an irretrievable harm and could do no more than that, and I would not move him to disturb it further, if that was what he wished. In the absence of anything else, this was a small comfort for him I hope, especially during the night, when he lay alone. I can do nothing about it either, until he asks me otherwise. I'd like if that were to console him, like an artefact of childhood. A small and reassuring weight; a cold jade stone to hold close to him as a shield, torn from the mouth of a jealous lion.

Crone Mountain

After Lorca

Moon—chrome tear on the cheekbone
of Cruach Mhárthain—seeping through
skylight, roof tiles and concrete,
swimming the room in silver: like a tide
pouring out in spate, the stranger I hold back
from watching daily, new planets
travelling at speed over water. Moon.
Madness of spring tides. Stillness in the head
like a hurricane. The bed is a white space
that is travelling, travelling. My body's a cut-out
on the Sea of Tranquility—mercury dappling
of night swims—making it beautiful
to the one who isn't here: tall, dangerous
white lady—outside the door now,
turning the key. Eyes: crescents of glacier,
breasts of polished tin.

David McLoghlin

42nd and Park

In Memoriam, Aedan O'Beirne

I'd like now to be going out the walk you told me
—the Liffey to the Dodder through city byways.
North Wall, East Link, Irishtown—can I hold it in my head?
A heron in the sloblands under Edwardian bridges.
The South Wall to the Poolbeg. I walk four miles out
into grey pointillism, then filigreed dark, and look back in
—bracelet of shore light—to nights you were alive
and I was walking to the DART to Sydney Parade.
'David—everything good now.' I knew you'd stand a while,
counting light houses' returns. It was your Mount Saint Victoire.
In the peloton near Grand Central, I achieve the glide
of separation. Walking out to Howth—the tide pooling
between the sandbars maps a river delta—
I never thought to be a fast walker.

David McLoghlin

Prosinečki
Adrian Duncan

I'd hooked the ball over my shoulder, hoping it would land just inside their box, because for the last twenty minutes their centre-halves had been pushing up the park and our right-winger, an earnest young man on loan from a large Scottish club, had been making a succession of diagonal runs across their defence. But the older centre-half, Thirlwell, a guy I played with years ago, had seen immediately what I'd tried to do. He'd backtracked and hacked my pass back over our heads, returning it down the field. The ball, a sphere of ivory in the night sky, had gotten lost in the floodlights, re-appeared, bounced, and our keeper, Arterberry, had come out to catch, but had been up-ended by their centre-forward, a lanky and sly operator called Cooper who is top scorer in our division and on his way up the leagues to a more prestigious club and enormous wages.

Arterberry is out cold. That frightening dead-man inertia came over his body when he landed and the ball just rolled off his stomach. Our medics rush to him. I jog towards the sideline for water and to loosen out my knee, which is stiff with painkillers and permanently destroyed. It mocks this puerile comeback of mine as a half-time substitute in a mid-table game on a wet, pointless night in late March. Our manager, a tall, bellying Londoner looks at me as I trot over; then he looks away. I'm thirty-five next month and returning from a recurring injury that most would have retired on. It's not that I need the money as such—I've been careful over the years, but if I can get another contract at even half of my current wage I'll be able to buy a fine two-bed apartment back home in Leeds, one I've had my eye on for a while now, one I can rent out and make a few extra bob off after I retire. I skoosh water into my mouth, and onto my face, and peer around at the crowd of seven thousand or so. The few hundred of travelling support are tucked away up in the North Stand, but the whole place has gone utterly quiet with everyone fixating on Arterberry splayed on the ground, amid plumes of vapour and hunkering medics. Our stadium is an old thing in the middle of a small city in northern England, a city surrounded by long-stilled steel and iron works and a network of congealing canals. I often think the fans come here just to be among the decaying trusses that hold up the roofs of the deep single-tiered stands. Old men and women with their grandchildren people the seats, and pockets of pale and overweight blokes on cheap season-tickets who obsess over transfers, gather in a sprawling sky-blue-and-white horde across the South Stand. This club was never great, and seems to exist now only out of the ghost of some habit.

The rain is spinning in thin films down out of the black, over the edges of the roofs of the stands, and through the large rectangle of floodlights that frames the sky. My breathing has modulated and my heart is thumping coarsely. Our home supporters' voices come up as Arterberry gets to his feet. They are chanting one of the club's old classics, something about being on a beach in Bari. It's a sort of over-unionised chorus that has begun, of late, to sound like a lament. I have been here six years, but for the last three I have been more injured than not. Yet the supporters love me, their limited but committed midfielder; I play as they would play. I scored on my debut in a cup quarter-final against their rivals, a club across the city now two divisions above us. I played well the first two seasons, scoring double figures and keeping us in the middle of this lower league. Then I hurt my knee during pre-season—a torn tendon, a repeat of one I picked up when I was twenty-three.

That first knee injury came days before I'd been meant to sign a contract at a big club in the top division. When I left, emptied out, the club recommended a knee-specialist in Munich, to whom I went for ten months, over and back, with no club and no wage and diminishing savings. I regularly bumped into another young midfielder there. A German guy called Michael, a polite, slight, muscular chap who played in the second division for a small club outside of Berlin. We chatted about swimming and gym work and the Bundesliga, and went for lunch on occasion. Once my knee repaired he convinced me to travel up to his club, and with no other offers on my plate I decided to trial and do a pre-season. I got fit again, became strong, and played well, so they gave me a two-season contract. They were an old East German club with a large following of what looked like mostly neo-Nazis to me, but they had a beautiful stadium, in the middle of a vast forest that shoe-horned around a dark, deep and peaceful lake.

I was in my mid-twenties then and after eight months finding my rhythm I became as rapid, nimble and healthy as I'd ever been. I never really drank and almost none of the Germans did either. Some of them smoked and a Turkish player, Umit, would sometimes take me to his parents's café in Wedding where we'd puff happily for hours on a shisha. Other than that I spent my afternoons after training sessions visiting erotic massage parlours in town—local, Thai, Latvian—after which I would drive back out to my spacious apartment, prepare dinner, read and sleep. Being injured and being a good professional over the years had taught me how to suppress my energy between games and to live as a lesser god. I soon learned some football German and began dating a local girl called Stefanie, but during winter break in my second season, while on holiday with her in Kos, I slipped on the tiling beside the hotel swimming pool and ruptured a ligament that, in the murk of my knee, neighboured the one I'd torn before. I didn't play again for a year. I blamed Stefanie and stopped seeing her.

I focused furiously on getting well again, but what disappointed me most was that it had happened at a time when I'd been dictating games, when my circle of influence around the team had widened and become more intense. My personality, then, had been extending through the field of play, sometimes into the opposition's shape, and my opponents couldn't dismantle it, no matter how hard they hit me. My Englishness had become exotic, and my range of passing had broadened in that forest in Brandenburg, short quick unlikely passes and long cross-field pings that switched play emphatically. I'd been casting out nets of influence over the pitch that allowed my inner-city Leeds swagger to appear, and when it did—a nutmeg, a no-look pass—it was was cheered brutally by the loving crowd. I'd wave to them at the end of games and they'd howl back at me. I'd learned each team-mate's preferred foot and how they liked to receive the ball. My tackling had become crystal, I almost never went to ground—staying on my feet and waiting for the opponent to panic at the gaps I kept filling. I once went three games without losing a ball. I scored eight times during the first half of that season, but more than anything else, my footballing intellect had begun to develop at a great rate. I wasn't just picking out passes before the ball came to me, I could see the pass after that as well, imagining the game three vectors ahead of the fluxing present. I'd become a roving pivot between our defence and attack, and had begun to intuit when the opposition started reading me and would mix my play up between: passing, or keeping the ball, or turning on it, or holding. I'd begun playing from a viewpoint at once far above and deep within the eddies of play—in short, at this lesser but accomplished level of football, I'd approached some genius.

Before each game I'd watch the grainy videos I'd collected since my teens of my favourite player, the tall blond Croatian Robert Prosinečki. Then I'd lie on my bed, close my eyes and re-visualise his movement: when he lifted his head, when he controlled the ball, rolling it under his foot, the way he used his body to shield himself, and how he spun away from bewildered defenders at the least likely moment. I analysed him when he was young and turning out for Red Star Belgrade, then-kings of the soon-to-crumble Yugoslavian leagues. I modelled my play, as a young man, on the brio I detected from him. But once I'd recovered from that third knee injury I found that my body had tightened and I couldn't meet the demands of his style. I fell away as a footballer, and changed from a creator of good ambition to one of near none.

One night, two weeks before I snapped my ligament in Kos, we had been playing a team from Cologne. Mid-way through the second half of a tight nasty game I received a pass that had been zipped at me from our left-back. I'd been on the midway line, with my back to the opposition's goal, and as the ball sped to me through the sleet I feigned right and clipped the ball with the inside of my foot, back across my body and past my left knee. Then, feeling the entire earth rushing over my right shoulder, I spun left, and the pitch, the stadium, the lights, the forest cleaved open before me. The crowd's voice surged as I pushed the ball towards the developing frames of possibility. Both of their full-backs were way beyond our wingers. One of their centre-halves got drawn left while the other advanced on me—a tall aging Pole, Grigor, who once played for his country at the Olympics. I ought to have shown him more respect, but I was young and full and I knew my midfield partner, Michael, would be running hard in a shallow arc behind me, so I made eyes left and shaped to pass but instead slowed, leaned back and scooped the ball high and right, and as the ball arced insolently over poor steadfast Grigor, Michael sped past me and advanced irrevocably beyond him. The ball bounced softly and Michael took a touch with his instep, looked at the keeper chasing out and rolled it to his left. The crowd bellowed.

Grigor slumped on the edge of the box, head down, but Michael was off, swinging his shirt in the air, sprinting to the corner flag where the ultras had poured down savagely through the stand. Our left-back jumped onto my shoulders and roared at the top of his voice while hurling his fist in the air, then he landed beside me and we chased towards Michael and the rest of the players. I jumped onto the huddle and bared my teeth at the corner of broiling white men, and roared banal non-words into them all. As I jogged back to the centre circle the same thoughts I always had when I was playing well in Brandenburg appeared: that I could run like this forever, that there was no limit to my Cartesian aptitude, that I was a conqueror here, that I was showing my football culture to be finer and that I was ready to return and present myself again in England, the only place where any of this had worth, or made proper sense to me; it was the only place where the admiration was appropriate, and, as my heart pounded and I tracked down their kick-off I thought: it is the only admiration that will last satisfyingly beyond my career, where I might be recognised for my deeds as an ageing, broad-shouldered and bronzed ex-pro in my forties and fifties and sixties, entering a café, perhaps, in some quiet West Midlands town, or a restaurant in Newcastle, or the clubhouse of a cricket club on a quiet Tuesday afternoon in a suburb in northern Leeds.

Arterberry has had to lie down again. They are calling the stretcher from the sidelines, and an ambulance pulls up at the mouth of the tunnel of East Stand. Our substitute keeper, Wilson, a young Northern Irishman, is warming up with a heartless vigour. I wonder how many times he has wished Arterberry dead. Along the sideline the goalkeeping coach drop-kicks shots at Wilson, who catches with a conspicuous mixture of method and what looks like instinct. He will never be a great keeper, he is too in love with technique, but he will earn well and convince many. I imagine when he is much older, should fortune offer him a moment of lucidity, he will look back on his sporting life as a mechanical insult to his trade. He runs onto the pitch fisting his gloves as Arterberry is carried off. Arterberry, prone in the stretcher, lifts his arm to the crowd, who cheer as if he were a miner lifted from a blast. The referee gives a drop-ball, which Cooper steps up to and hoofs disdainfully into the crowd behind our goal; they jeer. Cooper jogs, then strides back up the pitch and turns for the kick-out, and as the players gather around the centre circle, like steaming cattle awaiting feed, he looks over his shoulder, smirks and makes a what-can-you-do? type shrug at me. If I were younger I'd aim to nail him before the end of the game, but there's too much at stake, and though the crowd may bay their approval, the manager would see through it and if I get a red card he'll strike me from his reckoning for the three games I'm banned for and then, most likely, for the rest of season too.

I look to the seats above our dugout and spy an ancient Irish gentleman, Lawrence, who has not been to the ground for some time. He used to be a coach at my old schoolboy club. He was a goalkeeper then and had large beautiful hands and white, slicked-back hair. After training one day—I was fourteen and Leeds United had invited me to their academy for the summer—I stayed behind to practice with one of the other boys, Graham, who was as sweet a footballer as I have ever seen but never came to anything. As we walked back to the clubhouse to change, Lawrence appeared and asked me to walk with him.

It was raining heavily as we strode over and back along the centre line of the pitch for almost an hour, him advising me about going to Leeds at this age, and the sort of lads I'd be up against and how many people fail there, but that it is how you take the failure and what you learn from it that contributes to you as a footballer. As your body and mind develop, he continued, particularly in your central position, and if you are wise and lucky, you will get a sweet spot in your career when your body can carry your developing footballing mind, and your mind will in turn push the body beyond what you thought possible, creating new positions, new patterns, new time, he said, with rain pouring down his face, and you will feel this moment for a brief period in your life, son, and you must remain limber enough to feel it, to act and expand on it. This sweet spot, he continued, will happen during a game when the contours of adrenaline, exhaustion, familiarity, daring, and a recent history of good physical condition coincide, and you must treat that moment, or these moments, with a cavalier preciousness, and make them your own by making them memorable for those looking on, and if you can do this, son, even once, truly, then, he said, you will have achieved something as a footballer.

He is sitting in the stand now under a sky-blue-and-white hat. He looks old and cold. My stomach turns. My knee trembles. I think how wrong he was. I think how foolish I have been too, for believing for years in that crap and for believing too that that moment against the team from Cologne was the high point of my vocation, when in fact, I realise, jogging across the centre circle of the pitch, barking orders at our left-winger, that it was my lowest point. Throughout my career I'd so focused on moments in games when the aesthetic effect took precedence over the pragmatic decision, that I'd failed to realise through watching Prosinečki, for all of those hours, that it is the pragmatic that serves the aesthetic—that it is only from the core of good service that any beauty can bloom. If I'd analysed Prosinečki properly, I'd have seen that his decisions were always at the service of what was necessary, as he faced the manifold problems emerging before him on the pitch. Even though the most beautiful pass might be available to him during a game, he always chose the most effective, the one that few footballers ever see, or do see, but are too vain to take, playing in clichés of what is great, hitting entertaining passes—passes that are similes without sentences. But Prosinečki, as if playing for no crowd, always made the most moral decision on the ball. He solved the problems on the pitch in a way that developed the moment back upon itself, but with one small alteration that split the game open, and each alteration he made was balanced and fair and furthered an abundance that each game was already germinating, an abundance that did not require an opponent to be humiliated, an appropriate abundance that I and everyone else who speaks of him has misinterpreted as flair.

This and what I up to now have perceived as the high point of my career are two shades of the same ugly daub, and, I realise, my very worst crime was what I thought was my very greatest moment, the one those supporters in that small club near Berlin will remember me for forever. I would do well to go back and apologise to Grigor and to everyone who witnessed it, and to disown everything in my life that led to it, and beyond it, to now; but, there is nothing I can do, and no way for me to repent. I am a spent, age-thickened footballer mooching around a large circle with a line through it, in the middle of a city I care little for.

Wilson is shaping to boot the goal-kick up the pitch, but he spies our right-back dropping deep to take it off him. He rolls the ball out, and because Arterberry didn't try this during the game our opposition is out of shape to receive the attack. The right-back turns out with the ball, raises his head, and with a dumb, morphinic excitement, I spy a gap opening towards the right side of their box. I take off, and our right-back floats a cultured back-spinning pass up the channel and as I sprint I can see my fellow midfielder come across to meet it. His shoulders arch, his neck muscles slacken and he glances the pass off the top of his head. The ball loops gently into my bending path and skims out in front of me, and I sense my opponent behind as I chase towards where the ball will bounce again, and skid and roll, and I feel like I am clear and free. A silence comes over me as I take a touch, but the touch is terrible, and has put me too wide and the ball is gone too long and my right leg has been clipped and I should really go to ground, and I can hear the crowd scream for me to do so, as if nothing would make them happier. But to my left I glimpse our striker—a young, athletic Liverpudlian—powering alone into the box, and if I can clip the ball across to him he will surely score. I know if I fall I will be reconnected with my past, so I straighten, and my legs, out of dumb momentum begin to gather and re-coordinate beneath me and I realise that if I propel myself and stretch for this disappearing ball and dink it back across the box, that somehow I will have done enough. I lunge, feet first, and scissor my right foot desperately at the base of the ball. As I connect and slide over the line, I can see the ball spinning handsomely back up and away from me, towards a space in front of our striker, whose eyes and mouth have widened, his arms have spread, his feet have skipped, his knees are bent and he lifts himself diagonally up to where my cross is going. The ball begins to slow into its languid arc, and as our striker's body coils and as his eyes wince shut, bringing him into the great pre-impact dark that every footballer knows, I gasp deeply, once more, at the impotent, incidental and unforgiveable beauty of it all.

The Good News

Monarchs
are the color of Halloween—they should be in Texas, not in Canadian cold
and dead leaves. By November they should be in Mexico—flying over the
wall.

Two years ago
I wrote a poem about the monarchs, how they were reappearing—I wrote
it from the psych ward in Nanaimo, BC. It was a metaphor for hope in a
place that had little. We ate plastic scrambled eggs for breakfast and
played Bingo. It was Spring, but it's always Spring in psych wards. I had
no socks until somebody gave me some—black and warm like
redemption.

Monarchs
are back in the news, this time because the new warmth has created more
later in the season—who've not flown south soon enough and will
probably freeze. They're running out of time, the article says, but ends
with, 'Not all is lost.'

Meaning
you'll be able to feel the hunger dig into your gut like a knife carving a
pumpkin into a happy face. Meaning this is the good news. Meaning you
better save the bad for a hospital blanket and a meal listed like a poem—
looks better than it tastes.

Nevertheless,
the monarchs are back, and are still here—for now—carving their way
into our broken psyches, ever reminding us that the biggest loss is the
tinge of knowing what's to come. And the price of pumpkin spice lattes
has tripled, but you don't have to suffer through it alone—there's always

Oprah.

Jill Talbot

Revivalists
Sophie Mackintosh

The contestants filed out one by one and stood behind their column. A glowing button, red, in front of them. He talked to people with a great fluency. My father in this life had a direct manner that he had not possessed when I had known him. He was rapid and witty. He was physically changed; sturdier, a cleft chin, hair greying at the sides. He was American, not Swedish. He had a catchphrase: *Time for you to push it!* He meant the button but maybe also maybe their personal sense of what was doable. What was worth the risk. A woman won five thousand pounds and started to cry with joy. All the tears lit up red across her face. Her throat was chugging up and down. Goodbye, and until next time, my father said to the camera.

-

At the support group, we drank lukewarm coffee from one of those industrial aluminium dispensers. The button jammed and I fought with the urge to kick it over. Many of us were angry all the time. There was water, too, in dissolving paper cups. Somebody had brought coconut-and-jam macaroons that flaked all over us. I was very into details, the noticing of them, as if the noticing could prevent disaster or at least allow me to prepare for it. Hyper-vigilance. It is a formative trauma, the head of the support group told us. Accept and honour it. I did not want to, belonging as I did to the section of the group that did not like to talk about their parents. We were a slouching, antisocial few. It was good to remember that I was not alone, at least. But when the others stood up and recited their stories (some of which had been performed for us before) I realised I would never tell them about my father sliding batter around in a hot pan or tying up my shoes, let alone his appearance one evening on the television when I was moving from channel to channel, the automatic motion of my thumb on the control. Flick. Flick.

-

At the beginning of the discovery, I spent a whole weekend watching old clips of the gameshow. I downloaded everything I could find and watched in horror, in love. I recognised him at once, despite the differences. They said you could do that. A spark was left. The same spark responsible for déjà vu and for love at first sight. A neurological doubling. Lots of things had found themselves explained across the last few years. It was good to have the mystery squeezed out of things, to leave the dry husks lying where they lay. Yes, I was unromantic. That weekend I cried many non-cathartic tears. I also tried to make a list of evidence, but there was nothing concrete to write except for something in my brain lurching towards his, an imprint somewhere primeval. He laughed a big and chesty laugh, almost a cough. He waved a fist happily through the air. Somebody had won the jackpot and he had orchestrated it. That was purity. That was benevolence.

-

There was no denying that, the death of my parents aside, the boom had been good for me personally. My role was Future Resting Executive. I worked closely with those near to death and together we came up with a show-stopper. People went to funerals the way they had gone to weddings in the past. They accumulated ideas in embossed leather folders for their ceremonies and discussed caskets, fireworks, dining options. If the client was wealthy I would work with their end-of-life consultant, the professional figure who helped orchestrate those last moments, doling out the pills or perhaps putting their hand on the trigger in a soft guidance, perhaps even ministering the lethal injection themselves, although the ins-and-outs of it all were still sort of hazy and needed hammering out, legally speaking. But whether you could afford a consultant or it was just you, alone in a room with your quick last breaths and your fear and excitement, shadows playing on the wall—the outcome was the same. You went somewhere else. You disappeared and reappeared. It was my responsibility to orchestrate those plans we had picked out so carefully. I remained a person left behind.

-

It was important to have a vibrant social life, the head of the support group told us, so we sometimes got together of an evening and tried to pretend that we were friends. The others were mostly younger than me and earnest. We went dancing, or drank cocktails, or sometimes would watch a documentary on a projector at someone's house and then it would lead into a debate about the ethics of the personal revivalism movement, but we were all on the same side so it was never really that much of a debate, unless I decided to throw a grenade in. I knew how to push people's buttons. I would invent a scenario and then sit back and watch them worry it like dogs with a chew toy.

-

How often could you do it and remain spiritually uncompromised, a question on the movement's official FAQ page asked. I checked the website all the time, looking for new research. It was ostensibly part of my job. It depends on the revival, and the person in question, the answer came. As with so many things regarding health, we believe it depends on constitution, genes, and more. I clicked off and went to a YouTube video where a sweating man talked about the soul in terms of a shoe with fragile leather. You can only put it through so much, he explained. Each time, you lose shine. The material will crack irreparably, in the end.

-

I liked to talk to my father when I was cooking. I switched the sound off on the television and looked back over my shoulder occasionally, listing off what I'd done that day. I wanted him to look right into the camera. Sometimes I thought about the strange luck of his being recalled to this time period, when the options were literally infinite. Again, the neurological doubling; the invisible fish-hook of another connected spirit. It was more common than you would have thought. At the support group, Sad Keith talked about going to church and seeing a baby hefted up by a stranger, a baby that was definitely his mother. He had asked to hold her and been refused. He said the whole episode had really set him back. We had all found ourselves running back along the road at some point, chasing somebody who had passed us. Once I even thought I had seen my own mother in the jaunty tail-swing of a bird, a drab tan and grey one. Anything felt possible of the dead. Was there a limit to how much they could amaze and dismantle us? I didn't think so.

-

A client was assigned to me, a woman my age, in the expectation that I would provide an empathetic and on-trend experience. Lucy. She was jittery, even though it wouldn't be happening for a few weeks. I looked at her soft face and wondered whether she would return as a pure, new baby or an old person gasping back to life after an episode of sleep apnoea or a cyclist, grievously injured, coming to from a road collision. It was impossible to tell. It was not really my place to wonder. Instead I brought out my mood-boards and colour schemes, some sample menus. We sorted everything out and by the end she was beaming. I was good at my job. Afterwards I went into the bathroom and cried rare tears for a while.

-

My parents had done it quite close to the start of the boom. My father had gone first, walking off into the snowy forest that surrounded our house one winter day. My mother had followed him, a month later. She was less on my mind because she had never returned to me. Maybe our bond had never been that strong. I was seventeen years old. I stayed in the house for another year, alone, feeding sticks into the woodburner and hunting birds with a pellet gun and foraging for morels when I wasn't at school. It was that sort of resilience that made me good at my job.

-

Are you going to be bold? my father asked the contestants, but also me. I was eating a microwaved dinner of wild rice and meatballs. I had overcooked it and there was a crisped wedge of sauce attached to the edges of the plastic dish, the sort he would have been horrified by. Sauce burnt on at the edges of the tray, probably carcinogenic. Are you ready to press the button? Will you be fast enough? Will you be the winner? I abandoned the food and went into the kitchen and put white wine and ice into a blender together so that it became a delicious alcoholic slush. It was this kind of innovation that I wished I could share with another person, but when I raised my glass to the television screen nobody could see it, of course.

-

Lucy came in again. She was going to die in two days' time. She wasn't jittery any more, just pleased and excited. What a great adventure I am going on, she said to me, like she was going to climb Everest or visit Rome. We discussed her method. I had a gallows humour that I tried to reign in unless I could sense that the party in question would be into it, but I didn't get that vibe off her. Lucy's funeral was going to be elegant. She had asked for linen drapes, everything in cream and ecru. Baby-blue and lilac peonies and hydrangeas. Afterwards there would be a sit-down meal with chilled garlic soup and madeleines served afterwards on silver trays. She was from a rich family. 'I've picked up a lot of ideas from my friends' weddings,' she told me. 'It just needs to be classy. I want them to weep until they drown.'

-

Sometimes, I had read, it was possible my father dreamed of me. It is possible he awoke from some distant memory of squeezing a child's fat leg and looked in the mirror the morning with the edges of the dream still upon him, somewhere, and felt unknown to himself.

-

Before the support group I went to a bar and drank three vodka martinis alone. Everyone in the bar was young and precious, fitting their lives like a glove. They looked like there was no reason for them to seek spiritual growth elsewhere. There were chrome lamps drooping from the ceiling, small plates of elaborate food. When I got up from my stool to go to the meeting, the room dipped and righted itself. Everyone seemed very disappointed in me.

There was a person missing from the support group. It was Sad Keith. 'He has gone to a better place,' the group leader told us. 'Or maybe a much worse one!' I shouted back, and everyone looked at me as though I had sworn. 'I think you should go home now,' the group leader told me. She was right. I walked home with my arms swinging. I switched on the television. There were only re-runs of the show, no new episodes. 'Can't you see that I need you,' I told my father. He couldn't see. I poured another vodka into a small, dirty glass. I smashed the glass when I had drunk it. I ground it under the heel of my shoe. Something began to uncurl in my thoughts.

-

'Trouble sleeping—we see that a lot,' the doctor had said to me as he scribbled the prescription, a long time ago. He'd winked at me as he'd handed it over. 'Hope that helps.' It was a huge prescription, for three hundred pills. I still had most of them.

I stood in my living room with the TV on mute and stared at the wall. There was a patch of mould just above the bay window, and it had bothered me vaguely for months, but in that moment I fixated upon it, hated it with a million volts of hatred electricity. The patch of mould seemed to sum up everything wrong with my life, the dirty tenaciousness of it, the sadness of it, the fact that even though you could find solutions and be positive, ultimately there was no making things clean and good. It was only a matter of time. I took the pills.

-

And then—there was a light. It was pale pink and pulsing, like I was inside a giant ear, listening to the throb of blood. I was lying on something soft. It was so comfortable, I could have stayed there all day. The soft thing started to cocoon me. I started to become the soft thing. All my cells were dissolving. I was a liquid hovering in the air, and suddenly I was the light, and moving quickly down a plughole. I wasn't scared at any point. It was sort of like the time the bad ones in the support group had thrown an unofficial Out Of Body But Still Ourselves party, and I had taken a lot of ketamine and lain underneath a blanket, warm and paralysed. Now when I twitched my fingers, there was a shimmer of light around me, still descending down this strange red plughole. The pulsing turned into a thudding the further down we got. Boom. Boom. Boom. I closed my eyes and felt the sound become louder and louder, pressing in on me until it was the roar of a jet plane, until I was squeezed into a pip, a drop of blood.

-

And then I opened them. And I was in hospital. A hard white bed with the covers all tucked in. A tube down my throat. My head hurt. By the side of my bed was my father, but not my father. He looked exhausted. At his side was a tiny blonde woman with a sharp face, a person I assumed to be my mother, though I didn't feel the same pull, the neurological doubling, the whatever. Thinking about my father-not-father made my head hurt more, so I decided not to worry about it. When the woman noticed my eyes upon her, she burst into tears. 'Look,' she said, pulling at my father's sleeve. 'She's alive!'

'She's alive!' my father called out, jumping to his feet. Other people echoed it too. Lots of nurses and doctors ran in and started doing things to the machines surrounding my body. I could tell from their voices that I was in a different country. My new mother touched my knee very gently, over the covers. My body felt very small. I had no idea what age I was.

And already the person I used to be was fading quickly. I shut my eyes again and called it up. Soon there would be nothing there for me to remember. I thought *Godspeed* to the human whose body I lived in now, wherever their own soul, their little scrap of ether and mystery and fizz, had gone. I remembered, I remembered, I remembered. This is what they were all talking about, I thought to myself as a deep rush of joy flooded my entire body. Then like that, as if the joy had replaced everything—though it would remain in some shape or form for years, the memory of that warmth, puzzling, which the doctors would attribute to my miraculous recovery from the injuries sustained in an accident I could not quite remember—I forgot, and I was gone.

Dromomania

Brian Davey

1

One day in 1886 a man named Jean-Albert Dadas was admitted to hospital in Bordeaux with acute fatigue. Having suddenly left his job as a gas factory worker he proceeded to walk across the South of France, before ending up in the Hôpital Saint-André. A young medical intern named Philippe Tissié was doing his rounds in the hospital when he encountered a distraught and weeping Dadas. Tissié gave the following account of his condition:

> He had just come from a long journey on foot and was exhausted, but that was not the cause of his tears. He wept because he could not prevent himself from departing on a trip when the need took him; he deserted family, work and daily life to walk as fast as he could, straight ahead, sometimes doing 70 kilometres a day on foot, until in the end he would be arrested for vagrancy and thrown in prison.

The destination itself was unimportant to him—just hearing a place name was enough to send him on his way, like a wind-up clockwork toy. Strangest of all, Dadas would often have no recollection of how he reached his location, as if he had been lost in a fugue for the entire journey. Curiously, his case was not unique at the time, with many instances of similar fugues being recorded throughout France. By the end of the nineteenth century the condition was so common it had given rise to its own term: *dromomania*, meaning a compulsive need to walk aimlessly or take flight.

2

Several years ago I found myself unemployed and living at home with my parents in the west of Ireland. The bright future that was promised to my generation evaporated like a mirage as we graduated into a recession. There was little chance of finding a job, so I played video games to pass the time and only left the house at dusk. I hoped that I wouldn't meet anyone I knew. Most evenings I went for a stroll along a quiet stretch of country road and if it was a clear enough I'd walk with only the moon to light the way. On one occasion I stopped to look at a hill on the edge of town, a gnarled knuckle of rock with a bone-white glow in the moonlight. The only sounds to be heard were the cattle cropping grass in the anaemic fields beyond. I knew that life must be happening elsewhere, so I decided that it was time to move.

3

Dromomania emerged at a time when anxiety was growing about vagabonds in France. Borders between European states were extremely porous and communities were nervous about strangers in their midst. As a result, convictions for vagabondage increased steadily as the nineteenth century progressed and aimless wanderers became enemies of public order. One proposed solution to this problem involved sending vagrants overseas in service of the state. As the historian Kristin Ross wrote:

> Later in the [nineteenth] century the French government would learn to apply to vagabondage—'that nervous mania of locomotion and laziness that appears to be one of the ways in which the free life of the savage is preserved'—a more effective, if homeopathic, treatment. From vagabondage would come organized wandering in the form of geographic exploration and colonial expedition.

A distinction would thus emerge between merely useless wandering and a more economically productive form of exploration, sanctioned by the government.

4

Less than a week after arriving in London my plan of sleeping on a friend's sofa indefinitely was quickly dispatched, along with any self-serving bohemian aspirations. It quickly became clear that I was outstaying my welcome so I repacked my suitcase and took the Tube across the city to a hostel in Swiss Cottage. With my funds running low I couldn't stay for long, so I anxiously cast around for somewhere cheap to live. Not yet having a job meant that most enquiries lead nowhere and any offers I did receive seemed a little suspicious. One response from a landlord took an entirely metaphysical turn:

Note that i have several properties around the world & am well-to-do and that is why i am offering cheap rent to those in need of cheap & affordable rent especially students as i am not really after the money because i am aware that what shall it profit a man to gain the whole world and lose his soul

So I was surprised to eventually find a nice place in a upmarket postcode. I knew that a few prospective tenants had been to see the room but I couldn't understand why no one had snapped it up. The apartment was located on the second floor of a converted Victorian building and the interior was newly refurbished. The owners, a weathered-looking couple, would be the only other occupants. In any case, they seemed happy to believe me when I said that I wasn't unemployed but in fact writing a PhD (which was an outright lie).

The boyfriend was unnecessarily tall with long hair and he wore the same purple paisley shirt every single day. His accent was a dry drawl from the north of England and he only ever said what he meant. He would tell stories of how successful he was in 'the cupcake business' and never seemed interested in anything other than drinking White Russians. Even my appearance in the house didn't seem worth noticing, as if his own presence there was provisional too. When I got up in the morning, he would already be sitting in the living room, watching *Antiques Roadshow* with a drink in hand. I began to doubt that he ever slept.

5

The emergence of dromomania is concomitant with the appearance of the *flâneur* in France, although they represented different approaches to walking. Whereas dromomania involved detachment and walking as sheer mechanical compulsion, *flânerie* signified a more active, attentive engagement with your surroundings and is irrevocably linked with the spectacle of modernity. As Charles Baudelaire, who gave the term its first and fullest expression, wrote in his essay 'The Painter of Modern Life', the *flâneur* is someone who 'gazes upon the landscapes of the great city—landscapes of stone, caressed by the mist or buffeted by the sun'.

6

Not long after moving in I discovered that the couple regularly fought with each other, great big stormy screaming matches.

Late one night the boyfriend came home in a rage having being kicked out of The Wolseley. 'I was just sitting down to dinner when these three twats in business suits sat behind me and wouldn't stop talking. City arseholes, you know the type. I turned round and politely asked them to shut the fuck up and you know what happened? The restaurant told me to leave! *Me*! So I asked for my pheasant to go and then really gave those prats a piece of my mind.'

Lying in bed listening to this, I remembered that the boyfriend had had his driving licence taken away after he was found passed out behind the wheel of a parked car while the engine was still running. Without his licence, he must have had to carry the pheasant home on the Underground, I thought. The girlfriend managed to calm him down by promising a walk together to a nearby petrol station to buy more drink. Pacified, he went with her and the apartment fell silent. A couple of days later I discovered the uneaten pheasant had been left forgotten in a kitchen cupboard, its mummified carcass a grim totem of that night.

In the end I only stayed in the apartment for a month, leaving after another of their late-night rows became so intense that I considered calling the police.

7

In 1876 the poet Arthur Rimbaud was enlisted by the Dutch Colonial Army and despatched to Java. After less than two weeks he disappeared into the jungle. Eventually, he turned up on a vessel called *The Wandering Chief*, bound for Ireland. Landing in Queenstown, Rimbaud took the train to Cork before making his way home to Charleville-Mézières.

What must he have thought about while travelling through the Irish landscape? Perhaps he reflected on his time in the jungle, daydreaming about mangroves and tigers.

8

The first thing I noticed when I went to see the studio apartment in south-west London was its high ceilings. Or I should say, the first positive thing I noticed—as I tried to ignore the sizeable gap underneath the door, or the fact that the communal toilet was behind a flimsy partition in the hallway, or that the entire building had a murky, unctuous quality, as if it had been salvaged from the depths of the sea. I was too desperate to ask why the landlady needed a photocopy of my passport but I got the feeling that tenants had a habit of suddenly disappearing on her. An old sign above the entrance declared that the building had once housed a publisher but I had no idea what kind of books could have been produced here. I imagined that it was probably just a front for clandestine meetings or the printing of illicit materials. But I had no other options and the rent was cheap, so I moved in straight away.

Without anywhere in particular to be and with no money to spend, London felt cold and hermetically sealed, like a mausoleum or a bank vault. As winter started to consolidate its hold, the freezing weather brought with it a significant increase in rodent life. I had recently noticed a mouse darting out of the disused fireplace beside my bed, which I ended up chasing around the room with one of my cheap boots before it escaped again. From under the door and the cupboards, mice would run into the room, freeze stock-still as if suddenly remembering something, then take off again at high speed. On the advice of my landlady I covered the old fireplace grate with broken glass before sealing it with orange bin liner bags and cardboard, all of which was held in place with bright yellow masking tape. Although the mice still kept me up at night, with their flurries of scuttling in the skirting boards and ceiling overhead, at least they were no longer in my room.

Each day, I would submit to a crushing round of job applications, filling out endless forms detailing my skills, qualifications and ambitions. I found it difficult to believe that I had ever had a job. My old life seemed unimaginably remote and I couldn't envisage a way out. It would just be me and the mice and the covered-up fireplace from now on.

Looking to escape these thoughts, I took to the city streets to try and cover as much ground as possible. There was no particular aim to all this activity, except to keep me occupied and tire myself out. I allowed my walks to carry me like an impulse through the nervous system of the city, delivering me to its extremities. As the weeks passed the skin around my feet hardened and my boots fell apart in the rain, their soles slapping comically with each step. I had the ingenious idea of repairing them with the remaining yellow masking tape.

9

Rimbaud, whose own travels were almost contemporaneous with those of Dadas, would often use the term 'fugue' in his writing. In his youth he travelled vast distances on foot and in 1873 he fled to London with his lover Paul Verlaine, where they spent their time walking ceaselessly around the city and its surrounding areas. Verlaine wrote in a letter to a friend:

Every day we take enormous walks in the suburbs and in the country round London... We've seen Kew, Woolwich, and many other places... Drury Lane, Whitechapel, Pimlico, the City, Hyde Park: all these have no longer any mystery for us.

10

I developed a feeling of antipathy towards London and became frustrated with its inscrutability. Londoners were always impassive, helpful when asked for directions, but would start to panic if it seemed the conversation was entering casual environs. Maybe it was obvious that I was hungry for conversation. As a remedy, I started to use terms like 'mate', as a sort of bloke-y affectation, but these words always felt cold and unpleasant to me, like a mouthful of crushed ice.

The city began to grow monstrous in my imagination, like some sort of primordial beast that could crush you underfoot without knowing that you'd ever existed. Its sheer sprawl was unnerving: here was a place with no centre and an incomprehensible circumference. I missed the rambling vistas of the countryside, as everywhere you looked in the city your sightline was enclosed by a tessellation of concrete and glass.

The only means of escape was through walking. When you travel London on foot, you are no longer confined by the commercially defined transportation networks. You're free to disappear down the slipstream of an alley and be discharged onto streets too narrow for buses or suburbs, too obscure for tube stations: Atalanta Street, Pilgrim's Lane, St. Julian's Road.

11

Saint Julian, patron saint of travellers, is the subject of a short story by Gustave Flaubert entitled 'La légende de Saint-Julien l'hospitalier'. Featured in a collection called *Trois Contes (Three Tales)*, it was published in 1877, just a few years before the dromomania phenomenon came to prominence. This tale recounts the story of Julian the Hospitaller who, in Flaubert's version, is predicted to achieve greatness but, in doing so, will also end up murdering his parents. In order to avoid his fate the noble Julian joins a group of wandering vagrants and becomes accustomed to a life of illness and hunger. In the end, he fulfils his destiny by accidentally murdering his parents, who were in disguise, but is redeemed by a final act of kindness: he embraces a dying leper who turns out to be Jesus Christ himself.

12

Walking is a form of communion with the city, where you're guided like a divining rod. In our infancy we have to practice how to walk effectively until it eventually becomes an unconscious act, like breathing or blinking. Every day we stand up, orientate ourselves and put one foot in front of the other, propelling ourselves through time and space until the end of our lives.

13

Alússein: The repetitive motion of walking means that it can be a hypnotic act; one that invites daydreams and visions. The word hallucinate came to English from the Classical Greek alússein, meaning ill at ease or restless, via the Latin term ālūcinārī which means to wander in thought. Not only do we speak of minds wandering; they can also be lost.

Solvitur ambulando: 'It is solved by walking'. This Latin phrase was apparently coined by the itinerant philosopher Diogenes the Cynic and was quoted approvingly by the travel writer and Hellenophile Patrick Leigh Fermor, who had walked across Europe in the early 1930s. It was eagerly adopted as a personal motto by another inveterate traveller, Bruce Chatwin, after he heard Fermor recite it.

But what is the link between walking and thinking? Walking can help you to think; however, like Jean-Albert Dadas, you can also walk to obliterate thought through sheer locomotion.

14

One of my preferred walking routes took me through a small, Victorian cemetery. Its boundaries and paths were lined with trees sprouting various fruits and flowers: cherry blossoms, limes and, most intriguingly, medlars. The fruit of medlar trees are known for looking like they've rotted before they've ripened, and hang in fleshy auburn clumps. Looking at the tree, I imagined the course its roots had taken underground, as it felt its way through the dark earth. I thought of the roots disturbing graves, tendrilising their way around bones and drawing nourishment all the time. It was disturbing to think what its fruit might taste like.

15

In the winter of 1974, upon hearing that his friend, the German film critic Lotte Eisner, was seriously ill, the film director Werner Herzog set out to walk from Munich to Paris.

> German cinema could not do without her now, we would not permit her death. I took a jacket, a compass and a duffel bag with the necessities… I set off on the most direct route to Paris, in full faith, believing that she would stay alive if I came on foot.

During the journey he slept in barns, tool sheds and even a model mobile home that was on display for prospective buyers. A few weeks later Herzog arrived in Paris, filthy and exhausted. But his pilgrimage had worked its white magic: Eisner's illness passed and she lived for another nine years.

16

One day, I crossed the bridge to Putney in search of fresh sights. I spent the morning in a small gallery, which was pleasantly heated, before moving on to a secondhand bookshop. I picked up a book and read for a while before placing it back on the shelf. Gradually, I became conscious that the clerk had been following me around the shop. Had my boots been leaking again?

17

Flaubert's *Three Tales* was a great favourite of Chatwin's, who admitted on his deathbed that he had planned to write a similar triptych of stories. They never materialised, but he did help create an opera based on the life of Rimbaud towards the end of his life.

His death in 1989 as a result of AIDS-related illness was incredibly brutal. After visiting with Chatwin shortly before he died, Herzog gave the following account: 'He was lucid, but eventually became delirious and would exclaim, 'I've got to be on the road again, I've got to be on the road again." Finally, in a brief moment of clarity Chatwin admitted to Herzog: 'I will never walk again'.

Herzog has talked and written at length about the virtues of walking which sound, at times, like a classic description of a fugue:

> When you come on foot, you come with a different intensity. Travelling on foot has nothing to do with exercise… I do not dream at nights. Yet when I am walking

Dromomania   41

I fall deep into dreams, I float through fantasies and find myself in unbelievable stories. I literally walk through whole novels and films and football matches. I do not even look at where I am stepping, but I never lose my direction… I find myself twenty-five or thirty kilometers further on. How I got there I do not know.

18

Gradually, my situation improved. I moved into a different house and found a place to work. At lunchtimes I would stroll through Soho, where most of the sleaze had long since been sluiced away, or around Chinatown, whose layout felt like it constantly transmuted so I could never quite get a handle on it. I had a handful of regular routes but I remember one particular walk more clearly than the others. One summer evening, I ducked out of the sweltering heat to watch a film at the BFI, which was running a Werner Herzog retrospective. Released the same year as his journey to meet Eisner, Herzog's film *Jeder für sich und Gott gegen alle* (which literally translates as *Every Man for Himself and God Against All* but is better known as *The Enigma of Kaspar Hauser*) tells the true story of Kaspar Hauser, a mysterious 19th century figure who one day turned up in Nuremberg, unable to account for his origins. Hauser is played by Bruno S., a street musician who had no acting experience up to this point but still gives an otherworldly performance. When Hauser is recuperating in bed after being attacked by an unknown assailant, he begins a gnomic soliloquy, describing a strange vision he had. We see a misty, indistinct landscape with a series of figures making their way up a hillside. We hear Hauser's voice: 'I saw a mountain and many people. They were climbing the mountain as a procession. There was a lot of fog. I could not see clearly. But up there was death.' In fact Herzog used footage of pilgrims climbing Croagh Patrick to accompany this vision and, watching the film in a cinema on London's South Bank, I wondered if I knew anyone who had climbed the mountain while that sequence was being filmed. I had relatives who made the journey annually so there was a good chance that someone from home had been there but it was impossible to recognise anyone through the fog. Away from its original context the pilgrimage looked strange and sinister. However, my family in Mayo never thought twice about performing this ritual each year. I liked to think that this was an atavistic journey, like the migrations made by birds, as the tradition of making a pilgrimage to Croagh Patrick had most likely existed before the appearance of Christianity in Ireland. But walking was also significant for St Patrick, who was a self-described *peregrinus*: a wandering, stateless individual. His example, along with other saints such as Columbanus, gave rise to a whole group of Irish *peregrini* (or pilgrims) who criss-crossed the continent during the seventh and eighth centuries. They weren't missionaries; rather, their aim was to go into voluntary exile, becoming strangers in an unfamiliar land. A desire by the church to create a more stable administration meant that these wandering Irishmen had to be restricted. By the ninth century the days of free and easy *peregrinatio* were effectively over and Irish pilgrims were restricted to journeys in their home country. A millennium later, Dadas travelled across Europe with relative ease, walking in defiance of the enclosure of the state. I thought about all this as I continued my stroll through Middle Temple at dusk. All the barristers who usually thronged its streets had fled to the pub for the evening and as the sun set, turning all the old stone buildings a pale glaucous, I had a vivid sensation, for a fraction of a second, of what it must have been like here during the medieval period. I decided to walk along the Thames towards home. The entire sky was darkening and the air was particularly clear. There were few fellow pedestrians around. Looking across the river I could see lights coming on in a mansion block opposite and as each yellow light came on, it revealed another life inside the building. They were reflected in the dark waters of the river below where the whole scene seemed to leap and glow like a film projected onto a screen.

19

Fugue: The term fugue comes from the Latin fugere, meaning flight or to flee. Fugere also gave rise to the words fugitive and refugee. One of the last notable *fugueurs* was a man named Henri C., a depressive who was prone to compulsive journeys. On one occasion, he escaped from a military hospital in Montpellier and wandered as far as Barcelona, before returning to a small town on the French border. As Ian Hacking wrote in *Mad Travellers*, a definitive account of the dromomania phenomenon:

> That is great fugue country. There on a flowery slope or on a wind-blown outcrop you may still encounter a nervous man who was hoping not to be seen. Today he is more likely to be a confused Moroccan making his way gingerly through to Spain than a dazed French infantryman heading for the safety of Spain. Today he is just a mixed-up illegal immigrant. Ninety years ago he suffered from a distinct mental malady, ambulatory automatism.

Dora Maar quits smoking (and Pablo)

He's a raconteur, promising ember and gold; in reality
he delivers blue and cold purple.

He's mercurial, magnetic. I pray minutes towards him
(He, as always, stays epicural)

He jumps, I breathe (both inclined too deep). Histology,
pathology; he is my heart and lung.

He introduces at the door *Dora—meet calm*. We clamour
in conspiracies of two plus fire.

He mimes thin air to blow le petite mort, boasts
You will remember me and deserve it all

Lost in anecdoche of who said what, who started this,
it goes on and on. Neither of us stop to listen.

The opposite of me is disconnection he mourns.
One of us is addicted to the other.

Jo Burns

Scenes from a Private Life
Ridwan Tijani

When they finished eating, Yadichinma started to roll a joint.

'Where is she getting all this from? In this Lagos?' Kayode said.

'I've been asking oh,' Roland said.

'Obalende, I got it from Obalende. There's this guy there that sells it from a bookshop, which is actually very smart—a bookshop is the last place SARS will go to raid. I took a picture there and he was smoking a cigarette and I made a joke like, is it only cigarette he smokes, and he says no, he does marijuana too. I said, in an ambiguous manner, that since I returned from America I haven't smoked weed, and he kind of looks at me for a while to figure out if I'm joking or being serious in the form of a joke. Then he says in a quiet voice that he sells it here if I'm really looking for some, and he went on about how it's good that people can smoke weed in the streets of America anyhow, and I told him it's not so and we talked about that for a while. It's very sad that drugs are hard to find in this country. I mean most people are already convinced of the country's nightmares, at least let them have that while high. I'm sure he's scamming me on the price, but for now I don't really care,' Yadichinma said.

'That's true it's very hard to get high, I had never got high until Sweden,' Kayode said.

'Wait, you got high in Sweden?' Roland said.

'Yes, I got high in Sweden,' Kayode said. 'I think it's how we were raised you know, all of us were raised a bit on the middle-class line and you know how hampering that line is, it means conservative parents—conservative because they go to churches or mosques because they're praying to God for more wealth, and since they realize that oh we're not rich now, we may be later, but we're not rich now in money, but we're rich in our children. That's why we see names with wealth in their meanings, this causes restrictions on the children because the parents want a certain kind of future for the child, it affects the life of the child, affects school. I mean my mother put me in science class at the beginning of secondary school because she wanted me to be a doctor, and I suffered every day.'

He said, 'I've said this before and you guys didn't agree with me then. To really exist—I don't mean survive—in this country is to be very rich or very poor. The rich child has a certain step to his walk because that has been bred into him by parents that control this country, they're not going to attempt to shape him into an idea, they're not going to police him saying, oh if you don't pass this Jamb you're not going to get into that big university. The rich person has already decided that he's going to send his kid abroad to MIT or something. The poor has it because he's already hardened by what he's been through, you know this is true, look at our friend Wale, they're the ones that are the geniuses in secondary schools and university, while we're the struggling ones. The poor parent already knows their kid might not even go to secondary school, this is true. And we don't get anything, we don't get it, we're not connected to the zeitgeist of the country—take Lagos for example, isn't that what we've always been sad about? That Lagos has always eluded us? Because middle-class parents like ours move to places that they want to become suburbs because they think the city will corrupt us, and they plant mango trees in the backyard and they destroy our lives because in schools the kids mock us and call us Ajebota thinking we're rich, and say how can you be from Lagos and you don't even know any place in Lagos or anything that's happening. They speak and we don't understand them and they laugh at us. The rich kid laughs because he knows he's the rich one, not us, and the poor laugh and shake their heads and wonder how people can be and not know things about anything. They laugh because they own Lagos, the real Lagos.'

He said, 'They talk about the Premier League and football and new dances and we don't get it. We don't know how to play sports because we're not allowed to, and we always go to after-school lessons and when we come back they tell us go do your homework, there's no TV. So when the people the next day are talking about Drogba and his chest pass, you just nod and avert your eyes. It's people like us that later move abroad because we feel we don't belong here, and when we get there, we find that they don't want us and we don't belong there. I'm looking at you, Yadichinma. How can you expect Nigerians to get drugs easily when most of us are like this? We're in Lagos yet we don't even know Lagos. Of course now, being independent, we've been around Lagos, but

I'm talking about those seedy spots, those facial cues from the men hanging around the Mallam shops and football fields and Fuji music shops… Maybe all what I'm talking about is not true for everybody, but I think it's true for the three of us. That's part of why we were drawn to each other in the first place. I think this is distinctly a Nigerian problem, I don't know. Maybe I'm crazy and I'm rambling, I don't know. I just know I'm really sad when I think about it.'

They passed the joint around without talking for a while and Yadichinma noticed that there were a lot of cobwebs on the yellow walls.

The next day, Kayode awoke before Yadichinma and Roland. He slipped from the room where they'd slept—Yadichinma on her bed, Kayode on the floor because he preferred that and Roland beside him because he talked in his sleep. He went to wash his face in the bathroom. He realized he had started to grow a moustache—he'd never been able to grow one before and he felt that affected the way he wanted people to see him. He tiptoed back into the room to grab his phone and he watched Roland sleep for a while, marveling at the way a person completely changes when they're asleep and you can't see their eyes.

He slipped out of the room quietly, took a drink from the kitchen and then headed out the door.

The sky was like a Picasso painting—in that if you peered long enough at the grey sky, you could see a bit of yellow, like someone up there had previously under-painted yellow and the grey was starting to crack.

There was a shop that did hair in the corner as he passed and another one that sewed clothing. In the front of the clothing shop, he saw a mannequin that he thought resembled Roland—in the flare of the nose that made him look irreproachable, the full eyelashes, the aristocracy of his neck. Sometimes he thought it was a lie that Roland was Igbo, no Igbo man looked like that, or maybe all Igbo men looked like that and he just hadn't noticed.

He flagged down a Keke Maruwa, entered and gave the driver directions. As the Keke picked up speed, he leaned back and held the seat. He'd always hated how Kekes seemed feeble, even a motorcycle seemed stronger on the street and looked like it could withstand the blast of air after a bus had sped by.

He thought of Plato and the utility of poets. He wondered what came first, Plato's morally inclined reason to ban poets from his ideal state—since he thought Poets copied God's revelations in their cadence—or the idea that they lacked utility—the notion that they contributed nothing, they were not good in war, they had no dignity and so on.

Everything was poetry in this country. There was poetry in the dance, at the market when the old women haggled, in the way the conductor called out routes, in the colours of the buses and taxis, in the people at the edges of the society, in their veined eyes, in the blistering tribal marks on the faces of children, in football, the way it skids and bounces on the dusty ground hitting stones and condom packets and Ribena cartons, in the way kids give themselves nicknames on the pitch.

Still, maybe Plato was right, what good had poetry done in this country, what good did the legends do? Wole Soyinka, JP Clark—and the rest.

Didn't they fail? Didn't they invent new mediums and still fail? Didn't they fail to show the people that there was poetry in their blood?

Kayode recalled during one of the numerous strikes in university, he had gone to teach English at a secondary school and had asked one of the pupils, do you know the work of Wole Soyinka? The first black Nobel laureate in the world? And the pupil said, isn't that the man who knows so much English that makes up his own dictionary?

They don't even know him, he thought. They don't even know him.

Is that the failure of poetry? The poet? Or the place where the poet hails from?

He thought of lines from Marianne Moore's 'Poetry':

> I too, dislike it: there are things that are important beyond
>   all this fiddle.
>   Reading it, however, with a perfect contempt for it, one
>   discovers that there is in
>   it after all, a place for the genuine.

He too hated poetry, didn't understand it sometimes, feared that it wouldn't be enough, that it couldn't save anybody, that it was worthless, that it would be his doom, why is he even trying, but he couldn't do without it.

He was just getting off the Keke Maruwa when he got a text on his phone. He paid the man and checked his phone. It was Roland, *you've gone for the usual abi? You could have at least woken me up*

The usual? He hated the way Roland talked about it. He'd only started doing it when he came back from Sweden.

How Roland came to know about it was still befuddling to him.

The 'usual' was the fact that Kayode every day, from 7: 30 to 12:00, excluding Mondays, regularly performed sexual acts—including and not limited to fisting, deep-throating an eight-inch red dildo, spanking himself, gagging himself with a cloth in his mouth, oiling himself from head to toe literally, stripping, spitting, farting (once), inserting a butt plug deep into his ass, using nipple clamps to hold his coal-dark, short stubby inadequate nipples—for tips (Tokens, which converted into Dollars, which he then converted into Naira) on camera, on a site called Chaturbate, an adult webcam website. Plainly put, he was a cam model, a cam boy. And he liked it. He liked how it changed him, how it showed him, to himself, how it taught him things about humans and their desires, about hypocrisy, about eroticism, about how the black skin was fetishised and yet also vilified.

It excited him—sexually and anthropologically—that people were watching him. He liked watching the counter at the left corner of the website rise: 200, 201, 400, 800 people are watching me?

The first day he felt there was an openness in his head—an elongated feeling that seemed to stretch even through time—that propelled him to fill in the details on the website and to strip down to only yellow Chelsea football club shorts and take different pictures, posing in alternating stances to upload in the picture tab on the website.

It all began with poetry.

After his poem 'Machinations of Malice' was published on the African literary virtual space Brittle Paper, he started receiving emails. One of them was from someone named Mercadante:

Date: 7/12/2015 12:30
From: GabrielMercadante12@gmail.com
To: Kayodelanaire77@gmail.com
Subject: PRIMAL RESPONSE

Hello, I read your poem in Brittle Paper and I felt something I've not felt in years. The last time I felt this was when I was reading Don Delillo's Underworld. It's a kind of recognition you know? Like something is so far away from you but you still recognize it. I'm gay also, so your work really affected me. Your work is very rich and I just wanted to message you to tell you what it did to me. You don't have to reply.

Kayode, who didn't usually know what to say to responses to his work, supposed he was feeling a bit bold the next day, so he replied:

Date: 8/12/2015 9:00
From: Kayodelanaire77@gmail.com
To: GabrielMercadante12@gmail.com
Subject: Re: PRIMAL RESPONSE

Hey man, Thanks for your comment on the poem. I understand completely what you mean. I've not read underworld, but I've read Mao II, I found it in a carpenter's shop just laying there, I take it everywhere now. My work is very 'rich', who talks like this? Where are you from? My work is rich but I'm not, so if you have a few Euros you're not using—or is it Dollars where you're from? Send them my way. The artist is poor but his work is very rich. It's funny.

Date: 10/12/2015 5:00
From: GabrielMercadante12@gmail.com
To: Kayodelannister@gmail.com
Subject: On the theme of having one's own

Now you're sounding like a Nigerian prince that I hear on the news that scams Europeans out of their money. Send me money, send me money, that's the Nigerian prince. Are you a Nigerian prince? I would have sent you money, but I'm not rich. Have you heard of camming? I know a guy that does that—he's my nephew actually and he's on camera and he's naked and he's doing all sorts and he's making money. He's making money. He's naked and people are watching and paying him money. So maybe you can give this a try. I'm not serious or maybe I am. I'm from Norway, a real Viking me, I don't know probably, my dad migrated from Russia, so maybe I have some Asian in me too, who knows, the globe is a tennis ball of interconnected lines.

Not serious, seriously, Kayode went to the Chaturbate website and read through it. He liked the layout of the site, the sleek yellow-coloured minimalism.

He clicked the tabs, absentmindedly imagining himself stripping in front of a camera, expectant men—and maybe some women who knows—fondling their genitals, and the thought made his dick hard.

He read the columns: Female, Male, Couple, Trans, Login, Broadcast yourself.

He clicked on Broadcast yourself. The window that came up asked for authorization to access his camera and microphone. When he saw his face on the computer, he shrank back and peered at himself. He closed the website after a while, then he cleaned his house, moved the furniture around.

He had a bath. He felt he wanted to propagate an image when camming, that of a cool bookish youngster—someone that knew what to do with a dick and could recite passages from Infinite Jest offhand.

He oiled himself more than normal. He put on a yellow shirt—which he'd always felt was made especially for the black skin. He went to the kitchen to drink some water. He came back to stand in front of the laptop. He felt so nervous and very self-conscious standing there; the feeling that he would soon be exposed to the world threatened to flatten him.

He walked to the bathroom, locked the door and paced around. He liked doing this because the small space calmed him.

He looked at himself in the mirror. He took out a comb from the bottom drawer and combed his beard. He had not cut his beard in six months, because he wanted to grow a beard, because he hated how people still mistook him for a teenager, how people judged him with their eyes when he smoked cigarettes in bus stops, some even got to the point of saying: Ahan, Ma wo omo yi sha, on fa cigar ehn?

He went out to the kitchen and ate something from the pot. He drank water from the tap and went into the room.

He stood in front of the laptop again. He grazed the touchpad with his finger to wake the sleeping laptop and he went to the website and clicked Broadcast yourself.

This time he did shrink back but he didn't close the site, he just admired how the room looked spotless. He chose a username: Kyleyeswhy, because Kyle Xy was his favorite TV show.

The text below his username said: For us to age verify your account so you can receive tokens, you and any other person who will appear on your cam must complete an age verification agreement.

He clicked the Tokens breakdown page and a list came on the screen:

100 tokens = $10.99
200 tokens = $20.99
500 tokens = $44.99
750 tokens = $62.99
1000 tokens = $79.99

In his mind, he calculated, $10.99=3000 naira. Not bad for the minimum baseline.

He was doing this for the tokens, was he not? For the money? But in some part of himself—that part that revealed him to himself—he thought he wanted to also do this because he would like it.

So, when he gave the site access to his camera and microphone, and the counter on the left side started to rise, he raised his eyebrows and waved at the camera, feeling stupid, yet excited. He thought he could feel something at the base of his chest, some sort of wobble.

1, 2, 5, 10, 20, 53—it went on increasing until it was finally 79.

> ratface12: What's he doing? Why is he not naked?
> starsndbanners: Nigga dick!
> justindon: Is that the new Paul Auster novel in the back?
> roisinman: Do something man

Kayode waved at the camera and said, Yes that's a Paul Auster, but it's not a new one, here we don't get new books early. Hey guys!

> pleasecallmez: It talks!!
> spicymeatballs: English motherfucker! You speak it?
> justindon: What accent is that?

Kayode said, Nigerian, where are you guys from? I'm new to this so you might notice the outward face of confusion.

> aquaman: The sea, jk. Australia
> pleasecallmez: Do you have a mod? I can mod for you if you want.

So it began.

It came as a shock when Roland texted him one evening: *I saw you online*

My poems? Kayode texted back. *What website is that? Rumpus accepted my new stuff so I don't know maybe they've uploaded it.*

No I saw you on this cam site

He was trying to decipher the message, wondering if this was real and not a dream, when Roland called. The ringtone, his favorite song, sounded jarring and stupid. He realized right there that he very much cared what Roland thought about him.

'Yes, Hello,' Kayode said.

'Hmmm.'

'What?'

'You know now.'

'How did you know?'

'I was on the site, so…'

'You were on Chaturbate?'

'Oh, that's how it's pronounced? I was.'

'What were you doing there?'

'What people do when they go on there?'

'What's that?' Kayode swallowed. 'What's that,' he asked again.

'See, why are you making this about me? Well, I was there cause that's what I like, you know, I don't like the lavish kind of porn where everything is gleaming and you kind of see how many takes they did to actualize that certain position. I like a certain realism, so cam I feel is a bit real. You know it's live, so I was there and since you know I'm attracted to Africans, there was a hashtag there that said Nigerian and I was like that's more real, a Nigerian person that's camming. I feel I can imagine myself with her, you know, instead of a porn star, you know? So, I clicked it and different people came up. I was trying to decide who to click and who did I see, you, you there, you were wearing a shirt and nothing at all, my shirt, the one you wore and have not returned… and yeah…'

'What did you see, how long?'

'Quite a lot man.'

'How do you feel about that?'

'Well, you're quite a maverick.'

'Are you being sarcastic?'

'No hmph, come on, you know I don't mind, I'm just saying it was interesting. You had a thousand-plus people in there, even more than some rooms I visit, and you were funny and… many… things I didn't know a… body could do, so.'

'You don't mind? You're not disgusted?'

'No, why would I be? If I was attracted to you I would have probably enjoyed it sexually and I hope you're getting tokens! Cause there's people like me on those sites, people that just go there to masturbate and watch everything for free without tipping the models.'

'I get tokens.'

'That's good,' Roland said.

'It takes a while to enter my account, but yeah.'

'That's good.'

'Don't tell her,' Kayode said.

'What?'

'Don't tell Yadichinma.'

'Why?'

'I don't know, I suppose I want to tell her myself or something, I don't know man, just don't tell her,' Kayode said.

'Alright.'

'Yeah.'

'Thanks.'

'For what man?' Roland said.

'You know, not judging me.'

'Stop that jor, why would I do that, that would be stupid.'

'Still thanks.'

'Okay, sha if you want to really thank me, you'll treat me to something with your Chaturbate money, abi?' Roland said.

'Chaturbate money—sounds so weird when you say it.'

'Chaturbate money.'

'You're weird, you know?'

'In what way?'

'With your porn tastes, I don't know. It's kind of weird now,' Kayode said.

'I just feel really connected to the kind of stuff I like. Like before I discovered places like Chaturbate, right? On Pornhub, I'd search Nigeria or Ghana in that white box and it just made me feel connected. Part of watching and masturbating is the act of creating a story in your head you know? Transporting, connecting yourself through the virtual space to the physical one, you know, so I click a result that the search brings up and in the background as the girl is rubbing herself or something, I hear a Wizkid song, that's connection. Or maybe on the walls I see a calendar that has NNPC on it, connection. I can imagine myself there and then in the video, I can imagine what she would sound like to me, cause I can already hear her and because when a Nigerian person records a video or does porn, you know there's no fancy equipment there that's recording, it's just as it is and it's very stimulating to me, you know? That's why I like the cam rooms I guess, the simplicity of it and the starkness, so I don't... I really don't think it's weird. There's this thing I want to say but I'm feeling weird about it.'

'What's that?' Kayode said.

'You know this girl in Lasu that we knew? Like I know I'm not supposed to be watching that shit, you know, it's revenge porn, and I know it's dehumanizing to the women, without them giving consent, and it's all part of the hegemonic patriarchy but I don't know. You know the girl I'm talking about, Anu?' Roland said.

'Oh yeah, the one with the lecturer, that had sex with the lecturer?'

'Yeah, yeah, it made her famous and the lecturer leaked a video of it and people were sharing it around then. I still see her, you know, in the bus park or in the streets and I go home and there she is on Xnxx. And sometimes I click it and it really makes me feel guilty and I feel like I'm part of the oppressive system, I mean, I am part of the oppressive system, as a man, but I feel like I'm an active part of it, if you get what I mean.'

'Then stop watching it.'

'It's easier said than done. It's there and I'm seeing it and I click it and I'm seeing her face, I'm not even seeing the lecturer you know, I'm seeing her—and in a paradoxical way, it's very exciting yet I'm also feeling guilty. That's part of the reason why I looked for something else, like cam sites, because I know if I continue on Xnxx, I would click on that video. Why do you think writers masturbate so much? I read something online about a famous writer, I've forgotten his name but it was about masturbation and writing.' Roland said.

'I think it's therapeutic,' Kayode said.

'Probably. I do it when I'm blocked, like I'm writing a story now ehn and like, I know what I want to write, but I can't write, nothing's coming. I hate being blocked.'

They talked long into the night, and Kayode thought the reason he'd told Roland not to tell Yadichinma was because he liked this—liked having a secret with Roland, a sexual secret. He liked that Roland had watched him and whatever Roland may have said, he told himself that Roland must have liked it, must have liked what he saw.

He went to the kitchen to drink water. He looked outside the window. The moon hung blue and big, like in Spielberg's *ET*.

He stood near the entrance to his room. He could hear his neighbor's dog barking, the sound mixing with the sound of his own generator. He thought he had read the article Roland was talking about, the one about masturbation. He thought: I can remember the writer's name. He trailed his fingers across the panel of his room's door.

'It's Mark Twain, I think,' he said to Roland. 'It's Mark Twain.'

Lounge
Fiona O'Connor

The new room with its modern shape. Clean rectangle you walked its length, her green chair by the fire again, his matching alongside, slightly staggered, big window Venetian blinded. The nights spoke through the breeze block walls, war, politics, car doors slamming on city streets far away, the sea then, fog-horned sea; it all spoke as she adjusted the fire, selected and placed the coal lumps by tongs like a duchess adding sugar to her tea.

Or the space was an envelope, business-sized, not the compaction of *billets doux*. Their life an ease of folded length inside a generous warranty—that was what the room intended, and no fault to *it* if not fulfilled. Under yellow light bulbs she hugged her fire, eternity soaked them up.

The boy lounged in his father's chair. He could hear her out in the kitchen, running water, slotting plates and saucers onto their metal rack. He drew up his knee, sandal bold on the cushion, his two arms splayed over the curved wooden arm rests, flopping the bent leg side to side, waiting for the afternoon to move towards something, out of its deadpan anything, held in a grey lassitude infusing the room.

The phone rang, that was something. He moved quickly to get to it before her. *Hello?*

He heard her turn off the tap to listen.

No, the boy said. *He's at work*. After a pause he said: *Yes. Alright, hold on, I'll get her.*

She was in the room before he could yell. Her frown demanded, who is it? The boy shrugged, handing over the receiver. She indicated for him to get her

her cigarettes. *Hello? Oh, yes. How are you? Yes, that's right. I'm not sure, I expect him when I see him.*

The boy set her up with her cigarettes, lighter, and the pale blue saucer ashtray she usually carried from room to room with her. She sat down by the phone and the boy resumed his place on the armchair to observe her.

Her head bent towards the phone in its shallow corner, the management of her cigarette, the cautionary flicks of imagined ash from her crossed knee, long silences as she listened, responses then, harmonious, insignificant to him, only the rhythm of sound on breaths, exhalations short and long, smoky or pure he dwelled in, with her preoccupation taking her further into the corner, even as she looked at the boy, coolly, as she listened, as she smoked, not seeing him but registering the entity of him across from her.

Light was fading but she didn't seem to notice. The visitor had a beard and silver-framed glasses that interested the boy: the way he would shove them up the bridge of his nose with a stretched index finger. To make a point, the boy thought. The voice was low but loud, Dublin accent like a bus man might have. When she offered the visitor a cigarette he leaned forward out of his chair to take it from the box. She lit his and then her own.

They were waiting for the boy's father to come home. As usual. The house was always waiting on the father to turn his big old car into the driveway.

She didn't put the light on. They became insubstantial, fading into the room, with the open spaces of the Venetian blinds darkening between the slats. Their talk had substance though. Politics: boring to the boy, all they ever talked about, the adults. The left they were always on about, as against the right, which was bad. At some stage he crawled under the low wooden coffee table that ran along the big window, lay on his back looking at the underside above his head. A few words were scribbled there in another language, factory note probably, and a five digit number—meaningless but meant all the same: a sign not to be seen that always intrigued him.

She was not that long returned to them. She'd been in hospital. The boy didn't know for how long but it seemed a big distance separated their life in the new house from her breakdown in the old one, when she had gone away. Twice, if he thought of it, she had gone away. There had been a day, prepared for with a great clean-up of the new house, which had fallen into chaos in her absence and told of the despair that had moved in. His older sisters, his father, stuffing dirty clothes under the beds, rubbish over the garden fence into the field beyond. *Because she was coming home.* His father driving off in the car to collect her. His eldest sister sending the boy out because he was *useless and no help but a hindrance.*

Hours later the car pulling in again with that familiar sound, a final cadence of thrum and the engine switched off. He was idle in the garden, gathering dry clay from between the paving stones. The car drove up beside him. They did not get out. She in the front smoking, looking at him standing in the grass, his hands pouring sifts of small fine-grain stones onto his bare toes in the sandals. She had dark circles under her eyes. She spoke to his father, in the driving seat next to her. He could see her mouth moving behind the rolled-up glass. Looking at the boy, smoking, looking, speaking, dark-eyed, thin-faced, speaking what could not be heard.

The hall door of the house opening, his sisters emerging, excited, unsure, coming to stand with him. She mouthed something important. To them, not to their father, that's how they saw it, shaking her head slightly; her lips pressed together was a sign that said a lot. His father starting the car again, twisting to look over his shoulder as he always did, with that sound his breath made at the pressure on his big frame, backing out of the drive, twisting as he did, the sound he made the boy imagined. Backing out, the shift of gear a pullback in eternity, then forwards and they drove away.

The light was going but she didn't seem to notice. She reached for her packet of cigarettes and matches in their place on the mantle ledge, opened the box, slid up its row of pristine soldiers and offered one to the man, which he took, leaning out of his chair.

She lit her own cigarette then his, blowing smoke as she continued her conversation, relaxing back.

The old house had hung on the severity of her nineteen-fifties' beauty with its austere rationing of space and permanent cold. The old house of their marriage aspired to, but never occupied, the state of wifely satisfaction. It had furniture that seemed important to her then, suites of mahogany carefully polished, double beds both coy and servicing. She took to her marital bed like a mood takes hold, in for the long haul.

Alien nation, the man said.

His socks, the boy noticed from his eye-line on the floor beneath the table, were striped. Thin horizontal red lines against a dark grey ground. His father would never wear socks like that. But this man was younger than his father, and his mother. He noticed the socks when the man pulled them up. The crossed leg first, and then, uncrossing, the other one. Pulled them up although they were fine, not in any need of adjustment. The boy thought that, caught himself thinking and repeated the thought: not in any need of adjustment. Where had it come from, such a thought? It was like the glasses, the boy understood, the socks, done for emphasis as he talked loudly, filling the room. *Class war*, he boomed, pushing the glasses up this time.

At first the new house had resisted her return. Its shapes, its open plan against the tight corners of their marriage. She had not wanted to go back to her old life but could not find herself in this new one either. Going through her husband's suits to search out his true self then. She found it in dockets, bills, bailiffs' notices, folded unevenly and taking the shape of his body in the breast or hip pockets.

Surplus value, the boy heard, *according to Marx*.

She laughed a little. What were they talking about? The boy could not follow. He felt uneasy as he often did when she was talking to men. She was annoying him; he wanted to tell her to shut up. *Shut up woman*, he wanted to shout out at her from under the table.

As though she had heard his thought she glanced over at him. Her blue eyes in the murk were like the sea, lonely. She looked away. The boy bent up his bare knees so that they pressed against the underside of the table. The feel of the wood through his kneecaps was cool and solid. The pressure he was exerting felt good. Because her laughter was not good, it made him anxious. He was angry with her but shameful for her too. With her crossed legs, pink slipper hanging, her pleasurable cigarette cocked in her ring-finger hand, and the gaps from her missing teeth showing when she laughed at the man's jokes, her head thrown back and her teeth gone and this man watching her from behind the silver-framed glasses.

The boy pushed his pelvis forward slightly so as to take the weight of the table onto himself. He'd returned from school the day she went missing from the old house. His granny there instead. When she had never even visited their house before, not liking them, his mother said, because of taking her son away. His panic then, *where are you?* Screaming it, running through the small rooms downstairs, upstairs. No one would tell him where she was.

Stretching his arms above his head, his hands against the wood, he tipped his hips forwards again. The table lifted a fraction, balanced between his knees and hands. He lowered it, raised it again. The heavy press of the long low table, the balance he achieved with its layer of objects, the big cut-glass ashtray, the pile of newspapers, a teacup, all safely suspended by his efforts, lifted and lowered imperceptibly by the movements of his pelvis from the floor, were satisfying against her irritations.

Stop that, she said sharply.

The man was surprised, as though he'd forgotten about the boy and didn't know what her clipped command referred to. He'd been explaining reproductive labour. She'd seemed to be following.

Doesn't look as if he's remembered, the man said, reaching across to stub his cigarette in the ashtray on the table above the boy, looking down at him as he did.

Any second he could arrive, she said. *Have you far to go?*

In a certain sense his father was always not there.

Not too bad—meeting a few comrades down in The Old Shieling. He pushed up the glasses again.

The boy rolled out from under the table, went to lean behind her green armchair by the fireplace, draping his arms heavily around her neck and looking at the man, who had sat forward in anticipation of making his departure.

The pub?

She removed the boy's arms from her, as expected, leaned forward to tap her cigarette ash into the blue saucer. He held the back of her chair instead. The room was like a charcoal sketch of itself, with the cloudiness of dusk swirling around, objects seeming to phase in and out of distinct shape as though you were seeing their molecules in movement and they might become anything at all.

Revolution has to start somewhere.

After a few pints, she said. The man laughed and she didn't.

The new house had resisted her return to them; its light, its open plan tending to maroon her.

He's probably just delayed in the traffic. You know what it's like this time of an evening.

It might be raining for weeks on end, lashes against the big picture window, gusts flattening the fire flame, drafts under the doors. *The bird has flown*, he thought he heard her say.

The boy tipped her chair back, suspending her slightly as she spoke, her feet dangling off the ground, slipper slipped off.

He'd seen her getting ready earlier. Her cigarette idling smoke in the saucer as she penciled in her eyebrows, backcombed her hair in front of the bathroom cabinet with its speckled mirror.

Stop it, she snapped. He tipped it a fraction further.

Out, she shouted. He let the chair fall back forwards with a bump.

Tell him I'll phone him later in the week. The man took his opportunity to stand.

The room would be wasted by her death in a few years. The boy a young man studying architecture in New York, just in for the funeral, standing by the window. Glaring monotony of light through the blinds, he was thinking, savaging the mourners in their blacks, standing around murmuring.

The man with the silver-framed glasses, he remembers, as the light went down between them, with the stripy socks and all his adjustments against her far-from-shore eyes. And her laughing.

.

To that other me behind the looking glass

Go! To that backstreet & graffiti something obscene,
To Machu Picchu, to Milan. Go obsolete. Go back to your
Teens & piss in the teachers' toilets. Go wear a top hat
In the afternoon & spend days thumbing old photographs.
Go sideways, upways, timeways to your birth. Go sift through clouds
To find your worth. Go to your father's grave & leave nothing
On the earth. Go far. Go further. Go brave.
Go to sea & wave at the moon, beyond the finish line & start again.
Go to womb. To a home that never existed. Back to the farmer's warehouse
& burn it down to ashes. Go alone. Go on. Go to your bedroom
& open your curtains & lay on the floor, eyes to the stars, to the unknown.

Be! That silver painted boy juggling traffic cones. That black man with a swag
& cigar. That father who knows how to balance the world on his shoulders.
Be ash. Be bones. Your mother at the hob, burnt arms,
Humming & cooking. Be a country, be an island, be a lost boy in Neverland.
Be Hook. Be lippy & leggy & ready to fuck (& be fucked);
Be the fuck up, the fuck over. Be a candle, a pullover, the main course
& leftovers. Foam. Be a mountain dressed in white. Be an X chromosome,
Be the fight & the fought & the fought over. Be thought.
Be older, wrinkled & veiny & eyeing up death with a smirk.
Be nothing more than breath.

Live! With death in your pocket, with jupiter in your eye. Live with that tattooed
Boy your parents disapprove of. Live on the streets asking why; live without
Asking, live without withouts. Live on music & dancing & beats in your feet.
Live long. Live reading & writing & forgetting it all; live like a song, off-key,
Live like synchronisation, with fascination at all that is unknown & free. Live
With her, & him, & him & him & her. Live with a middle finger to the sky.
Live poor & poorer until you're rich with living; live inside your skin, inside your
Fur; outside your life & soul; live within. With your heart in your hands,
Pumping & bleeding & ready to throw, live it all, what you've done &
Haven't & know & unknow. Live today. Live tomorrow. See how it goes.

Patrick Holloway

Looking for Business
John Harris

The phone on my chest woke me: a text from Helen.

'Pouring here. Worried whether we'll actually be able to play.'

'Pity,' I texted.

She was back straight away. 'You managing ok? Making decisions about the day? Not drifting?'

'Fine. You don't have to keep checking.'

The tone might have been a bit off, but I didn't have the energy to fix it.

I was lying outside the duvet with my clothes on. It was cold, the wind blowing the light curtains back into the flat. I rolled off the bed and went to make tea. It was Saturday and I was stuck in Dublin for the weekend.

The phone again. 'Just like to know where you are. We're disconnected enough already.' She liked to send long messages, with careful punctuation, proper capitalisation. Before I had time to reply, there was a follow-up.

'Just an affectionate little thought, that's all. Getting petrol here outside Galway. Since you didn't ask. Anyway x.'

I imagined her standing in the forecourt, sheltering from the rainy wind. I hoped she wasn't texting near the pumps. Just looking at her car, you knew she had teenage kids. But she still got these quick scans from men all the time, even men in their thirties. She claimed not to notice. But of course she did—and she didn't mind me noticing either.

This weekend, she was taking part in a tennis tournament down the west and the kids were at my parents' house. I was staying put in Dublin because I had a hard deadline on Monday afternoon and I needed to spend a day in the office over the weekend. Normally, I headed back to Cork on Friday night. Both Helen and I had been solicitors in the same firm in Cork, mainly conveyancing. When the recession hit, the work dried up and I had to look for something in Dublin to keep us all going.

'Sorry. I want you to have a good time. Please don't text near the pumps.'

I put down the phone and went around the kitchenette wiping surfaces and jotting down items on my list. My plan was to do a pile of jobs I had been putting off for weeks: get a haircut, do a big Tesco shop, buy new underwear and shirts. And a new kettle: neither of the two I had in the flat was working, so here I was boiling water for tea in a saucepan.

I sent a follow-up text: 'Going to have a Big List day.' She would know what I meant.

I was down in the hairdressers in Rathmines, thumbing through the clammy *Hello* magazines, when a woman came over carrying a black gown for me. Do other people find this strange? The stagy consultation about what exactly is to be done: the hairdresser picking up wads of hair and dropping them again, as if some complex assessment is going on. Then you're supposed to gather your gown and stumble to another chair to have your hair washed. Finally, onto yet another chair to have it cut, all the time parading around in this camp fashion with the black gown, led by this ill-at-ease stylist.

But the woman I had that morning was new to the salon and she went through the usual motions in an easy, amused way, saying just what was necessary. I had a few passing views of her pale, composed face as she moved about, cutting my hair, looking pleased at how it was turning out. She was tall and somehow familiar. Although she said a few predictable things, hairdressing talk, there were also long silences.

'Getting away at all yourself?'

'Hard enough nowadays, isn't it? So much to do before you go. Nearly takes the good out of it.'

She wasn't trying too hard. She cut and combed slowly, patting my hair all over, viewing it from different angles. Just an expression of satisfaction with her own work, nothing more. But I felt distinctly included in her approval, grateful to have been admitted into her care, even for this short time, for this mundane task. I would have liked to tell her how good she was at her job, say something a little warmer than usual. But you never knew; she might get the wrong impression. Think I was weird.

'Thank you very much,' I said. 'Great job.'

'It was a pleasure,' she said, smiling directly at me, carefully picking stray hairs from my shoulders as I stood there in front of her.

On to Dunnes Stores. I grabbed five basic white shirts before heading over to underwear and socks. The usual bewildering range of boxers and trunks in packs of three, all showing amply-endowed men in their 20s. It felt slightly furtive to be spending so long handling pictures of bulging crotches. When I found the right size, I decided to throw in four packs of three so I wouldn't have to make this trip again soon. I was a little short of breath and avoiding eye contact as I shovelled the lot in front of the woman at the checkout.

An hour later I was finishing up in Tesco. With an overloaded trolley of groceries and other jobs on my list still to be done—the kettle, the car wash—I suddenly felt dispirited. Halfway up the ramp, I wedged the trolley against the side in order to check my phone, and then I became aware, right beside me, of this huge photographic mural advertising Irish food. It stretched the full width of the store, well beyond the ramp. Despite its scale, I had passed it for months without really seeing it. A glorious, intensely immediate picture of farming countryside. Nine or ten square miles of fields sloping down to trees, the suggestion of a river just out of view. Tall grasses and crops, all blown at a slight angle. Cattle and a halted tractor. Beyond the fields, the greater Irish landscape.

It was countryside that seemed really familiar—maybe East Cork, South Tipperary or West Waterford. Up this close, it felt as if I was standing in the nearest field. I was flooded with emotion as I traced the details: hundreds of crows at random in the stubble of a freshly cut field; an almost hidden one-lane road; a rusted but serviceable gate; people working here and there on their own land. The sense of an ordered existence, of plenty. A picture of how things are, in some realm, perfect. And, all of it, offering itself up.

I had abandoned my list for the moment and brought a cappuccino and croissants back to the flat. I looked out the window at the military barracks. I'd spent a lot of time staring at these bleak spaces in the last few months. I used to think my time as a student in Trinity would give me a connection to the city, that I would feel at home here. But my old contacts had not amounted to much in the end: a few rounds of golf, two dinner invitations. The trouble was I was always back in Cork at weekends when things were on in Dublin.

I put my coffee on the bedside locker, lay down and thought back to the Scholars' Dinner in Trinity last Monday. I had been invited as one of the 'Scholars of the Decades', since I had won my scholarship in 1983. As a Scholar, I had lived on the north side of New Square. Arriving in Front Square last Monday as the light faded, I felt I was truly back home. Privately, I have always thought that being a Scholar was my earliest, and probably greatest, success as an adult. Helen made me buy a dark grey Canali overcoat for the occasion, something of an indulgence given our finances. She said I must arrive looking the success I am. Ha. At the end of the evening, full of wine and good cheer, I put on my Canali and began walking home to the flat. Near Fitzwilliam Square, I stopped to text her.

'What an evening. So sorry the invitation didn't include you. It would have been worth coming up for. Love the Canali.'

I realised I had been swaying slightly and set off briskly again. A woman in her mid-to-late twenties was crossing the road towards me from beneath the trees. She was tall, wearing something like sports or hiking clothes. She had a slim, shiny, out-of-the-shower look, with lank, slightly curly blond hair. Someone's sister.

'Are you looking for business?' she said faintly as she passed close by. I paused and she swung around. She said it again, more distinctly this time, standing about ten feet away, blushing slightly as she met my gaze. Looking properly now, I saw she was fairly dishevelled, her face exhausted. She had a small scab below her left eye, the index and middle fingers of her right hand stained with nicotine. An addict.

'Ah no, I'm grand,' I said, feeling foolish.

There was something wild and vigilant about her that I was no match for. She didn't seem crazy or vindictive or anything, but I didn't want to think about her chaotic life. I felt exposed for a moment, a dart of anxiety. There might well be someone else around, a man she was working with. She must have seen that there was something marginal about me, something I thought was well disguised: that I was on my own, looking boozy and flushed, wearing this ridiculous Canali overcoat, obliviously texting away.

Once I was on Leeson Street, I recalled the things I had noticed. A collar opened wide at the neck and a slim bust. An attractive mouth, regular lips, no lipstick. Ankle-length suede boots, very worn. Her left foot turned inwards. Her mouth closed, covering up a missing tooth maybe. Presenting her best self even in this odd encounter.

I phoned Helen as I walked up through Rathmines. She had been asleep and she allowed long silences develop as I tried to explain what it was about the brief exchange that had made such an impression on me.

'It's not anything exciting,' I explained. 'Or erotic or sexual. It's the intimacy and connection.'

'I am glad you didn't get excited,' she said drily. 'I would have expected nothing less from a Trinity man.'

'I didn't choose it,' I said. 'It just happened. It's not that I feel flattered. Of course, she made exactly the same approach to the next male passerby, irrespective of age or appearance. I'm not stupid.'

A group of teenagers were drinking cans near the fire station in Rathmines. I crossed the road, phone to my ear.

'I think you need to go to bed, Jack. It's midnight. Go home so I can stop worrying about you wandering around Dublin. I have four highly-sexed teenagers here to keep in check.'

'Ha ha,' I said. 'I've drunk nothing. One glass of white and three red.'

'No port?'

'Yes, yes. A small port, of course. It's Trinity. You know the score. I gave away the dessert wine.' I took a deep breath. 'Here is someone who is prepared to allow you into their ambit. When you're on your own a lot, you know…' I knew she would be grimacing at the other end. 'The fact that, however remotely, they would entertain the idea of you. In that way. Even if it's for money.'

Silence.

'Anyway, I found it… moving,' I said.

'Hmm.'

'Ah come on. Don't pretend you don't understand.'

After a moment, she said, 'I have to sleep.'

'I like you when you're sleepy,' I said.

Silence.

'So phone sex is out of the question?'

'That's for Christmas, if you're good. Listen, Jack: why don't you go back to Harold's Cross and imagine me tucked in in the bed behind you. That's what I am going to do here anyway.'

'Night,' I said.

'Night darling. Watch your phone.'

Turning up Leinster Road, I began to think about Helen herself, how she had been the first few times we went out together. Helen Doyle. Really dark hair and eyebrows, pale, pale creamy skin. Doyle. Ó Dubhghaill. Dark-haired foreigner.

Something had woken me. As I tumbled off the bed, the bell downstairs buzzed furiously. No one ever called here. Most of the students in the other flats were gone for the weekend. I went down quickly. Helen was at the top of the steps with a weekend bag.

'Surprise, surprise,' she said, throwing up her hands a bit nervously. 'I had to ring twice.'

'Oh great,' I said, my heart thumping. 'Surprise is right.'

I was so taken aback, I forgot to kiss her. I led her up the stairs.

'Maybe I should have texted first but I didn't want to spoil…'

'… the surprise,' I said. 'Of course.'

She began a tense, studied monologue. 'Couldn't leave you in Dublin for a whole weekend like that, as well as the Monday to Friday. Your phone call about the hooker the other night clinched it. Ha ha.'

'So the tennis thing in Galway was all a cover?'

'Yep,' she said. 'Yep' was not a word she normally used.

She was breathless and a bit panicked by the time we reached the open door to the flat. We embraced rather woodenly before entering, as if I were meeting her off a plane.

'I feel like I'm intruding,' she said, taking a few rushed steps ahead of me into the room, then wheeling around. We kissed in a perfunctory, embarrassed way. Estranged relatives at a wedding.

'I'm sorry,' I said, 'The place looks pretty sordid. But you gave me no notice. I haven't even put away the groceries.'

'I tell you I had a bad moment below there at the door,' she said.

I couldn't help noticing her Cork accent. Posh Cork.

'What if I have totally misread you, and you actually have some Latvian beauty hidden away here,' she said. The tone was uneasy, striving for a kind of: 'We're best friends here, right? We can say anything to each other. Sure it's all a big laugh anyway.'

'Obviously, you see me as an exploitative middle-aged gent.'

'But it's what you'd really like, isn't it?' she said, jumping in. 'Someone young. Okay, just challenging enough to be interesting. But hanging on your every word.'

She laughed in what she clearly intended to be a good-humoured way. 'Admit it. That's what you really want isn't it?'

I knew that she was saying all this in spite of herself. In normal circumstances, she would see it as letting herself down.

'Nothing compares to you,' I said.

'You're actually doing ironing?' she said, ignoring this banality. She was looking at a pile of shirts on the board.

'I like the smell of freshly ironed shirts,' I said. 'It's homely. Reminds me of special occasions. Getting ready to go on a school tour. I iron just one or two things each night. For the atmosphere.'

She looked appraisingly at me while I made this little speech, as if I were a candidate for a job.

The bed was huge in the middle of the room, beige and joyless. She swung her weekend case onto it. I began tidying the duvet and pillow. There was a terrible silence for half a minute while she struggled to unzip the case. Everything inside was neat and compressed. Womanly.

'You obviously don't want me here,' she said, not looking at me.

'I'm delighted you're here, ' I said. 'Delighted. I'm just a bit in shock, that's all. You look fantastic.' I glanced around at the flat. 'And all of this looks seedy.'

She abandoned the case and began to move my MacBook off the kitchenette counter and on to the bedside table.

'There's no room on the counter to unpack the groceries,' she said. She got down on her knees, grunting as she tried to find a socket to plug it in. 'Just moving your stuff around like this feels like intruding.'

Things were dying fast.

She went to the window and looked wildly out. 'This could be great. It's all what you make of it.'

I could almost hear her mind racing. She turned back to the room and threw herself down on the bed.

'I'm exhausted,' she said, as she tucked her hands behind her head.

I could tell she already regretted lying down.

'It's bound to be a bit awkward initially,' she said in a loud voice, her elbows flapping like wings as she tried to settle herself. 'We have hardly been alone together for half an hour in three years. Well, except for sleeping. Now we're suddenly stuck together in the middle of the day.'

'You look stunning,' I said, staring down at her from the end of the bed. Which she did. 'Desirable,' I added, probably a little less certainly.

'Jesus,' she said, jumping to her feet. 'Creepy.' She threw her hands in the air as she turned her back. 'Don't touch me.'

I felt a bit breathless.

After a second, she resumed unpacking. I watched her, feeling as if something was about to happen. It was like a long sequence in a French film. Then she noticed the Dunnes bag behind the door.

'What's this?'

She got down on her knees, rifling through the packets of new socks and underclothes. This was the second time she had been on her knees in as many minutes. For an odd moment she looked like a stranger, less familiar to me than the hairdresser or the drug addict.

'All this stuff?' she said. She was scattering images of crotches on the floor.

'What?' I said.

'Just,' she said.

After some more rummaging, she picked one up and began to read aloud. 'Large, to fit waist 36-38 ins. Grande, Para La Cintura 92cm... There's tons of it here. Like some serial killer's stash. I only got here in the nick of time.'

'I won't even dignify that,' I said.

She was relieved to have got a handle on things, an emerging theme. Standing behind her, I saw that she had new high heels on, the soles barely scuffed. And the skirt: I couldn't remember her wearing anything that short in years. It made me feel protective about her, seeing how much effort she had made. I caught her glancing at me as she scrambled to her feet. She had noticed.

'Lighten up. It's a joke. I'm trying to lighten things up.' Then she added: 'They'll all have to go back, though. You should be wearing Canali or Calvin Klein.'

We were heading into town by taxi. She had suggested making a day of it—going to the National Gallery, doing some shopping, wandering around. She said we needed to escape the 'suffocating intimacy' of the flat. I thought 'suffocating' was a bit much. She rolled her eyes as we got into the taxi. It smelled sour and unhappy, the interior stifling and junky.

I texted her: 'Am I imagining it, or is the taxi speeding up and slowing down in an odd way?'

'It is. It's making me feel car-sick.' She looked quite pale.

It seemed easier to text her like this, more intimate than talking. That's just for the moment, I told myself.

We sat in silence. It was a strange pleasure to hear her breathing quietly beside me as she went through her voicemail. Of course, we were together in Cork every weekend. But to have her here beside me in Dublin was something else. I desperately wanted to reach across and take her hand tightly. But my previous efforts had failed so badly.

'Who are you texting?'

'The kids,' she said, passing me the phone with a questioning smile.

He's in a state of shock. Like I caught him with his hand in the till. Horrific squalor. Fraternising with hookers and transients. Speech and cognition just about threshold functionality. Wouldn't be surprised to see Paddy O'Gorman outside with a microphone and a radio crew. Be careful. Mum x.

'Don't send that, Helen, please. It's over the top.'

'You're not hurt surely? It's a joke. A joke. Totally harmless.' She looked punctured. 'They understand my sense of humour. I actually thought you'd like it.'

'Sorry,' I said. 'Go on. Go on, send it off. The Paddy O'Gorman thing is clever.'

She pressed Send and then started going through her email.

'I wonder if we should both switch off our phones,' I said.

'Jesus,' she said. 'Goody, goody. It's not some kind of personal indulgence. I'm a mother.'

She turned it off, looking like she could have said a lot more.

In Trinity, I pointed out the window of my old room in New Square.

'You remember the exact one?'

'You don't forget something like that,' I said.

We looked at the faint greyish squares appearing on the grass where the marquees had been dismantled after Trinity Ball. There was a fair bit of construction noise in the square, so we moved across to the cricket grounds and sat on a bench.

'So, tell me about her,' she said.

'Who?'

'You know who. Your hooker, of course. What did she look like? What was it about her that got you going?'

This felt like a trap.

'I told you—it was all about connection and intimacy. Not what she looked like.'

'Jack. Just get on with it. What did she look like?'

'Well, one of the things… she had her shirt collar open wide, showing her neck and the top of her rib cage. Lovely and flat. And then the suggestion of softness below that, under her anorak. Just something that stuck in my mind.'

We looked at the seagulls prancing on the grass.

'You're much more lyrical about her than you ever are about me.'

She was the one who had insisted on getting into this.

'I'm worried about the flat chest, though. Three years on your own in Dublin. Are you sure this was a woman at all? A lot of them are men.' This was self-consciously jokey.

'Trust me. She was a woman.' I mentally checked back over the signs: throat, voice, wrists, the foot turned inwards. I couldn't actually recall any curves.

'Well, you were confessing on the phone the other night to having inappropriate feelings for a young woman. Now he sounds more like a courier from Doneycarney, with dirty fingernails.'

'I confide in you, something private and...' I was struggling. 'And this is your reaction.'

'It's just that I'd hate to see you deceived. In that way.' She looked down towards the Pav. 'I know how important she is to you.'

'You're such a bitch,' I said, turning her face around and making her kiss me. She kept her hands resting on her handbag. Her colour was improving.

'Well here we are at last,' she said, her eyes flashing across my face for an instant. 'Like a date.'

We had decided on a late lunch. It was the first time we had sat face to face. I felt a bit of a thrill that she was avoiding my gaze. I loved the way her front teeth overlapped slightly, how she composed her lips to accommodate them. It gave an intensity to her presentation of herself.

'Do you mind if we sit at one of the tables outside instead?' she said. 'I have a terrible mind for a cigarette.'

She smoked a single cigarette a few times a year, always when the kids were safely out of sight. Outside, she lit up awkwardly, looking up and down the street all the while. When the wine arrived, we both took urgent gulps. She picked up the bottle and stared at the label.

'Montepulciano,' she said. She went on looking at the label.

I took the bottle from her.

'13.5%,' I said. 'Not too bad.'

She turned her phone on. There were texts from all four kids. The messages were scrupulously even-handed, supporting me, subtly praising Helen, discreetly pushing us together.

'God. We have such an attentive audience in Cork,' I said. 'Aware of...'

'They're so civilised.' Her face was super serious, which meant she was holding back tears.

'They're being so parental,' I said. 'Makes me feel irresponsible.'

'Glad they can't see me then,' she said, blowing smoke away from our table.

It had grown cold, but we liked where we were. We didn't want to break the atmosphere.

'What was that thing you were saying there earlier, about the Merries down in Douglas?' she said, still not looking at me.

'The Merries was the very first place that we spoke, when we were only fourteen.'

She knew this, of course. But she wanted to hear what I had to say. She listened without interruption. I went on for a while.

'When your friend Susan went over to talk to her Dad that time, I walked up to you and said "You're Dekka's sister." The first words I ever spoke to you. "Yes," you said back to me. "And you're in Dekka's class."

'Neither of us spoke the other one's name. I said that I had seen you in the bumpers. You said that Susan thought I was going to ask you to go in the bumpers. "But it's only what Susan thought," you said.

'And then we ran out of things to say, but you looked straight at me, like I was meant to be there. You just stood waiting, as if I was entitled to look. Your eyes and face, your arms stretched straight down in front of you, your white socks and perfect shoes. I had never seen a more perfect girl.'

Helen inhaled, her eyes half closed.

'I liked that you were so serious.' She blew out a long, slow line of smoke. 'I wanted to be really, really nice to you. Really nice.'

'I'm worried about your smoking,' I said.

'Jack, will you just go on,' she said. 'You're ruining the story. One isn't going to kill me.'

'Anyway,' I said, 'do you remember Susan running back and saying "Helen, my Dad has to go. He says there's room for Jack if he wants to come."

'"He does want to come," you said, looking at me. "Don't you, Jack?" "Yes," I said. "Helen."'

There was silence for a moment. Helen was feeling the cold. I could see goose pimples on her arms.

'You're a sly one,' she said. 'You come up with something sweet like this every... I don't know... ten years? Wasn't I such a great kid, so sensitive? I've always looked out for you.'

'The idea of being entitled to you,' I said.

'I know,' she said. 'I know.'

She leaned forward and kissed me lightly. I loved the wine and smoke on her breath.

'Are you looking for business?' she said, her face still close.

Amhrán an Fhir Óig

Mo dhá láimh
ar do chíocha,
do dhá nead éin,
do leaba fhlocais.
Sníonn do chneas
chomh bán le sneachta
chomh geal le haol,
chomh mín leis an táth lín.

Searraim mo ghuaille
nuair a bhraithim
do theanga i mo phluic,
do bhéal faoi m'fhiacla.
Osclaíonn trinse faoi shoc mo chéachta.
Nuair a shroisim bun na claise,
raidim.

Mise an púca
a thagann san oíche,
an robálaí nead,
an domhaintreabhadóir.
Loitim an luachair mórthimpeall.
Tugaim do mhianach portaigh
chun míntíreachais.

Nuala Ní Dhomhnaill

Song of a Lad (Inclined to Wander)

My two hands
on your breasts,
your bed of cotton,
your two birds' nests—
your skin so white
you'd have to squint,
whitewash bright,
sheer as pure lint.

My shoulderblades rise
and arch as I perceive
your tongue's on my tongue
and I receive
the full weight of your mouth.
A furrow opens under the jolt
of my plow. When I reach
the far end of the drill I bolt.

I hit and run. I'm the Bogey Man
who visits in the dark,
the nest burglar
and the plowing world's brightest spark.
I ravage the rushes all around—
aye—with my weather eye
on your plot in the bog,
the one that I'm planning to suck dry.

Peter Fallon a d'aistrigh

Ó Thuaidh

Féach romhat in airde
Go bhfeicir fíor na spéire
Á nochtadh chugat aduaidh
Taobh na fothana den chnoc.

Ach tá fraoch is aiteann
Le dó agam ar learga sin
Na haimsire dúchaite
Chun an talamh a shlánú.

Na toir stóinsithe sin
Nár ghéill dom i mo neart,
Driseacha cosáin romham
Le glanadh as mo chuimhne,

An poll portaigh le dúnadh
Mar ar slogadh go ciúin
An bhodóg thórmaigh
Ab fhearr dá raibh agam.

Tá garbhlach is screathan an ama
Le tabhairt chun míntíreachais
Sula dtabharfad aghaidh ar an bhfaill,
Sula séanfad fírinne na feisceana.

Seosamh Ó Murchú

North

Look up and make out before you
the horizon rising on, exposing
the inland slopes…

It's time, if the land is to be salvaged,
to burn the ancient whins and heather
these hills inherited, obstinate shrubs

which just get in the way, now (as then,
when the resources were there for them).
They need cleaning up, and to be set aside,

like that fine springer (the best animal I ever had),
who was swallowed in the silent boghole
which needs to be blocked off, plugged.

Time, all rough growth and gravel,
must be owned up to, before I face up to
what I cannot credit, this new light.

John McAuliffe a d'aistrigh

the soul has no skin
Wendy Erskine

Guys who've messed up and gone off track, they'll work in the place for a while but once the boredom seeps in, they'll get themselves sorted out with something else. Years later a guy like Phil will call in to buy something, a car seat for the baby say, and it'll be, Barry, you still here mate?

Yeah I'm still here.

Said with a smile, a smile and a shrug, because it isn't that bad. It can be a laugh when you do the thing where you pick what you hope to be the most obscure item from the catalogue, and if anyone orders it you have to pay all the others a fiver. Has to be pricey enough because otherwise somebody could get one of their pals to come in and buy the thing so you have to shell out. And it has to be something that could reasonably be ordered and picked up in the shop. Dishwashers or tumble-dryers are out. A Scuderia Ferrari Men's XX Yellow Black Chrono Watch maybe. Or a Haven Fresh HF710 Humidifier—Black. A Tefal ActiFry Fryer—Silver. Barry's had a good streak so far with the Flower Flush 8 Light Ceiling Fitting; he picked it over eighteen months ago.

People steal stuff from the shop, as you'd expect. A box is brought to the collection point for a customer but then it gets swept before anyone has a chance to do anything. The security guard in tassels and epaulettes stands at the door. He says the trousers are cut that tight he can hardly move in them. That security guard always seems to be at the other end of the shop when it happens. People settle themselves on the display sofas like it's their own personal living room in the city centre. Bring a packet of biscuits, why don't you. Kick off your shoes and get yourself comfortable. I'm putting the kettle on, anybody want a cup of tea?

Fair amount of hassle some days. The product doesn't work and they want a refund. Some old guy hands you over a toaster that doesn't work and when you take it a load of crumbs drop out the bottom. Sir, I am sorry but since you've used this, I just can't give you a refund. You haven't used it? You both stare at the crumbs, saying nothing, before you sweep them off the counter with the back of your hand. Uh huh, uh huh, I do hear what you saying but I'm sorry I can't give you a refund. I don't make up these rules. The best I can do, Barry says, is to send it back to the manufacturer for you. No I don't know how long that would take. Not too sure about that. If I could give you a new toaster I would, he says, because if he could give them a new toaster he would. The old guy looks murderous.

A bank of ten sleek tellies on the shop floor, the repeated image crisp and saturated. In the staffroom out the back there's a radio, a kettle and a microwave. Barry'd rather mooch round the town for half an hour in the lunch break, smoke a fag in the lane, rather than go to the staff room. Even by two o'clock the town feels tired like it can't be bothered with the afternoon either and longs for the shutters down.

Some of the others, Phil and all that, sometimes say after work to come for a drink, just the one like. But he'd prefer to get back to the flat. Not much to see at his place. Living-room bedroom kitchen bathroom. Bathroom's full of his creams, Vitamin D analogues, corticosteroids. Flakeybake they called him in school, Flakemeister. Slather on the skin stuff morning and night: just one of the things you have to do. Walls here are wafer thin and he hears his neighbours fighting sometimes: she goes guttural, he goes squeaky. They throw things about before they make up and Barry sees them heading out somewhere, the woman's hand in the back pocket of the fella's jeans. They're alright; they lent him a corkscrew when Annie brought wine one time. And if they find his music annoying, they've never said anything. They're not bad at all.

Annie looked around the place and declared, Well Barry you haven't exactly embraced the concept of interior decor. Grand Designs this ain't. Alright, the flat's pretty spartan, can't deny it. There's only one thing on the wall, a picture torn out of a magazine of a Gibson Les Paul guitar, bleached pale because it's near the kitchen window and that spot always catches the sun. Barry used to play the guitar, messed around on it anyway, a good few years ago now.

Annie had been one of the bosses for a while, an unusually well-liked one. Everybody knew she drank, but they didn't care because she wasn't operating heavy machinery nor was she personally responsible for any individual's safety.

It was never a massive problem that she often had to be busy with administrative tasks out the back until after midday. Only a shop after all, where everyone was an adult. In her younger days she had been into the whole rock scene and she still dressed in that style all the years later: poodle perm, floaty scarves, a biker jacket although now she went with cheap, fake leather. They called her rock hen. Phil started it then everyone else joined in. Never mind those there rock chicks here's the rock hen. She'd liked it though, thought it was funny. Annie was married to some Scottish fella who had one of those illnesses where basically everything shuts down slowly over time. Annie said he used to be in the Hell's Angels, except this crowd were called the Blue Angels.

The first time Annie and Barry got together was after a Thursday late night in the run-up to Christmas. Town was tinselled up with rain and lights and they swigged from a bottle of brandy near the waterfront. Cold enough down there so the brandy was welcome. Back at his place they were leaning on the door as he tried to find the key and when it opened they tumbled into the dark hall. How long had he lived there and he couldn't find the light switch! In the bedroom he did know where the switch was, but he didn't put it on.

There was another time when they both had a day off and she came round at about half ten in the morning with a bottle of wine.

Is it not meant to be maybe a coffee and a biscuit at this time of the day? Barry said.

According to what? Annie replied. Barry Young's Guide to Modern Living?

They borrowed the corkscrew and because he didn't have any wine glasses they drank out of mugs. The rock hen was just a bird with nowhere where you couldn't feel the bones, whereas he seemed to himself a crude and hulking lump. Barry didn't feel guilty. Why should he? It was nothing to do with him, nothing at all, the husband in the wheelchair or whatever it was. He had a fleeting thought of him surrounded by wires and monitors, a skeletal ghoul in motorbike leathers.

Afterwards, when they were lying there, Annie's hand reached out to touch his hip.

Barry, she said. Come on. It's really not that bad. Seriously. It's not.

Yeah, sure, he said. And he reached for his t-shirt and trousers squashed at the bottom of the sofa.

She looked around the room. You know what it's like in here, it's like a monastic cell, she said.

Just the way it is, he said.

Well if it suits you.

It does—you live in a palace yourself? he asked.

You know I don't. You know I don't, Barry.

She half put on her top and then took it off again. She wasn't wearing a bra. Look at me, she said. I want you to look. You seen the, well I hardly need to point any of it out to you, I would rather not give you chapter and verse here, but what you are looking at is not really babe material. What's in front of you isn't exactly a hot piece of ass. Barry. You taken a look? Look.

He said, There's nothing wrong with you.

Course there is, she said. And the she did put on her top, and her jacket. She needed to go. Someone was looking after her husband for a few hours but she needed to get back so that they could head on. Her time was up.

Barry's morning routine: out of bed, do the creams, get dressed, get a takeaway coffee from the garage, get on the bus. It's the same people, more or less, on the bus each day. Tinny beat of that guy's cheap headphones, the woman always doing her makeup. Some, like him, are tagged with the logos of their work. The uniform's alright. A polo shirt with a sweatshirt for the winter. When he gets off the bus and walks round, he always has at least ten minutes to spare.

Barry has a usual spot for a smoke. He sees his own cigarette butts when he looks down. Looks up and there are empty rails for clothes on the first floor of the building opposite. Beside him the hoardings surrounding a vacant space are covered in weathered, flaking posters. Building on the space was meant to start months ago. They advertise long past club nights, a psychic who visited a hotel on the outskirts of town.

This morning there's been a big delivery so that means lots of stuff for them to unpack. They have to slice through the cardboard and ties with blades. Some of the other guys were there early this morning for the van coming through; you need to go on a day course if you want to be able to unload the lorry but Barry hasn't attended it, nor does he want to. The new manager won't be around for much longer because he is looking to move to a bigger shop. It's alright unpacking the stuff: you get into a rhythm as you work away. You think about things. Don't think about things. Think about things. Barry goes through the track listing of various albums, tries to remember the back cover of *Second Helping*, Lynyrd Skynyrd, the guitar listing. That new woman on the bus, Polish maybe, the line of her jaw as she wiped a circle in the condensation on the window, but now it's Annie and he feels her leaning against him and laughing as they tumble in his front door. Don't switch on the light.

But didn't everyone say the sun was great for clearing up your skin. The good old sun works wonders. Lying in the park, first summer after he'd started tech, trying to see if everyone was in fact right and that the sun could work some magic. He was down by the old bandstand on one of those early July days of melting tarmac and yellow grass. There were a few fellas from the college going through the park. They came over, sat down for a while, then headed off. They were going off to a party that night.

You wanna come?

No. You're alright.

You sure? What the fuck's the point just hanging around here by yourself?

Hot, hot day. The guys from tech ambled off but then another bunch came and started throwing a frisbee to each other not far from where he was lying. When the frisbee hit him for the second time he thought about the cool of the kitchen and going home.

Two playgrounds in the park, one at each entrance. The new one had a zip-line and fresh rides, the old a rusty climbing frame and forlorn couple of tyres.

Hey, she shouted when Barry was walking past. Hey there, can you help me?

A girl was dangling there in the old playground, fat legs a few feet off the ground. She was maybe nine or ten. Her hands clung to the rusty bar above her and she couldn't get free because she was hooked to a broken pole by her pants. Face shiny from crying and the sun. Barry reached up and freed her. He held out his hands so that she could take them and jump down.

What happened you? he said. How you get stuck?

They'd all been messing around, she said, but then one of her big brothers had gone and done that to her. They'd all cleared off on her after that.

My brothers are always doing stuff like that on me, she said. They have me tortured.

She fixed her skirt which had got all twisted, pulled up her socks.

Well, Barry said. That's you down now anyway. He felt around in his pocket and found a 50p.

Take it sure, he said. Get yourself something. Away on, off you go and get yourself something. Get an ice-cream or some sweeties.

She took the coin and walked off towards the gates, breaking into a skip as she got closer.

Did none of yous think when you were unpacking all this stuff that there seemed to be a bit of an excessive amount for us? James the manager says. None of yous boys think about that?

Some of the stuff they have just unpacked should have gone to the other shops. They are overwhelmed with ironing boards.

Not really, Barry says.

Nah, never thought, Phil says. You told us to unpack the stuff, so that's what we did.

Well I'm gonna have to arrange for them to be taken away again, James says. So don't be doing anything more with those ironing boards.

They stack them in the only empty space in the store and get back to unpacking more stuff but James comes back through again and tells Phil that he needs him out the front. Annie always said, would you mind, in work. Would you mind giving me a hand. Would you mind coming out the front. Nobody ever did mind. When Annie didn't appear in work for the best part of a month nobody knew what had happened. Barry tried to phone her but there was never any answer. One night he was going to bed when she appeared at his door. How could you be skinny and bloated at the same time? She said she wouldn't stay long, she'd come in for just a minute or two. He made a couple of cups of tea in the mugs where they'd once had the wine.

When you coming back? Barry asked. Place is going to wrack and ruin without you.

Oh yeah, right enough.

Yeah. We got all these temporary managers, haven't a clue. Everybody misses you big time.

She said that she wouldn't be coming back to work again because it had all got too much.

You know what I'm talking about, she said.

He asked if they were moving her somewhere else.

I don't think so Barry, she said. There comes a time when I think you just have to call it a day.

Well, said Barry, yeah. Suppose so.

I do though, he said, I do miss you.

Yeah well. Something for you, she said. It was a set of glasses. They were popular those glasses because they only cost £8.99. They were the four pack Belgravia wine glasses 38cl. On the cardboard there was a soft focus shot of a pretty woman holding one of the glasses to her lips. Barry knew he and Annie probably wouldn't see each other again unless by chance.

Thanks, he said. I'll make sure that these are used next time I've got somebody round for a drink.

Well Barry, Annie said, I would love to hear that you were using those glasses.

Back from the park the house was still and dark as he knew it would be, and the water from the tap tasted so cold. After tea he was lying on his bed listening to something or other with the headphones on when his ma opened his door.

You need to get downstairs, she said. Quick, Barry.

Why?

There's a policeman! she said. She was untying her apron, fixing her hair in the mirror on the landing.

The police?

Yes. You better go down Barry. What on earth's it about? They want to speak to you. You haven't even got your shoes on, where's your shoes?

Here's Barry now, his dad said when he came to the door. The policeman was young and smiling. He said that all they needed was just a quick chat with him, wouldn't take long at all they hoped.

Me?

The policeman nodded.

You need to speak to me?

The policeman nodded.

Had there been a terrible crime that he'd not noticed himself witnessing? He didn't know anybody that got in trouble with the police. One of the fellas from tech that he saw earlier had been smoking a bit of grass in the park. Had somebody seen that? Was that what it was?

He asked the policeman what happened. Was it something he'd done?

The policeman was pleasant. He smiled. We just would like you to attend the police station for the purposes of assisting us with an investigation, he said.

Excuse me sir, are you arresting Barry? his dad asked.

Oh no, we're asking him to attend the station voluntarily.

His mum came down the stairs holding his old school shoes. The policeman watched him as he put them on. Old school shoes and jeans. He felt suspicious already.

In the car the bulk in the front seat was another policeman. He said nothing when Barry got in and the three of them drove along in silence. Then the car stopped at a garage. The young one went in to get something so it was just Barry and the other one in the car. He turned round slowly and deliberately to give

Barry a long stare. He put down the window and spat onto the garage forecourt before giving a weary sigh. Barry started to rub at one elbow and then the other.

They turned out of the garage and drove back down the way that they had come. They passed the bottom of his road and suddenly it looked beautiful. The sun was hazy in the trees and there was a guy out washing his car, clots of suds gleaming on the road. Barry thought how he never knew before that he loved that road. It was just the road. All those people at the bus stop. You could see the cranes and beyond them the hills. The adverts in the estate agent's window set out in a grid, all those little houses, he loved everything about it, and the people coming out of the Chinese with their takeaway. It was all so fragile, who would have thought? His ma, at the kitchen sink, doing the dishes, holding up a bowl to the light to see if it was clean.

At the station he was put in a room. They told him they were waiting for his dad. He needed to be there before they could ask him any questions. They hadn't realised his age, that he was under eighteen. It smelled like the changing rooms in school in the room. They all knew his name, Barry this, Barry that. Then they took him through to another room where his dad was sitting, now wearing a suit. An eternity ago his dad had got up to answer the door, only maybe forty minutes ago, and now here he was at a police station wearing a suit he never usually wore. Stapled on the cuff there was still the dry cleaner's pink paper after the previous time. The woman on the other side of the desk thanked his dad for coming.

Barry, she said. Do you want a coffee?

He said yes even though he had never drunk a coffee before. He needn't have worried because the coffee didn't ever come anyway.

She explained that they would need to record the interview and then a door opened and another man came in.

So, she said we need to ask you a few questions. And you've come here voluntarily. We need to ask you about a girl who's gone missing. Young girl of eight by the name of Megan Nichols. Now Barry have a look at this please. I am showing Barry a photo of Megan Nichols.

Looked straight off the mantelpiece, still in the brown cardboard frame of the annual school photo. She was wearing the same primary school uniform that he wore himself when he was a kid.

Do you know Megan Nichols? the woman asked.

Yeah, she's a kid I saw today, Barry said. She's a kid that I saw, I saw her today, but I don't know her. So, no, I don't know her.

She's gone missing, the woman said. Every parent's worst nightmare. Can you imagine?

No, said Barry. I mean, yes I can.

But you saw her?

I saw her in the park. In the kids' playground. The old one near the way in.

The kids' playground, the woman said. Alright. Would you have any idea what time that was at?

Maybe a bit after four, Barry said.

The woman leaned back in her seat.

And where exactly were you when you saw her? she asked.

I was in the kids' playground.

You were in a kids' playground?

No I went in to the playground because I saw her there.

Barry swallowed hard.

You spoke to her?

Yeah.

Why were you speaking to this little girl Barry?

He felt his dad turn slightly to listen to his answer.

She shouted at me to come over because she was stuck on a climbing frame. She was crying and she was stuck.

Yes we know you spoke to her. You were seen speaking to her. Speaking to Megan Nichols.

There was a knock at the door and then the woman left the table, and then the room.

Dad I'm sorry, Barry whispered, I don't know what's happening here, I've done nothing wrong at all.

Nothing wrong at all, years ago now, years ago, and so much in between. He cuts through the orange ties on another delivery that is stamped This Way Up. All the cardboard cut, all the items re-stocked, the notes taken, the cards read, receipts given, marking the distance between now and then. Displays rearranged, the garden furniture and the barbecues, wood-burning stoves with their artificial in-store fire, Christmas trees and the year's new toy, engagement rings under glass, wedding rings under glass, things put in bags, things pulled out of bags, times stepping on to the bus, times stepping off the bus. Washing your clothes, drying your clothes, getting them dirty again.

The woman came back in, apologetic. The guy looked at her and she nodded.

So, the woman said, you say that Megan Nichols was stuck.

I got her down from the climbing frame. She was stuck on the climbing frame.

So why couldn't she just get down herself?

Because she was stuck. I had to get her down.

How, stuck?

Her knickers were caught.

The word hovered somewhere above the table

Her pants, he said. They were caught on the frame. That's why she couldn't get down.

The woman leaned in a little. Did you touch her pants, her underwear Barry? Did you touch her pants?

The guy coughed and put his head down.

I couldn't not have touched them when I was trying to get her down from the frame. She was hooked on by her pants.

The woman said, You couldn't not have touched her pants.

No

You just said that you couldn't not have touched her pants?

To get her down! Barry said. For Christ's sake. I'm trying to tell you she was stuck on the climbing frame, the other ones had wedgied her there and I got her down. There was nothing funny about it.

And it was all being faithfully recorded.

The woman said, That was the only physical contact you had with her?

Yes, said Barry. It wasn't really physical contact though, that sounds bad, it was like, three seconds, getting her down.

And you're sure about that?

Yeah I'm sure about that, Barry said. Totally sure.

We're asking questions because a child is missing, the man said.

So after you touched her underwear, the woman said, what happened then? When she was down on the ground? What happened, Barry?

I, and he didn't want to say it, I gave her some money.

What did you do?

I gave her some money.

A child you didn't know? Why would you give a child you didn't know money?

Because she was upset! Because she was by herself and her friends had left her and she was upset and crying. 50p to buy an ice-cream or a can of coke and then that was it, she went off and I didn't see her again and that is all I can tell you.

The woman sat back on her seat. Fact remains though Barry, she said, fact remains that you seem to be the last person to have seen this girl. Look at her photo again Barry. Look at Megan Nichols's picture and let's start all over again.

Barry's dad spoke up then. He's told you, he said. He's told you what happened. Can I just check, is Barry under arrest or what is the situation here?

We're just asking him a few questions. He's come along voluntarily. To answer a few questions.

Her gaze was steady. So, she said, thank you very much.

We're meant to have a solicitor. We're meant to have someone else here, his dad said. Look at the state of him.

He hadn't realised that he had been working his skin, that his neck was up in weals. The crooks of his arms were on the point of bleeding.

What are you doing that for? the man said. Why's he doing that?

Stop doing that, the woman said.

She said they would take a break. Barry and his dad were shown through to a waiting room off where the main desk was. There was a man in a corner with the dregs of a black eye looking at his hands, one and then the other.

This is some to-do, his dad said. Some to-do indeed. I don't know solicitors. I've no dealings with solicitors. The only solicitor is the one we had to go to when your granny died and we were selling the house. It was a man in Carrick. He wouldn't know what to do here. He's all to do with selling houses. Selling houses and wills.

Barry wondered if he'd go to jail. It didn't matter if they hadn't done anything, sometimes people still ended up in jail.

Another policeman came through with a blue tub. Maybe you want to try putting that on, he said. She sent it to you. Our boss.

Should I put this on? Barry said.

If you think it'll do any good, his dad said. Stop that scrabbing.

There was thick silver paper on top of it and underneath gluey cream.

The perfume of it seemed to be everywhere in the waiting room. Did the guy with the black eye look over because he could smell it.

Barry felt he should put it on. The woman would maybe be angry if she came back and he hadn't put it on. That sort of stuff was pointless though. It was for women's faces. It wasn't medical. It clung to his fingers and he knew it would do no good but he put it on one arm and then the other.

You won't be going to that park again, his dad said. There's always bad sorts around that park. Around all parks. What's keeping your woman? They'll be bringing us a solicitor now no doubt. You'll have done nothing wrong son I know that, I know that. The solicitor will get it all sorted out. He looked around. Should I speak to somebody about the solicitor?

I don't know.

You hadn't even ever seen the wee girl before sure you hadn't? No? Well there you go.

No.

Her parents'll be beside themselves, he said. Bad people about.

There was the end of that film where a young fella in jail slits his wrists lying in his bed and you see the blood come seeping through the sheet.

The woman reappeared. She was looking different. Could she see he'd put on the cream? Was she happy because he'd used the cream?

We're letting you go Barry, she said. There's a sighting of Megan Nichols just shortly after she left the park.

Barry handed her the tub of cream.

But that's not to say we won't need to speak to you again. You understand that?

Barry had nothing to do with anything, his dad said.

His ma rushed down the stairs when they came into the house. His dad put his hand up and shook his head.

But what's happening? Don't go upstairs yet Barry, his ma said. I'm just straightening out your room. Nearly finished.

The police had been round. They had gone to Barry's room to remove some stuff. Although what were they going to find, his ma said, other than dirty socks and pants? Isn't that right Barry? You've not done anything wrong, have you? There was a police van outside. Mortifying, his ma said, them carrying stuff out. Never anybody on this road but suddenly there's a whole bunch all gawping.

The next day was a Saturday but there was still no sign of Megan Nichols, nor on the Sunday either. She moved up the order of the headlines on the news. Megan Nichols's mother was on the screen, her two dark-eyed boys beside her. People in the neighbourhood arranged searches, posted flyers through doors. But no one came to Barry's house. When his dad went for the paper on Sunday morning all talk stopped when he went into the shop. Barry knew what they would be saying. You see the bags came out of the house? Heard the polis held him for hours. No smoke without fire. Right odd-looking bloke, that fella, you'll have seen him about. Big guy with the skin. Don't judge a book by its cover, yeah I know, but even so. You heard about them taking anybody else in? No. No smoke without fire.

They were eating their dinner that night when the radio said that Megan Nichols was still missing. Poor wee pet, his ma said. Barry's dad got up. He said he thought he heard something out the front. What he saw was an egg running down the window. And then Barry and his ma were there too, watching one egg and then another. This was followed by showers of what sounded like gravel. Handful after handful.

Should I call the police? his mum asked.

No, said his dad. Don't do that.

On the Monday morning Megan Nichols was discovered. She was found by the caretaker opening up the primary school for the couple of teachers who liked to come in at the start of the summer to tidy up their rooms. Megan had spent the weekend eating old packets of biscuits left by teachers in the cupboard in the staffroom. There was a whole box of crisps too, from the end-of-year disco. Megan said she played with the school tortoise and messed about with the paints. She'd gone in to the school because she thought she'd seen Mrs Foster's car and she wanted to say have a nice summer to Mrs Foster who'd been absent on the last day. But she couldn't find Mrs Foster and then the place got locked up. Why didn't you use the phone in the staff room to ring for help? the woman on the telly asked her when she was briefly interviewed. She paused. I was liking the peace and quiet, she said. For a while that was a joke with people. If you wanted to take yourself off for some peace and quiet you were doing a Megan Nichols.

Barry's mum was out that morning, brisk and efficient, dealing with the eggs like it was nothing other than a spring clean. There was paint on the front door, pale green, the colour somebody might have used for a bathroom. His da had to go to the DIY place to get the remover for it. It was decided that Barry would go to stay on the other side of the town with an old uncle of his dad's. It was only ever presented as a temporary arrangement because sure didn't everyone know that Barry had done nothing wrong anyway? The uncle ate pies that came in tins and listened to the cricket on the radio. But Barry lasted a year in the old uncle's place until he moved out, first into a damp old house with some others and then, when he got the job in this place, into the flat. And now he meets up with his parents in the town every few weeks or so, somewhere that does a business lunch or an early-bird meal because that's what they like. They've started getting vouchers that they print off the internet, complicated arrangements involving arriving and leaving restaurants at certain times.

They've been to his flat, but they'd rather meet in the town. He goes back home for Christmas and that's alright because with the lights and the decorations and the empty streets on Christmas morning it feels like a different place. He always leaves in the afternoon. Can't hang about too long. Always working Boxing Day. Just the way the rota always seemed to work out. His dad gives him a lift.

Phil comes through from the front of the shop. Barry, he says. Barry, you wouldn't come out here would you? Only going to take a minute.

Barry puts down the blade and folds up the packing slips that he's laid out on the floor. They'll be coming again soon, the two of them, into the town for a meal. They'll ask about work. They'll ask about the flat. He'll say everything's alright, because it isn't that bad.

Glitch in the system, Phil says.

And where's James our manager? asks Barry.

Don't know, says Phil. Nipped out a couple of minutes ago. Said something about wanting to buy a shirt. Needs a white shirt. Got an interview for somewhere else this afternoon I think. Some amount of managers running through this place, him, that other guy the fat fella, Annie—

Yeah, Barry says. I know. Just the way it is.

Aye, so, two people have paid for the same item at exactly the same time, Phil explains. But there's only the one of the items actually in stock.

What they looking for?

Paint.

House paint?

Johnstone's Matt Emulsion in Cadillac.

You tried seeing if it's in the other shop?

Yeah, course I have, says Phil. But nah, no luck.

OK, says Barry. Well there you go. They'll have to decide between them who gets it.

Well they both want it.

That's as may be, but if there's only the one tin.

Oh Barry you go and speak to them, Phil says. You're good at all that sort of stuff.

Yeah right, Barry says.

You are, Phil says. No messing. You got the knack.

Okay, okay, Barry sighs. And he goes out to the front to deal with the customers who are both holding their receipts for Johnstone's Matt Emulsion in Cadillac.

My body, full scrape

across this pavement
towards you.
        The tide drags us
 out before it flows back
into the bay   the fullness
between distant cliffs.
Cut of water   carving
islands out of rock
    your body
its weight beside me
in sheets. Coffee in paper
cups and the whistling
that leaves my lips
in the morning as I bike
past the park—its flatness
under the dogs
and children. Coffee
in paper cups. Sunday
and God is wondering
where we are. Hoping
we have figured it all out
by tomorrow when he
opens his eyes, lets
thunder fall out of his mouth like
laughter.

Nolan Natasha Pike

How They Live Now
Wes Lee

'A dog is an impossibility. It will slow us down.'

'Dogs have been around for ten thousand years. They were the first domesticated animal. They lived around the campfires of prehistoric man.'

'A dog will need feeding, there won't be enough food to go around.'

'What if I gave the dog some of my food?'

'It won't work.'

'Would you give me your food? Would you share your ration?'

'Of course. I would give you my last bite.'

'Would you give me your overcoat?'

'I would give you anything and everything.'

She stares at her husband's thin red lips. His big square teeth. Too many for his mouth. 'Would you eat me? If it came to it, would you eat me?'

'Of course not… A dog is a frivolous thing, how can you even think about it in the days ahead.'

'That may be ahead,' she reminds him.

'We have to keep ourselves free, so we can leave at a moment's notice, at the drop of a hat.'

Yesterday she watched a dog running to and fro, back and forth to its master.

A golden Labrador, who had wriggled its way out through the car window when an old woman had parked. The woman had thrown a stick and the dog had jumped into the river. No thought of the cold, of being sodden afterwards.

'He's brave,' she'd told her.

'He's mad,' the old woman said, while the dog leapt and cavorted for the stick.

They will never own a house, they will not own bricks and mortar. *Nothing you cannot leave, nothing you cannot carry with you.* She slept on a camp stretcher for three months until she spit the dummy. They had a stretcher each, he would crawl to her in the night. She made him get a double mattress. He would not buy a bedframe. *No bed legs, no bedframe. Nothing so big we cannot carry.* We must live like travellers, he tells her.

She stares at the long cord around his neck, at his photograph dangling on the security swipe. She tries to imagine the door he swipes but never gets past the glass. It would be glass, they are always glass.

She doesn't actually know what he does. He wears a suit and tie and works from 8am until 5pm in the city. Of course she knows what his job is, but she doesn't know what he *does*. He's gone through a series of jobs that are all the same and not interesting to her. She knows he does something all day and that's enough, and in the beginning when he joins a new firm he seems to like it.

She grows most of their food on an allotment by the river while he works.

'Working for money doesn't mean anything,' he tells her. 'Having skills— being able to do things we will need, like hydroponics and smoking fish, trapping animals, being able to kill animals you can eat—that's what's important.'

She has tried to get a job, but there are no jobs. No one is hiring.

She knows he has a desk, and each day she asks him what he had for lunch. He tells her things that are ongoing with one person or another. She remembers some of their names. They are abstract figures he has fleshed out, but not too much, he doesn't describe people unless she asks and then he doesn't do a good job, not like she would.

She would know all the gossip. She would know the way they breathed.

'Did you put my photo on your desk?' she asks him.

'Not yet.'

'Why not?'

'You have to do these things slowly, show people a little bit about yourself at a time. You have to keep yourself safe.'

'From what?'

'Marauders.'

She imagines the plastic frog she bought him, and her photo in the silver frame. All the paraphernalia, the cards; each card she made and he made for her, crowding his desk, crowding out everything.

The man who sits at the desk next to him: his wife handed him a baby in the middle of the night, umbilical cord attached and everything, which she thought only happened in books.

'His wife woke him and said: *Here take this,* and she handed him a baby. She didn't even know she was pregnant… He tells it like it's funny, an amusing anecdote… He's from Norway,' he tells her.

She imagines salted fish; jangling reindeer bells; his ruddy raw-boned face.

'What does he look like?'

'Short. Dark… Average.'

'What's he like?'

'He's an okay guy.'

'What does he have for lunch?'

'Burger King. Every day, a double quarter-pounder with cheese.'

'What else?'

'He eats boiled sweets.'

'What kind?'

'Oddfellows mints. There's always a packet open on his desk.'

'Does he offer them around?'

'Not really.'

The last place where her husband worked, he came home from his leaving do and said:

'The biggest surprises were the ones who were larger than life. It was a bizarre thing… arms around these people, and they were so small, their clothes crumpling in on these tiny frames. Collapsing like balloons.'

She starts writing *Dog* on notes around the house, under his pillow, inside the bathroom cabinet. When he picks up his coffee cup he sees *Dog*. Folded inside the butter conditioner he reads *Dog*. Stuck to the bathroom mirror with Blu-Tack: *Dog Dog Dog!*

She imagines finding notes pinned to her make-up bag. Poked into the pockets of her jeans. Slotted beneath the tongues of her trainers: stick figures with their hair on fire, flames roaring out of their mouths.

'It was fine until they passed that ridiculous law,' he tells her. 'Now you have to carry a plastic bag, wrap it around your wrist or tie it around its collar. Imagine going out and tying a bag to your neck, always reminding yourself about shit, like you've got shit on the brain, that this is the reason for going out, for having a run, for breathing ozone, this little plastic bag waiting to be filled, then everything can go back to normal, then you can relax. All those rubbish bins filled with tiny plastic bags then bulldozed at the dump. Imagine archaeologists or aliens, excavating a thousand years from now, there will be layers and layers of squashed plastic bags with one dog turd, a little twisted-up plastic thing with the most foul-smelling shit, except for maybe the Tasmanian Devil, which I have never smelt, but I'm sure it's the worst, worse than a dog. Carnivores have the worst smelling shit. What will scientists think about the layers and layers of shit-filled bags, they might think it is ours, made by neurotics. All these neurotics squeezing their turds into plastic bags, they will come to the conclusion there were no toilets in the twenty first century…'

She watches his eyes, his quivering beard. The tight, anxious puckering around his mouth.

She takes his face in her hands, rubs the back of her hand along his cheek.

'It's okay,' she tells him.

If they excavate us in a thousand years they'll find all these rooms filled with bottled water and tinned food, she thinks. Cartons of matches and toilet rolls pushed under the bed, stacked in wardrobes. As if people were living in a siege.

They stockpile in the event they have to barricade. They keep everything light in case they have to walk. They have a handcart—a supermarket trolley he dragged from the river. They think about the creeping cold, the baking heat, ice floes, they think about ice breaking off the Arctic shelf, they think about weather far too much.

If nothing happens she doesn't know what will happen to them. She does not think that far ahead. She cannot allow herself to think that far ahead. For him it is out of the question, such is his resolve, such is his certainty that something is going to happen.

They watch a documentary about the men who work in the nuclear silos. They talk of their longing to launch the missiles. They want to see what the bombs can do. What they are capable of.

She can understand it. All that time waiting and wondering and then you finally get to see it.

The brilliant cascade.

America seems like a dream anyway. She remembers the Polish man who murdered his wife and child in America. He said from the moment he got off the plane, driving through America never seemed real, he'd seen it so much on TV, it seemed like a dream. He said he felt like he had never actually arrived in America, he was in the dream America in his head—so none of his actions had felt real. She could imagine that, landing there and feeling you hadn't really travelled, you hadn't got off the plane. Travelling on a plane seems so unreal anyway, you sit there for a few hours and you are supposed to be in China, or Dubai, or Fiji.

The children of the men in the silos are eating hot dogs. The American children. At some kind of celebration with banners welcoming a son home. A prodigal son who has walked out of sunlight. A car door opens, and he steps out. He's wearing a uniform with *Hazeltine* on his nametag. The uniform they wear in the desert. Older wars had different colours, having to blend in with the green of grass and the solemn bark of trees. He takes off his hat, runs his tanned hand over his hair, cut so close it is barely there. Cut with such precision.

If they had a war now in snow, she thinks, the uniforms would be white.

'We won't survive. The people with guns will kill us,' she tells him.
'We'll take their guns. We will *have* to take their guns.'
There could be a nuclear power plant melting right now as we speak.
Bottled water stacked in every corner of the house.

Having children is out of the question. It has never been a big thing for her. For him it has nothing to do with the apocalypse, nothing to do with the days ahead. It has everything to do with the past, and a certainty that he did not want to repeat what had happened to him as a child. Neither did he feel the need to manufacture a perfect childhood for someone else. So that was that.

Sometimes she thinks it would have been nice, if things had been good, to have people around who she had helped grow. The flesh of her flesh, people she felt strongly toward, people she could have fun with, or bring fun to, or news, news and fun, but she recognises it as an ideal situation, the news could be bad, the fun could turn sour, there could be such loss.

'How will we know?' she asks him.
'There will be a sound.'
'What sound?'
'I don't know, a big roar, a sound you can't imagine. An unimaginable sound. There will just be a roar and everything will be on.'
She thinks there will be silence. A complete engulfing silence where everything feels stopped, wound down, where there is no communication. The paths are all blocked. Everything is jammed.
In a disaster, she thinks, you stare into each other's eyes.

A wave comes to her in her dreams—giant, black, all-encompassing. She turns from the sun and there it is. A vast golden beach with a skyscraper shunted on its side, like a fallen tower, an archetypal tower, a tower from a tarot card.

She walks along it, so huge, monolithic.

People are still going about their business, not totally convinced that the landscape has suddenly become surreal, having watched too many disaster movies. It could be a stage set, scenery that has been moved in.

A girl follows a line of pretty snapped fingernails along the sand, dropping them in her pocket like seashells.

The road is moving up and down like a wave. Things are on fire and it is snowing.

She opens her mouth and green gas flows. She speaks in green gas and blancmange, jelly floods from her mouth.

There's a man selling ice creams. He smiles a big fat-faced smile, a last smile, a smile you see in old sepia photographs.

She begins eating the apocalypse food, right out of the can with a spoon or fork depending on her mood.

She eats the stockpiled tins, because it's not on the menu, because it's so white-trash, fatty, mundane, so terrible it's exotic. Spam, spaghetti hoops, ravioli, chocolate rice pudding. Shovelling it into her mouth like a kind of possession.

The textures are all the same, only the colours are different. Old people's food. Baby food.

'There should be more Spam,' he shouts one night when he gets home. Checking the cans for rust, shifting them from one side of the bedroom to the other.

'I heard they've stockpiled a whole palette of creamed corn in the basement of the library.'

His eyes flicker with approval.

'And tinned mince,' she tells him.

Her mouth starts watering.

She watches couples talking to other couples in the supermarket. They talk about ice cream flavours; holidays in Fiji; house prices.

'We've sold it but we haven't found anything.'

'We're still looking. You know how it is.'

They seem like exotic birds in the rainforest displaying their strangeness. She feels grey, homespun beside them.

Her hands move over the shelves, they come to rest on a pregnancy kit. She slips the cardboard pack in her coat pocket like a tube of toothpaste. Somehow it feels better not having paid for it.

'Everything is so hard now,' she tells him when they are lying in the bed with no legs.

'I know,' he says.

She wants to feel a dog settling in the gap between them. Its warm body attuned to any disturbance. Looking up for reassurance, searching out her eyes in the dark.

She thinks about the photograph he will put on his desk, the one she had framed for him.

The photo was taken ten years ago when she had long hair and did not think about the ice caps melting or ice floes or icebergs of any kind, or fire or volcanoes, or men with guns with eyes not like their own suddenly bursting in and roaring.

The photo was taken inside the crater of an extinct volcano, where she was sitting on the grass that had long taken over, the breeze running through it and through her hair. Her face slightly tilted to the right because she'd known that was her good side, how she would look, half-knowing and not knowing, and he had not taken it, another man had taken it. Someone else she was in love with.

That was me

I remember the first time I caught my head on a cabinet,
running full tilt through the kitchen
and the close heat,
while out of eyeshot someone was preparing a meal.
I remember the shock of the impact
and my ass thumping the ground,
dazed in a stupor.
That was me;
dumb as breadcrumbs,
down there
not understanding
the suddenness with which things sometimes happen.
That was me,
that teary-eyed fearful blinking around,
looking at people at the table
watching what I'd do next.
My fat little fingers were flat on the tile floor
and then trembling and wiping themselves on my pant-leg.
I was a little boy once—think of that.
I must have been four or five.
There were things I never expected.
Not things I didn't think would happen—
things I didn't think about at all.

Now an ex-girlfriend gets a new boyfriend
or someone I knew for a long time gets sick.
Something happens that doesn't change much
but seems to
and it's incomprehensible
for a long time.
First time being fired, first time getting hurt
first time I realised that I needed a cigarette
instead of wanting one.
I still sometimes have to walk in the rain
with wet socks
just like as a kid
and I just want to be little again
and safe
and soft fingers.
I miss the comfort of knowing I could run anywhere in the house
and fit places
and fall asleep in the car
without waking up there.
I want to be able to sprint under a kitchen cabinet
and slide beneath the table
playing with dinosaurs.

D.S. Maolalai

About my dad and his dad and his brother too in places

I had gotten my hands on a car
and it had a tape deck
and my dad
had dug
some old recordings
up from his mother's attic—the sounds of my uncle
practicing
playing
at blues guitar
(dead in africa
winds blow
long ago)
sang clumsy the wind
as we turned corners
like a ghost knocking over a piano
and I asked tactful questions
careful
as a child weeding grass
learning
by mistake
what flowers are.

D.S. Maolalai

Viewpoint
Eamon McGuinness

Tuesdays are quiet in Sorrento's. Kev is sitting in his car, scrolling and waiting for deliveries. Since his brother Paul was sent away, Kev's become obsessed with finding the Facebook pages of criminals. Recently, he found the page of a young man in custody for the killing of an elderly woman in North Tipperary. Before that, he'd been fixated on the page of a man who'd killed his parents, then turned the gun on himself. If the pages aren't set to private, Kev can read all the comments. He uses a fake profile. His first comment was meek: *dirty scumbag*. He got ten 'likes'. He became more confident and got fifty 'likes' once, for a long comment under the profile picture of a man in Donegal who'd killed his wife with a hammer, then tried to make it look like a burglary. In the picture the man is wearing boots and goggles, holding aloft his county flag and smiling on top of a snowy mountain. Kev was drunk when he wrote the comment: *Id love for u to be in front of me right now, the hack of ya, ya scaldy lookin mutt. Id blow ur fat head clean off ur shoulders with a belt of something u evil sick twisted cunt.*

Kev gets a one-ring missed call and shifts into the chipper, under the hatch, to the back heater, where the delivery orders are kept. The address is on the bottom of the receipt and he types it into Google Maps and heads off. The two staff members, Francesca and Bernardo, are watching the Nine O'Clock News. Paolo is the owner, but doesn't work Tuesdays. Kev's been on since six and this is his fourth delivery. He listens to the radio on his rounds and will, sometimes, text in a request for his mam. She worries about him, out delivering. He'll occasionally put a request in for Paul. Kev hasn't visited him in a month so isn't sure if he hears them. They used to listen to the radio together and send in fake requests.

Before Paul got put away, he and Kev had been working on their own version of Cluedo, with six local characters. The board is currently half-finished. Paul wants Kev to keep going but Kev lost heart doing it alone and hasn't touched it in five months. The last character they did was their neighbour, Brendan Burke, a retired plumber back living with his elderly mother after his marriage broke down. Burke is bald, active and sprightly. He cycles everywhere. The brothers had him strangling the victim, Molly Flynn, with his bike lock.

Couples in apartment blocks are the worst for tipping. Their food usually goes a bit cold by the time Kev gets up the stairs or the lift. They've no problem complaining or leaving reviews on websites. Rushed families are good, they'll throw any money at you just to shut the kids up. Tuesdays are mostly couples and bachelors. There's usually one or two curveballs, but none so far tonight. Kev only officially does three days, but Paolo doesn't care who works. The drivers have a Whatsapp group, where shifts are swapped. Kev is always up for being out of the house. Last week, he worked nearly forty hours. The chipper closes at midnight Sunday to Thursday and at half-one Friday and Saturday. He drives his mam's Micra for the deliveries. The car is sun-bleached with different shades of red. His mam doesn't drive anymore and there are scrapes and small dents all over the bumper and side doors from where she used to hit it off the front gate.

Kev is just back and scrolling when Mark from the Village Take-Away pulls in beside him. The windows come down.

'Story Kev, busy?'

'Fuck all, four so far, yourself?'

'Grand, just did a couple in their thirties, that apartment block near the M50. 16" pizza and a bag of chips each, fucking slobs.'

'Tip?'

'Three quid. Money to burn these cunts.'

Mark is a fitness freak who despises fast food, but more so, despises the people who order it. His fiancée is pregnant and he's working two jobs to save money. His goal is to be a personal trainer. Between orders, Mark does squats, lunges and stretches. Kev's never seen him in a jacket or jumper, and his t-shirts are at least a size too small for him. He keeps a wrist strengthener beside him and flexes throughout his shift. Kev is tolerant, but wary of Mark. He's an old friend of Paul's and used to spend a lot of time in their house.

'That's where this country's at,' Mark continues. 'Do you think in Haiti they've gobshites delivering food to cunts in high-rises?'

'I don't know, man, I doubt it.'

'Exactly.'

Mark's sister volunteered in Haiti for three months last year and he hasn't stopped talking about it since. Kev stays scrolling.

'Who's it today?' Mark asks.

'Your man who killed the Polish lad outside the nightclub in Donegal Town.'

'I heard about that.'

'Have a look.'

Kev shows Mark a picture of a young man at a music festival, the band on stage, a cigarette in his lips, arms in the air, outstretched in a state of victory, as if he'd just completed a race.

'What're the rabble saying?'

'The usual. *Bring your Vaseline with you buddy, you're gonna need it.*'

'You are one fucked-up cookie, my friend.'

'It passes the time.'

'There're better ways,' Mark says. 'Smoke in a bit?'

'Yeah, wait till Tsunami gets here.'

As a mark of respect, Kev never looks at the pages of the victims. When Paul was sent to jail, he gave Kev his passwords to deactivate his accounts. It took Kev a week to do it. He wanted to see the level of abuse Paul got. Currently, Kev is caught up in a two-day argument on the page of a Mayo woman who killed her husband. The papers reported years of domestic violence from the husband, but she's been attacked online. The comments on her page are predictable: *Burn in hell u sick cunt. You'll get what's coming to you in the next life.* Kev's comment, which started the argument, was: *This woman was clearly a victim herself, we need more resources to help the most vulnerable.* He was happy with that one and had retyped it a few times to get down exactly what he wanted to say. He hadn't responded in a day, not since he was accused of excusing the woman's actions and was called a *potential kiddy killer.*

Tsunami Jack arrives at half-nine and jogs over to the lads. After the 2004 tsunami, Jack put on a high-vis and, with an I.D. badge pinned to his vest and handmade signs on buckets, went around pubs in town collecting for an unnamed charity, until an off-duty Garda questioned him and had him pulled in. The money was donated to a real charity and he was let go with a caution. He spends his summer evenings in the bookies. Once the last race finishes, he hangs around the village, talking to the smokers or delivery drivers. Jack worked as the cellar-man in the Laurels before it shut last year. He lives half a kilometre away and lost his licence six months ago, when he drove from his house to the village after a few cans. Jack is thirty-five, ten years older than Kev, two older than Mark. He rubs his hands before resting an elbow on each car.

'Story lads, busy?'

'Fuck all going, Jack,' Mark says.

Kev drops the phone and scans the street.

'Story, Jack.'

'Smoke, Kev?' Mark asks.

'Yeah, fuck it, no one's around.'

Mark pre-rolls all his joints, four one-skinners, and keeps them in a small case under the seat. He's paranoid about the Gardaí stopping him. His joints are always the weakest and he keeps multiple packets of mints and chewing gum in his glovebox. Jack loves the dirty delivery stories Mark regales him with—lonely single mothers giving him phone numbers and invitations to slip back later. Kev gets propositions and invitations too, but he's never followed any of them up. Not even tempted. Even when it's raining he wouldn't step into a house. He always keeps the car running and acts like he's busier than he is. Kev and Jack know Mark calls into houses after he's finished, and they've heard him on the phone, lying to his fiancée about how busy the night is.

Jack passes the joint from window to window. Molly Flynn and her cocker spaniel walk by. She's late fifties, with wild scraggly hair. She walks her dog without a lead. She has thick red cheeks, permanently embarrassed, and waves over without really looking.

'Have you gone there, Jack?' Mark asks.

'Where?'

'Molly?'

'Once, New Year's Eve a few years back.'

'This cunt'd get up on a wet Monday morning.'

Mark looks over to Kev, who has his head down and dug into his phone.

'You and that fucking phone, man,' Mark says.

'What?' Kev asks, a dazed look in his eye.

'Molly.'

'Yeah, she's our neighbour. Look, this lad in Donegal is getting dog's abuse.'

Kev shows them a series of messages. Jack squints to read the text.

'Vicious stuff. Are you posting?' Jack asks.

'Not this one. Trying to take a break.'

'Why do you look up that stuff Kev?' Jack asks. 'Do you not think it's a bit gruesome?'

'A little, maybe, but it helps.'

'With what?' Mark asks.

'The papers tell you fuck all.'

'How's Paul?' Jack asks and Mark perks up.

'We haven't talked in a bit. We had a row about mam,' Kev says.

'Yeah?' Jack says.

'He's worried about her slipping and is giving me grief. I'm letting him cool off for a while.'

'I was talking to him a couple of weeks ago,' Mark says, 'gave him a fitness programme. The cunt lives in the gym.'

Paul got ten years. He used a weight on his father's head while he was sleeping. Their mam was in the spare room and Paul waited until her sobbing had stopped and his dad's drunken snores started. His face was crushed so badly they couldn't have an open coffin. Paul didn't run away. He sat and smoked and let his mam scream and ring the Gardaí. Kev never saw the body. It all happened quickly and the house has been quiet since. During the day, Kev makes sure he's out from nine. He tells his mam he's looking for a job or going to interviews, but usually he'll just drive to Viewpoint and sleep until lunchtime, then go home to eat. He goes to the gym until evening, comes back for dinner, before napping and going to work. His mam has moved into Paul's room. The master bedroom has been completely emptied—right down to the curtains, not a hanger in the press, the carpet stripped. She hoovers the house every day, top to bottom. All pictures of his dad have been removed. Kev is thinking of going away but he hasn't built up the courage to tell his mam yet.

The night passes. There is only one order between ten and twelve. Jack stays with Kev, chain-smoking in the passenger seat. Jack knows the estates well and helps Kev with directions and hard-to-find houses when Google Maps lets him down. Before closing, a big order comes in—the last of the night, a house in Mountain View Rise. They've ordered twelve bags of chips and six battered sausages. Because the stock is being cleared, five onion rings and two battered burgers are thrown in for free. Kev returns the float and gets paid for the night:

six hours makes thirty-six, two euro for each delivery makes twelve, a tenner for petrol plus tips leaves him with €64.50. They give him his dinner: a 16" pizza and chips. He takes two half-pints of milk. In the car, he gives Jack the food and a carton of milk. Jack digs in like a ravenous dog. Mark pulls up as Kev is about to leave. He looks at the hefty bag on the back seat.

'Who the fuck is that for?'

'A gaff party in the Rise.'

'Whose name's on it?'

'Gemma Doyle.'

'That's Fran Doyle's little sister.'

'I know.'

'He's a fucking dope. I'll spin up with yis, see the skirt.'

'Nah leave it, Mark.'

'Fuck it man, something to do, isn't it?'

They drive together towards the mountains. Kev is a slow and conscientious driver and keeps checking his mirrors, annoyed by how close Mark is. The Rise is the last estate before the suburbs give way to the motorway and then the wide stretch of gorse, farms and mountain paths. Paul went to school with Fran Doyle; they were friends for a while. Fran is another character in Paul and Kev's Cluedo. He's a trainee chef and they have him killing Molly with a frying pan. The driveway is full, so Kev parks a little away from the house. He zips up his jacket and takes the three bags up the drive. The front door is open. Two baby-faced lads are smoking in the doorway. He waits as the lads call, then scream Gemma's name. Mark is parked across from the house, like an undercover Garda, with his lights and engine switched off. Kev looks at his own car but can't make out Jack. Gemma appears, tipsy but in control. She's thin and pale, barefooted and wearing a black jumpsuit. Three of her drunker friends surround her and try to pay, pulling money from Kev's hands and replacing it with their own. They are all three to four years younger than him and he remembers some of the faces from school. He knows all of them through Facebook. Kev wavers at the door as they argue. He ends up with a clean tenner in tips, plus change. As they are about to go, Kev says:

'I threw in some extras for ya, a couple of onion rings and two battered burgers.'

'Nice one man, you're a legend,' one of the lads replies.

Kev asks him if Fran is about. The lad goes in. A minute later, Fran appears, heavyset in a blue hoody. Kev hasn't talked to him in person since the funeral. They shake hands. Fran asks after Paul. There's movement behind Kev and he turns to see Mark strolling towards the house, pushing his shoulders back and forth and bouncing his head, as if to some music only he can hear. He taps the bonnets of the two cars in the driveway. He pats Kev on the back and looks into the open door of the house.

'Story Fran, session, is it?'

'Something like that, Mark.'

Kev updates Fran about Paul but Mark keeps butting in and finishing his sentences.

'You should see the cunt man, he's gotten massive.'

Kev sees Mark gearing up for something and knows he's itching to go inside. Fran looks nervous and Kev glances towards the car. He can't see Jack for the darkness, but wishes he were here beside him.

'Stall it, Kev,' Mark half-orders, as he sees Kev's body shift away from the house. Kev looks at Mark's bald head—a shiny globe, full of veins and tension. Kev can feel the cold and knows Mark must too. The windows are full of gawkers and Mark is asking Fran if he has any weed or smokes. Mark has moved closer to him. Fran peeks back at his front door constantly. Mark keeps smacking his palm with his fingers, a one-handed clap.

'C'mon Mark, leave them at it, they're just chilling out,' Kev says.

Mark lunges at Fran, feints and shadow boxes on the spot.

'Cause ya can't, ya won't,' Mark shouts and laughs loudly.

'What does that mean?' Fran asks.

'You were always a dope, Doyler,' Mark says, watching Fran flinch.

'Here,' Fran says and moves into the doorway.

Kev is in the middle now, staring at Mark.

'Leave it man, that's how things start,' Kev says.

'Nothing's starting,' Mark replies, looking around him. 'Saps.'

Mark walks off and with the sole of his shoe kicks the door of a car. Kev turns and shakes his head at Fran, tells him he's sorry and that he'll see him again. They shake hands. As Kev walks away, he hears the door being locked and bolted. At the car, Mark is leaning in the passenger window, telling Jack what happened, giving a stretched out, exaggerated version of events.

'We go for a smoke, lads?' Mark asks while rubbing his hands.

Jack looks at Kev.

'I'm going home. I'm wrecked,' Kev says.

'You want a lift, Jack?'

'No, I'm grand with Kev, cheers Mark.'

'Fuck yis, ya saps. Go off and ride each other if you like.'

Mark gets no reply and sniffs the air around him.

'See ya tomorrow, Kev.'

'Yeah Mark, tomorrow.'

Mark spits on the ground and turns towards his car. Kev speeds out of the estate. He's in too high a gear for the windy roads. Jack looks frightened. Kev hasn't spoken since he left the driveway.

'You up for a smoke, Jack? Sorry, I never asked.'

'Course man, whatever you're doing.'

There is no traffic and Kev uses his full beamers.

'Maybe you should slow down, Kev,' Jack says, holding onto his seat. 'You seem a little tense.'

'That prick.'

'I know man, he's full of it. I think he's back on the bag.'

'No excuse.'

They arrive at Viewpoint with only one other car there, parked at the far end of the car park, its lights off, but with a faint glow of something being smoked. Below, Dublin is bathed in orange. Every time they're here, Jack tries to position himself, to find his house or street among the jumble of lights. He gets excited and likes to cross the road to the fields and sit on the low wall. Kev never leaves the car except to piss. He rolls a joint while listening to the radio: soft jazz, movie soundtracks and sean-nós songs. He takes his time, mixing the weed and tobacco, flipping the joint carefully, expertly. He opens the sun-roof and both the passenger and driver's windows. A cool breeze enters, which wakes and stuns him. Kev picks up his phone and goes to his drafts folder. He rereads the message he's been writing all night. As if he can smell the weed, Jack comes back in, panting.

'You wouldn't wanna walk too far out there, man. I'm telling you, dark as fuck,' Jacks says.

'Things turn very quickly, that's all I know.'

'You could be anywhere.'

'Yeah.'

'You feelin' better?'

The word better hits Kev and he looks at Jack, exhales upwards and passes him the joint.

'Yeah man, thanks for asking. I'm working on a message for this lad in Donegal.'

'The little skinny prick?'

Kev nods. 'I wrote it earlier and am thinking of posting it, listen: *If you are found guilty of this barbaric crime you should spend the rest of your life in a grey claustrophobic cell reflecting on your lack of humanity towards that poor lad. May God console that lad's family and friends and your family also because you have broken their hearts too.* What do ya think of that?'

'It's something man, it's really something. Is there any milk left? I'm all cotton mouth.'

'Yeah, here.'

Kev passes his unopened milk and Jack downs it in two gulps. The orange lights flicker and dance across the city. The other car speeds out of the car park. The night behind them is pitch black, away up towards the Old Military Road. They finish the joint in silence, no cars pass and the radio is so low as to be inaudible. When the joint is finished, Jack feels uneasy and slightly nervous. He sniffs the air and looks around him. Kev has his eyes closed and is leaning back in his seat.

'Kev?'

'Yeah?'

'What are we gonna do now?'

'I've no fucking idea, man. Not a clue.'

Autumn in Hong Kong
Naoise Dolan

Julian wasn't bothered coming out to meet me after work, so I often ended up going straight to his apartment in Mid-Levels at about 9pm. I told him I found this awkward and degrading. Actually I liked taking the outdoor escalator up. I got on at Queen's Road and passed over hawker stalls on Stanley Street, then the signs—Game & Fun, Happy Massage, King Tailor—and dingy high-rises and enormous windows on Wellington Street. Then came fishy air wafting up from Central Street Market and the old police station stacked with thick white bricks like pencil erasers. The whole thing took twenty minutes. When I reached Julian's building, I got a visitor card from the lobby and went up to the fiftieth floor.

Inside, his place looked like a showroom, the sort that had been unconvincingly scattered with items that anyone could have owned. His most obviously personal possession was a large grey MacBook Pro. Most days I watched Netflix on it while he ordered something on the phone. When the buzzer rang, he jumped up like a cat upon contact with a hose.

'Food's here,' I'd say. He rarely responded.

I did the washing up. I liked using the giant sink and the dishwasher, though again, I didn't tell him so. Then he'd pour us wine and we'd talk in the sitting room. The mantlepiece was bare apart from an empty silver picture frame and cream candles that had never been lit. By the window, there was a long brown corner sofa. I'd take my shoes off and lie on it with my feet on the armrest, crossing one leg over the other and alternating them during gaps in the conversation. Julian took the wingback armchair opposite me. The first time I stayed in the guest room was in mid-August when the tropical storm Dianmu hit. After that, he always offered to put me up when midnight approached. Depending on my energy, I accepted or left to get the green minibus back home—the covered escalator only went in one direction, down for morning rush hour or up for the rest of the day.

That was the shape of it, but it didn't have a name, apart from hanging out, catching up or popping in for a chat, which was, to be fair, the content of what we were doing. He was so stretched for time that I found it at least semi-plausible that he just preferred to meet in his apartment for convenience. Once I asked him whether bankers had time for relationships.

'Usually not at the junior levels,' he said. 'A lot of them just pay for it.'

The way he said 'it' made me uneasy, but there wasn't any point in taking things up with Banker Julian. He was too self-assured to notice when I criticised him. He registered that I'd said something, then continued a parallel conversation.

When he paid for my takeaway, or when he took me to a restaurant, and when in return I spent time with him, I wondered if he saw himself as paying for a milder 'it'. I liked the idea—my company being worth money. No one else accorded it that value. We sat in high-ceilinged rooms and he said Hang Seng was down and the Shenzhen Composite was up and the Shanghai Composite was flat. It wasn't like normal friendships, where I worried about whether the other person still liked me. He liked hearing himself think aloud and I reasoned that I was profiting from it, that you never knew when you'd need facts so it was best to collect as many as you could.

When I was a few glasses into the bottle, I told him he was attractive. I said it exactly like that—'I find you attractive'—to avoid seeming earnest.

'You're quite attractive, too,' he said.

'I guess that's why we get along.'

'Could be.'

In some moods he told me about markets. In others he'd fire questions at me, only attending to my answers to the extent that they could help him think of follow-up enquiries. Even when I'd already said something, he wanted to hear it again—the two brothers, the brown terraced house in one of Dublin's drearier suburbs, that I'd taken a year out after school to save up for college. That we got all our groceries from Tesco before Lidl and Aldi opened, and from Lidl and Aldi after Lidl and Aldi opened. That after 2008 I shared my room with my brother Tom so we could rent the other one out to a student. That none of this made us poor and was in fact pretty much what had happened to Ireland as a whole due in no small part to the actions of banks like his. (I did not choose to verbalise all these thoughts.)

He wanted to know whether my accent was posh where I came from. I'd never met an English person who didn't wonder about that. Most of them wouldn't ask directly—and he didn't, he just asked what 'kind' of a Dublin accent I had—but they found some way to convey their curiosity. I told him it was a normal Dublin accent. He asked what that meant. I didn't know enough about British accents to make a comparison.

'Well,' he said, 'what does the posh Dublin accent sound like?'

I tried to do one and he said it sounded American.

He'd ask what I proposed to do with myself when the time came to stop teaching English as a foreign language and get a real job. He was almost paternally adamant that I shouldn't waste my degree on lowly employers, and even paid convincing lip service to not thinking less of me for not having gone to Oxford. But when it came to which jobs he did consider good enough for me, he was vague. Law was glorified clerking. Consulting was flying to the middle of nowhere so you could piss around with PowerPoint. Accountancy was boring and didn't pay well. And banking, in some nebulous way, wouldn't suit me.

'Why not?' I said. 'I hope you don't think I'm too nice. I'm awful.'

'Good. But you need more than that. You need to fit into the culture.'

'That's what I said.'

'The culture isn't just about being "awful". There are other things.'

'Like?'

'It wouldn't be a good fit for you.'

I liked when he rolled his shirtsleeves up. He had big square wrists and jutting elbows. Sometimes I worried he could tell how often I thought about his arms. He was always calling me a freak for other, much less strange things, so I couldn't own up to it.

On Fridays he always had something work-related, and on weekends he was usually abroad. I kept Mondays, Tuesdays and Wednesdays free just in case, but mostly Thursday was the only day he could see me. Really we didn't know each other at all, or have much of a routine going. I thought of something as a common occurrence between us if it had happened twice or three times. We'd been friends for about two months, and in total I'd spent perhaps thirty hours in his company—little more than a day. But I was in the habit of thinking he was a habit.

'Thanks for your time,' he said when I left. I wasn't sure if he put it formally to give himself an ironic get-out clause like I did, or if he how stiff he sounded. 'I'll text you.' He seemed to think only a man could initiate a conversation. Worse still, his saying it meant I couldn't send him one first. It would look like I'd despaired of his getting in contact and was only doing it myself as a last resort.

I explained to the class that there were two ways to say the 'th' sound. The one at the start of 'think' and at the end of 'tooth' was the voiceless dental fricative. If you held your hand in front of your mouth, you could feel a puff of breath escaping as you said it. By contrast, the one at the start of 'that', 'these' and 'those' was the voiced dental fricative. Your tongue blocked the air when you made the sound.

As a Dubliner, I had gone twenty-two years without knowingly pronouncing either phoneme. If anyone had thought there was anything wrong with my English, they'd kept it to themselves. Now I had to practise dental fricatives, voiced and un-, so the kids could copy me.

'You stick your tongue between your teeth,' I said. 'And then you breathe out.' That was what the teacher's guide told me to say, but I tried it myself and produced a sound unlike anything I had ever heard from an English speaker, or indeed from any other vertebrate in the animal kingdom. I'd have to ask Julian to show me how to do it later.

At the end of September, he took me out with some of his friends. They weren't from his bank—he kept work and non-work people separate. But like virtually everyone he spent time with, they were British and worked in finance. You could tell they were posh by how difficult it was to make out whether they were saying 'yeah' or 'year', and by how slowly they talked. They never mumbled or hesitated. If they didn't have the next word ready, they paused until it came to them.

We met at a bar in a boutique hotel on Wyndham Street. The men were in suits, navy or charcoal grey, while the few women present wore shift dresses of indeterminate cut and unassailable office-appropriateness.

'What do you do?' one of them asked. The skin around his eyes looked ten years older than the rest of him.

'I'm an English teacher.'

He seemed to find this frightfully bohemian. 'That's gutsy. It takes balls to come out and do something like that. Especially here.'

Julian had said something similar when we had that conversation. Briefly, I wondered if he was actually as interesting as I found him or if he was just the first banker I'd happened to meet.

'Brave?' said another. 'I don't know about that. What's gonna happen? Will the building explode if she forgets to show up one day?'

'I'd take a lot more sick leave if I could make that happen,' I said.

They acted like this was the pinnacle of wit. Had Julian asked them to be nice to me?

He said very little to me all evening. I understood why, but it irked me—though not for the reason he would have guessed—to watch him conversing with one of the other women. I knew if I mentioned later that maybe he should pay me attention when I was his guest, he'd chalk it up to jealousy. It wasn't that. It was just that the people beside me were boring and I wanted to talk to him instead. At first it was hard to hear what he and the woman were saying, but an adjacent conversation quietened down and it emerged they were discussing the Hinkley Point nuclear project in the UK.

'It's low-carbon,' she said, 'and we can't keep relying on imported energy.'

'It's a lot of money when you compare it to electricity,' said Julian.

'But the market's depressed right now,' she said. 'You need to look at where prices will go over the next few decades.'

I wanted to keep following their exchange, but one of the men on the other side turned to me. 'Do you like teaching?' he said.

'No. I can't stand children.'

'You don't like kids?' He waved over at Julian. 'Mate, this girl is ice cold.'

'That's why we're friends,' Julian said. I agreed with him there.

I didn't often see my flatmates. On an average day, we shared little more than hellos and goodnights.

There were three of us. I'd booked the room on AirBnB until I could save up a deposit on something more permanent, but the others lived there long-term. Emily was the oldest and the most proactive. At twenty-eight, she'd been in Hong Kong a few years. Freya was around my age and her chief hobby was complaining about her job. She changed into her pyjamas the minute she got in the door and had four sets of house slippers: bathroom, kitchen, bedroom, other.

Emily always had something to say when I came in. 'Could you close the fridge more quietly?' was this evening's criticism.

'Sorry,' I said. I didn't see how you could make noise shutting a refrigerator, but it was best to go along with it.

'And eat those grapes soon. They're going off.'

That was what she said when she wanted to take something of mine without having to ask. I wasn't in the mood to humour her, so I said, 'Sure, will do.'

The fact that I started work at ten and not nine was a source of resentment. If I came back late, the assembled salaried rolled their eyes.

'Guess you don't have to be up early tomorrow,' Freya would say.

'Or get any ironing done,' Emily added. 'No shirts for you.'

I could have pointed out that because they came in to work at nine they got to leave at six, but it wasn't worth it. I was sharing four hundred and fifty square feet with two people I'd never have otherwise chosen to spend time with. I let things slide.

My lack of a 9-to-6 card also meant I had no right to use the flat during peak hours. If I tried to shower in the morning or cook dinner when I got home at 8.30pm, they said I could do it some other time while they were stuck at work. The noise of them getting ready woke me up—spoons clanging on bowls, taps protesting on being asked to produce water—but I couldn't brush my teeth until the bathroom was free. I lay there and ran my tongue over the night's accumulated plaque on my teeth. We often got cockroaches. I swore I could hear them in the dark, though I knew scientifically that this couldn't be true.

All this to say that spending the night at Julian's became ever more appealing. His guest bedroom was an ensuite and he had a washer and dryer that he never used. (Time, he said, is money. It takes me sixty minutes to do laundry myself, versus sixty Hong Kong dollars or six pounds to get someone else to do it, and an hour of my time is worth a lot more than that.) As soon as I woke up, I bustled around making myself clean. He'd left for work by the time I got out of the shower.

My presence was probably more of an imposition than he made out. But I thought it was fine as long as I remembered it was a favour and he was within his rights to make me leave any night he didn't want me there. He gave me a key, which I stressed wasn't necessary but which I supposed made things easier for him because he didn't have to be there to let me in. To make myself useful, I started cooking for him.

'What's this?' he'd say when he got home at night. I'd be frying tofu or baking vegetable dumplings. His kitchen was well-equipped in terms of fixed appliances but had next to no pans or crockery, so I was limited in what I could do.

'Surprise,' I'd say.

'Jesus. Gordon Ramsay turns herbivore.'

He was a better amateur chef than I, but he liked seeing me busy while he collapsed on the couch. Anyway, the food was decent—it's hard to mess up the kind of things I made—and I was comfortable knowing I'd contributed something.

'How did I end up taking you on?' he said once while I was doing the dishes.

'I think you're familiar with the history of it.'

'I know the sequence of how it happened, but I have no idea why it did.'

'You don't sound happy about it. Maybe I should fuck off.'

'Maybe you should.'

'I'm sure you've got banking to do or whatever. Is that what you're doing right now?'

He closed his laptop. 'Just checking emails. It's morning in New York.'

'It's always the morning somewhere.'

'And we're bound to have an office there, wherever it is. Funnily enough, they've all got those big world clocks on their desktops, but no-one thinks to check what time it is in Hong Kong.'

'Do you check what time it is for them when you're about to send an email?'

'Of course not. It's their job to be awake.'

I offered to clean his apartment, too, but he had someone who came to do that—I never saw her, perhaps by design—and anyway, he said I'd miss things. He didn't even like me wiping the stovetop after I was done. I left too much soap behind, he said. The inside of his bedroom was still a mystery to me, but I imagined everything folded and stored in optimised locations for speedy access.

After about three months, I was spending a few nights a week at his apartment. My bed had a soft twill houndstooth throw that I thought about asking if I could take home, but I decided I preferred having it in his place than in mine. On the wall in my room there were three black-and-white pictures of London. This small effort was the strongest evidence of personalisation I'd found in the whole apartment. One day at work I printed out an image of Dublin and asked him if I could put it in the empty frame on the mantlepiece. 'Be my guest,' he said. He often came back after I'd gone to sleep. He told me I was welcome to stay over while he was travelling for work, but I tried not to. The temptation to look around his room would have been overwhelming.

'We don't see much of you lately,' said Emily one day.

'There's more space for the two of you that way,' I said.

'Yeah, but maybe we should do something.'

'We physically can't all be here at once. It's claustrophobic.'

'Let's hang out somewhere else. We used to go for drinks all the time.'

It hadn't been 'all the time', but I thought it best to file that under 'battles not picked'.

'Sure,' I said. 'When are you free?'

'How's tomorrow?'

Julian was coming back from Singapore then. We'd planned to get pita flatbreads at a vegetarian restaurant in Sheung Wan. 'Sorry, I can't.'

'What are you doing?'

'Dinner with a friend.'

'Is this the same friend you stay over with all the time?'

'I mean, I don't have that many friends.'

Whenever Emily was annoyed, she started tidying up minor things as if she hoped I'd notice how good she was for not asking me to help. Right now she was fluffing up the couch cushions and picking off tiny hairs.

'It's weird living with someone who treats you like a stranger,' she said. 'I'm not asking for us to be best friends, but please be civil with us.'

'"Us"? Does Freya feel that way, too?'

'Yeah. You've dropped us for some guy and you won't even tell us about him.'

'I'm not with him.'

'Then why are you always at his place?'

'He's just a friend. We like spending time together.'

'Okay, whatever. I'm just saying it's selfish to ditch us because you've found someone else to hang out with.'

Selfish. I'd heard that one before. But it was unfair coming from someone I was doing a massive favour. She got more shower, kitchen and laundry time than she was paying for because I was washing and feeding myself elsewhere. If she wanted to complain that I was never there, then accuse me of taking up too much space whenever I did make an appearance, then it was no wonder I preferred Julian.

The next evening, I narrated the argument to Julian. He nodded and of-coursed in all the right places. 'She sounds like a bitch,' he said.

I flinched at that word but didn't pick him up on it. 'Have you ever had flatmates?' I said.

'Yes, of course, at Oxford, and when I was starting out in London. Most of them were fine. One guy was an absolute nutter. This was in my final year of uni. He was doing his dissertation on some existential quandary. You'd hear him pacing around all night muttering about it. And he never ate solid food—he put everything into this big fucking blender. Lived on smoothies. I think he got the best first in his year.'

'So having your own place is better?'

'Substantially better.'

Neither of us pointed out that he didn't live alone anymore. We finished the wine and he went to get another bottle. My jeans had a hole on the inseam near the top of my thigh. I picked at it, then jerked my hand away when I heard him returning.

'You never tell me anything about yourself,' I said. 'What was your last girlfriend like?'

He twirled his glass. 'She was fine. I was with her for about a year but then she got sent back to London.'

'How long ago was that?'

'We broke up a few months ago.'

'Any regrets?'

'No, none at all. I don't tend to look back.'

We drank our wine and enjoyed each other's silence. His cushions, I noticed, were beautiful: pebble corduroy, gold and ivory sateen. I picked one up and hugged it to my chest.

'That thing you said before about wanting to be a history teacher,' I said, 'were you really just bullshitting me?'

'Completely. I'm glad other people do it, but for my part I'd rather hang on to the dim prospect of owning a house.'

'What if that wasn't a factor? What if you could own a house no matter what you did?'

'I've never thought about that because it's certainly not happening in our lifetimes. Possibly I'd have stayed at Oxford and done more history. But there's no point dwelling on it. I have every respect for people who follow their passions, but I prefer stability.'

I wondered if he meant his comment to have point.

'It could be worse,' I said. 'You could have no passions and also no stability.'

'To be clear, Ava: in your estimation, we're both dead behind the eyes but at least I can pay rent?'

'Yeah, pretty much.'

'We really are the denizens of a new belle époch, aren't we.'

'Arsehole bankers and deadbeats.'

'Not all bankers are arseholes.'

'Yeah, just you.'

'Just me.'

'I like talking to you,' I said—quite stupidly, I realised while saying it. 'It makes me feel solid, like someone can confirm I'm real.'

'Good.'

'Do you like having me here?'

'Yes,' he said. 'You're good company. If I've got this space and I like sharing it with you, there's no reason not to.'

I frowned. 'You mean it just happens to suit you, having me here.'

'I wouldn't say it "suits" me. You're making me sound calculating. I'm saying it makes sense to ask you over, and that's why I do it.'

'If it stopped making sense, would you stop asking me over?'

'You mean would I do something that didn't make sense to me? Well, no.'

I leaned over to refill my glass. Our legs touched.

'Here, let me get it,' he said, and he hovered close to me as he poured it.

I waited. Finally he said, 'Do you mind if...?'

We kissed for a while. Then he led me to his room. He ran the errands—pulled down the blinds, dimmed the lights, shoved everything off the bed—while I took off my necklace, dropping it slowly on the nightstand so the steel wouldn't rattle against the wood. Conscious that he was watching me, I tried not to appear curious about his possessions.

My hair got in the way. Julian caught some of it in his mouth and then it got jammed in my zip at the back and he said: 'I hope this doesn't end in A&E.' 'Really,' I said, 'because I hope it does.' 'You say the weirdest fucking things,' he said. I liked that. It made me feel like a sphinx—lion-limbed, limestone-faced, ready to riddle him something.

Caution, Please

Do not look directly into the projector beam
or confront your dreams, not ever ever ever
Not everyone you know can see the colour blue
and this is problematic when it comes to self-analysis
Our own advice is to keep clear of others, though some—
despite warning signs—will always ignore advice
But if you hear one thing only then let it be Do Not Touch
at least, Handle With Care—and if the label says Fragile
and you're left wondering how easy it is for some object to break,
some secret to be shared and destroyed, some chance opportunity
or other to be squandered—And if you still need the scrutiny then
wear protective clothing and hold on, hold tight, hold out,
and do not lift manually, and please, with your notebook
and keys—Please do not operate without guards in place—
Make it safe, make it safe—My needs are unknown,
my hopes are unmet, I ask only for authorised personnel
And that sign does indeed read Heavy Plant Crossing
And now remember, to go and wash your hands, I'm all yours

M.W. Bewick

Bland God: Notes on Mark Zuckerberg
Roisin Kiberd

Sometimes at night, when I can't sleep, I think, shit, we are colder than they are.
The adversary.
—Philip K. Dick, *A Scanner Darkly*

A year ago, in a charity shop on Capel Street, I found an expensive hoodie. Not expensive in terms of its current price—the Goodwill Thrift Shop was asking for €4—but its original one. The hoodie bore no outward sign of branding, but its design was strategically luxurious, sewn from the softest cotton and dyed to a muted, achromatic grey. It had been designed to include the kind of thoughtful details you only notice on second glance, when you realise the person wearing it is a little wealthier than they first appeared.

Second-hand shopping is unpredictable. For every miracle find—that ludicrous, beautiful thing which has found its way to the charity shop by chance—there's the monkey's paw, the dybbuk box, or the mysterious, probably-cursed item donated gladly by its former owner. There are broken electronics, outwardly-fine appliances which won't switch on when you bring them home. There are shoes in your size, which will still pinch and leave your ankles blistered.

I might have laughed once at the idea of a designer hoodie, but touching its fabric I felt myself converted. I pulled the zipper, looked inside to read the label, and noticed spidery text across the back, on the inside lining. *Making the world more open and connected.*

It was a hoodie given to Facebook employees, likely donated to the shop by someone who had recently left the company. If walking around wearing

Facebook's mission statement was a squeamish thought, then walking around wearing it secretly, printed on the inside my clothes, made me feel even more uncomfortable. I put the hoodie back on the rail and moved on.

Late last year, a group of writers took Zuckerbergian semiotics—including the hoodies he wears for his public appearances—as the subject of a collection of essays. Volume One of *The California Review of Images and Mark Zuckerberg* was published in November 2017, edited by Tim Hwang, a fellow at NY research institute Data and Society whose CV also includes positions with the Electronic Frontier Foundation and Creative Commons, a journal of essays on the cartoon *Adventure Time*, and 2015's Kickstarter-funded *The Container Guide*, a field guide for spotting corporate shipping containers.

Each essay in *The California Review of Images and Mark Zuckerberg* addresses an image posted to Mark Zuckerberg's Facebook timeline, one pre-approved by the Facebook founder and his team before being published to his 101,047,691 followers. Zuckerberg's carefully stage-managed presence runs through these essays as a common thread, prompting questions about mediation and identity —both Zuckerberg's, and our own.

Mark Zuckerberg's identity is directly linked to that of every Facebook user, because Facebook, his product, is an identity machine. The site feeds on our identities and all the 'monetizable' ad data they generate, even as it encourages us to manufacture new ones. More than any form of interactive media before it, Facebook foregrounds the 'personal brand', a public-facing online self.

Amid the noise, the emotional and visual clutter of the Facebook experience, Mark Zuckerberg is notable for his absence. While the founder has made occasional public appearances over the years, and routinely publishes Facebook posts addressing his followers, his public image is subdued, carefully curated, and so ordinary as to be inscrutable.

One essay, 'Mark Zuckerberg's Significant Insignificance' by Dilara O'Neil, addresses this theme, using a 2013 Zuckerberg profile photo as its starting point: 'Here is Mark Zuckerberg, our current tech dude of the moment who presents himself neither as a businessman or a thinker, but as a Normal Guy.'

The image, a little grainy, and likely taken on a now-outdated phone, features the Facebook founder standing against a landscape which might be the surface of a distant planet. Blank, wide-eyed Zuckerberg poses before blank and rolling hills, under the kind of sky artists in Hollywood were once paid to paint as background scenery. His appearance could be called 'youthful', but Zuckerberg has not noticeably aged in the last ten years. He appears, then, the same as he always has.

This picture might be a selfie. It might have originally included people who were cropped out. It might also be revealing, but it's not: Zuckerberg's expression is placid, impenetrable, generic like a child's drawing of a human face. O'Neil looks for meaning in the landscape instead, casting Zuckerberg as its conqueror:

> Facebook is not just a website like the ones that came before, which stayed stagnant until consumers grew bored and moved on. With its constant updates and algorithmic strategies to infiltrate user's information, it unleashes onto untouched land and like nature, will continually evolve.

Mark Zuckerberg is defined by the community—the product—he has built. O'Neil compares Zuckerberg to 'MySpace Tom'; everyone's friend, the guiding figure who adds you on arrival on MySpace and leads you through the social media underworld. Certainly there are similarities; you get the sense that Zuckerberg would love to be everybody's friend, if only he could make himself more likeable.

But Zuckerberg is not likeable. He has middling-to-negative portrayals of himself to contend with: Kate Losse's memoir of working at Facebook in its early days, *The Boy Kings*, portrays him as young, guileless, and more than little bit entitled, while David Fincher's film biopic *The Social Network* casts him as inept, bordering on sociopathic. In interviews, Zuckerberg comes across as clear-eyed but lacking in self-awareness; another essay, Mél Hogan's 'Sweaty Zuckerberg and Cool Computing', takes as its subject a video rather than a picture, discussing a somewhat notorious interview from 2010. At the Wall Street Journal's D8, an 'executive conference' promising 'straight-up, unvarnished conversations with the most influential figures in technology', a twenty-six-year-old Zuckerberg is grilled by journalist Kara Swisher. Visibly sweating when asked about Facebook's privacy settings, he refuses to take his hoodie off, displaying the awkwardness which has come to define his public persona.

Beyond the images discussed in these essays, what do we know about Mark Zuckerberg, the fifth-wealthiest person in the world? What does he stand for, apart from the cause of Facebook itself? This question might connect to a larger one: what does Facebook itself stand for? The hoodie's slogan, 'Making the world more open and connected', has since been discarded as the company motto; in 2017 Facebook announced a new and equally innocuous intention to 'Give people the power to build community and bring the world closer together'.

The world was 'open' before Facebook, a time when communities existed just fine. It could even be argued, especially in light of the 2016 US election and its fallout, that services like Facebook actively narrow our perspectives on the world by only showing us what we want to see, reinforcing the effects of the internet's 'filter bubble', named by Eli Pariser in his 2011 book of the same name. In 'Zuckerberg and the Imaginary Cosmopolitan', Ethan Zuckerman argues that Facebook's effects are, in fact, often the direct opposite of an expanded worldview:

> Facebook welcomes us into its service by asking us about our past—our place of birth, our elementary and high schools, our colleges and jobs. For the 50% of Americans who live within 18 miles of their mothers, Facebook is more tool that deeply anchors us into our communities than connects us to distant ones.

Silicon Valley's Big Five (Google, Apple, Facebook, Amazon, Microsoft) and their 'disruptive' heirs (Uber, AirBnB and others) share a common response when faced with criticism. If a violent, bigoted or otherwise objectionable video appears on YouTube, or a hate group forms on Facebook, or if your Uber driver tries to rape you, it is never the fault of the company. This is because the company does not 'employ' this driver, or 'endorse' any of the content its users create. They may not even be aware of it, because the 'platform' is too big. This system acts against its workers too: an Uber driver does not have the rights of an employee, because they are not technically an employee at all. Lacking the grassroots values of early internet culture (where users were relied on to police themselves, but retained some right to ownership of their content in return), 'platform capitalism' blames the user when anything goes wrong, mocking them for being misguided enough to trust the service in the first place.

The modern tech giant is more 'platform' than company; it is a blank, hungry canvas which swallows up and monetizes its users. Facebook has long exemplified this approach: while Facebook's reps pressure media outlets into paying for more 'native advertising', the company denies that it is a media company itself.

Zuckerberg embodies this same absent quality, a resplendent blankness paired with power too prodigious to define. As instigator of an 'open and connected' world, little is known about his private life. We know that he dropped out of

Harvard, where he took a joint-major in computer science and, interestingly, psychology. We know he has a wife, Priscilla, and two daughters named August and Max. We know he jogs regularly, because he posts photos of himself jogging on his Facebook page. We know that he worries about surveillance, because he covers the camera on his laptop with a sticker (it appears in the background of a 2016 photo posted to celebrate the acquisition of Instagram, discussed in the essay 'Consequences of the Frame' by Melissa Lo).

We know that Zuckerberg owns a 700-acre estate on the Hawaiian island of Kauai and has built a wall around it, one mile long and six feet high. We know he has filed lawsuits against hundreds of Hawaiians in order to settle disputes over land. We also know that Zuckerberg enjoys hunting his own meat, because he announced in 2011 that his new year's resolution was to eat only what he hunted. Pictures followed, soon after, of Zuckerberg grilling shanks of beef on a barbecue and holding a dead chicken by its legs. Zuckerberg, apparently, is so fond of meat that for his birthday his employees gifted him a meat-shaped cake. In 2012, he announced that his hunting challenge was over, via a 'connected steak' app called iGrill.

We also know—or, at least, I know, and believe that it will eventually be universally acknowledged—that Mark Zuckerberg is the progenitor of normcore. Normcore, the millennial fashion trend, is what it sounds like: a celebration of mundanity in all its wearable forms. It involves ill-fitting denim, clumpy orthopaedic trainers, and oversized machine-worn cotton sweatshirts with ill-chosen fonts and dodgy graphics. First identified in 2012 by trend-forecasting group K-Hole, in their paper *Youth Mode: A Report on Freedom*, normcore involves wearing clothing so cartoonishly basic as to resemble a character from *Seinfeld*, or from Microsoft's 90s IRC client 'Comic Chat'.

Normcore is the look of an ordinary, gormless, apparently decent person— someone so generic as to not show up on CCTV. Normcore is at least in part a response to criticism of millennials as decadent, self-involved and lazy, because no one whose style is this utilitarian and bland could possibly be a bad person.

Zuckerberg's style is normcore at its purest: he wears fleeces, hoodies, dad jeans and Adidas sandals, christened the 'fuck-you flip-flops' in *The Social Network*. His apparently unintentional personal brand slots into an emerging archetype, that of the self-neglecting, socially inept Silicon Valley wunderkind. The idea is to dress like a slob, because you have no one to impress except other (invariably young, white, male) coders, who pride themselves on their ability to sit in darkened rooms for days on end typing and drinking Monster Energy.

Mark Zuckerberg spent the better part of his first decade in the public eye wearing those same 'fuck-you flip-flops', and managed to get away with it without attracting too much scrutiny. His normality placed him beyond surveillance: he dresses in the same grey t-shirt and Facebook company hoodie every day, though in recent years the sandals have been replaced with trainers.

K-Hole describe normcore as 'Youth Mode', the infinite newness of a world where history has been flattened by capitalism and the internet; where everything has been made 'open and connected' and has already been seen. Facebook, as a service, enacts a similar effect: the user is fixed in eternal distraction, present and past joined together on an ever-scrolling timeline which appears to stretch back, beyond the year you first joined Facebook, following its users into the womb. Facebook's algorithmic timeline means you digest 'news' and 'updates' on a timeline but not in chronological order; instead, Facebook calculates what you are most likely to want to see, and shows you this first.

'Fake news' breeds in these echo chambers, where stories too outlandish for the mainstream spring up again and again. They never fall down the Timeline, and they have no sell-by date, because they never occured in the first place. Confused, we return to Facebook looking for answers, scrolling and scrolling without satisfaction. Facebook lulls us into dependence on the very service which keeps us in the dark.

With Facebook facing scrutiny for its influence over politics, truth-telling and human behaviour in general, the blankness of Mark Zuckerberg becomes a model of millennial blamelessness. Like historical normcore (and tech) icons Steve Jobs and Bill Gates, Zuckerberg appears visionary, but not so idealistic as to hold political opinions anyone could disagree with. As a celebrity he tolerates a degree of surveillance, but his genius is that he is so fundamentally bland and uninteresting that we pay very little attention.

As of 2017's third quarter, Facebook had 2.07 billion users, easily enough to form a continent. In July last year, Facebook even started to make their virtual 'community' a physical reality, announcing plans to develop a 1500-unit social housing scheme in Silicon Valley. In his book Move Fast and Break Things, Jonathan Taplin identifies user 'interactions' as work performed on behalf of Facebook HQ, calculating an average 39,757 years of time spent on the network in a single day. He adds, 'That's almost fifteen million years of free labor per year. Karl Marx would have been totally mystified.' (This estimate is now outdated, based on figures from 2014, when the network had only 1.23 billion users).

Few of the writers in the *California Review of Images and Mark Zuckerberg* name Zuckerberg as Facebook's body politic, a boy king guarding the networks and collective memory of billions. But this medieval implication is what the collection seems to grasp at as a whole, by deeming pictures of Mark Zuckerberg worthy of study. Only 'Sweaty Zuckerberg and Cool Computing' speaks directly to the theme, likening Zuckerberg's on-stage sweat during an interview to a data leak, or to the mechanically-cooled servers which host Facebook's data in centres around the world. Hogan also discusses Zuckerberg's hoodie, which, like the one I found on Capel Street, conceals Facebook's mission statement in its lining:

> It's lost on nobody that this mission statement about openness is intentionally hidden from view, or that Zuckerberg is trying to hide his discomfort inside that hoodie. In fact, hoodies are wearable hiding places by design.

In 2010, in an interview conducted with David Kirkpatrick for his book *The Facebook Effect*, Zuckerberg made perhaps his most infamous public statement, saying 'Having two identities for yourself is an example of a lack of integrity'. This occurred shortly before the company rolled out its Timeline feature, which streamlines individual user activity into a single scrolling feed. The Timeline is curiously, yet satisfyingly simplistic: it presents identity as a straight line with no complications, a self forged in loyalty to Facebook, over a lifetime.

Sometimes I fantasise about interviewing Mark Zuckerberg. I would ask him the questions Facebook began asking me from the moment I first signed up. What films have you watched? What make you happy? Add your relationship status. Add a life event.

What we know of Zuckerberg himself is hardly enough to constitute a single identity. We know him purely by his luxurious blandness, his posed photographs and his lengthy, ultimately meaningless statements about 'community building'. We also know, if we read Kate Losse's *The Boy Kings*, that Zuckerberg used to work in a glass office, in the name of radical transparency, but kept a secret private meeting room in the back.

Where does the wunderkind go, when he gets older? Does he settle into public life? Does he save the world? Or does he disappear entirely?

Rumours abound that Mark Zuckerberg might one day run for US president. By touring America in 2017 and having photographers capture his visits with the ordinary people (posted regularly to Zuckerberg's Facebook page) he already appears to be moving in this direction. Li Cornfield's essay 'Fireside Chats, Tech Spectacle, and the Making of Mark Zuckerberg', brings Zuckerberg's presidential posturing full circle, comparing the 'fireside chats' staged at tech conferences to those by the originator of the trend, Franklin D. Roosevelt, who made regular radio broadcasts throughout the Great Depression and the Second World War.

Adopted by tech conferences like TechCrunch's Disrupt or SXSW, the fireside chat becomes a way to venerate powerful, fundamentally unknowable leaders while appearing to humanise them. The fireside chat is rarely revelatory, because those judged important enough to merit fireside chats are inherently protected from difficult questions. As an interviewing format, it conjures mediated intimacy, yet it takes place on a stage in front of thousands.

What Zuckerberg represents, then, is a hive of connections, a cybernetic black hole which swallows up human behaviour and regurgitates it as ad revenue. He is a seer, a keeper of memories. He pressures us to share, then ostracises those who refuse. He encourages us to watch each other, the way he watches us. In 2012 Facebook even instituted a 'snitch list', asking users to inform on friends who might be operating profiles under fake names (Salman Rushdie was targeted by the 'real-name' policy, along with a number of San Francisco-based drag queens who later took Facebook to court and won).

Writing in the *London Review of Books* about Facebook and its use of 'retargeted ads', a marketing tactic which follows individual users through physical space using geolocation on their phones, John Lancaster concludes:

> ...what this means is that even more than it is in the advertising business, Facebook is in the surveillance business. Facebook, in fact, is the biggest surveillance based enterprise in the history of mankind... that's why the impulse to growth has been so fundamental to the company, which is in many respects more like a virus than it is like a business. Grow and multiply and monetise. Why? There is no why. Because.

Neither Lancaster nor anyone writing for the *California Review of Images and Mark Zuckerberg* will go so far as to compare Mark Zuckerberg and Facebook to a Lovecraftian monster, so it falls to me to argue the case. Zuckerberg represents the familiar—we know his face, and we deal with his product every day—but also the sublime, the unfathomable, the potentially horrifying. Who can fully comprehend how well Facebook knows us, and how little we know of Facebook? In my relatively short career as a tech writer, I have personally approached Facebook for comment on a number of occasions. I've even taken part in conference panels where a representative of Facebook was expected to appear. The reps did not attend, and Facebook HQ never replied to my emails. Facebook operates as a multinational Wonka factory; limitless information goes in and nothing comes out, apart from quarterly profit reports.

Facebook's earnings come from our 'likes' and dislikes, our relationships and behaviours and connections. In this sense, Facebook is a machine which traffics in the things which make us human, and to understand its workings in full would mean seeing ourselves sold as bulk humanity. To understand in full the scope of Mark Zuckerberg's vision, his plan to mediate every moment of existence, would surely inspire bafflement or horror in the average user, or perhaps a Scanners-style explosion of the head.

One cannot understand Mark Zuckerberg by seeing him. It's necessary, instead, to see what he sees. This brings to mind the 'God View' enjoyed by many tech CEOs, the view of your users from behind a screen in the war room. In 2010, Google's CEO Eric Schmidt described Google's God View in a speech delivered at the Washington Ideas Forum: 'We don't need you to type at all. We know where you are. We know where you've been. We can more or less know what you're thinking about.' Uber, a more recent arrival in the pantheon of panoptic tech companies, agreed to submit to two decades of Federal Trade Commission audits last year after facing criticism for showing off their own God View of drivers and users on a giant screen at a party (reportedly, Uber management were also using it to spy in real time on politicians, celebrities and ex-partners).

Facebook has yet to face accusations that its employees spy on users directly, though the company has been criticised for emotional manipulation—in 2014, a team from Facebook published a study detailing how they had actively manipulated users with sad or uplifting posts, in order to study their reactions. The company also came under fire for a leaked pitch to advertisers offering the option to target users when they felt 'worthless', 'insecure', 'stressed' and 'defeated'.

It's a challenge to imagine Facebook's God View in full. Certainly it would include our physical locations, along with our web of relationships, our place in the 'community' Facebook claims to facilitate and build. But a map of what Facebook knows about us might also branch into the metaphysical; it might include our hopes, our fears and uncertainties, and the secrets which play out between ourselves and our screens. Their map would stretch into the past and future, reaching both ends of the user's mortal timeline, and beyond.

We may never know how much Facebook sees of us, but the site placates us with a miniature God View of our own, every time we log in. Facebook's UX is an overview of our lives: along the left hand side are our groups and events, the centre is a news feed, and the right hand column is a buffet of our friendships. Facebook imparts its dehumanisation of its users to its users in turn, encouraging us to view our social life as a game of alerts and dialogue boxes. Facebook breeds solipsism in the user. Everything is arranged for you to 'like' and acknowledge and comment on: everything is happening to you. You can pick up conversations with people and drop them again in seconds. You will never see yourself on a list, as part of someone else's menu: you will always be the centre of your own world.

Bearing in mind his God View over 2.07 billion people, perhaps it is useful to think of Mark Zuckerberg himself as a kind of god. Certainly there are those who already treat him this way; each of Zuckerberg's Facebook pictures, including those discussed in the *California Review of Images and Mark Zuckerberg*, attract thousands of adoring comments. The team of twelve employees who manage his public profile have likely filtered out all the negative ones. Those which remain are so adoring and supplicant and effusive that they make for uncomfortable reading. In one picture, taken during his much-publicised 2017 tour of America, Zuckerberg eats pie a la mode alongside truckers at a diner in Iowa. A comment, one of 310 posted below, reads 'Mark Zuckerberg you are such a down to earth & amazing person. That explains why God blessed you with so many things. Please stop by at North Platte, Nebraska. Take care.'

To 'see' Facebook one must register for an account, and eventually be owned in some small way by the service. For every image posted, or comment made on Facebook, the service claims you for itself. This kind of surveillance can't be negotiated in pieces; you're either in completely, or you're out.

What will happen when Facebook runs out of new users to convert? What will happen when Facebook's filter bubble begins to work against itself, when —accustomed to copying each other and 'liking' the same things as the rest— we stop demonstrating the unique behaviours and interests which once made us useful as ad data? What about when we have nothing to offer, when we— like Zuckerberg—become so bland, so beaten down by peer pressure, as to be 'normcore' and beyond surveillance?

Is Zuckerberg himself an augury of this future? Is he a benevolent god, a genius, or a warning? Is he Moby-Dick, a sprawling white void of American power? ('Is it that by its indefiniteness', Melville asks, 'it shadows forth the heartless voids and immensities of the universe, and thus stabs us from behind with the thought of annihilation… a dumb blankness, full of meaning, in a wide landscape of snows…?'). Might it be that Zuckerberg is not white, but 'cosmic latte', the distilled hue of the universe?

It's painful to think of an ordinary young man having so much power, and money, and information. Easier to think of him as a robot, a savant, or a meat-hunting superhero. Easier to conceive of Mark Zuckerberg as a machine.

To build a relationship with someone online is to draw them into a web of self-fashioning, and to consent to mutual surveillance. With Facebook, this has happened in reverse: Facebook has seduced us, and encouraged us rebuild ourselves. We've been welcomed into a placid blue-and-white world where someone is silently watching, organising our lives, making us feel like we deserve their attentions. It is as though Mark Zuckerberg loves us, more than anyone else ever will.

Perhaps this is why we tolerate the figure of Mark Zuckerberg. He will always be more boring than we are. He makes us feel like we are worthy of surveillance.

We accept the friendship of MySpace Tom, the all-seeing eyes of Zuckerberg, and the promise that Elon Musk will someday find a home for us on Mars. We sell our lives to Google, because in return they make life easier by breaking it into actions and data segments. There are those among us who bask in surveillance, who dream of an NSA agent out there watching, checking in on us from time to time.

A passage in *The Boy Kings* comes to mind here, written not about Zuckerberg himself, but about a video chat conversation between the author and someone she cared about. On screen the feelings are simpler, easier to access, and more readily extreme. It becomes difficult to separate human from machine, mediation from emotion, selfishness from love:

> I think we could tell him we love him because he was so far away, and to love him is to love the technology that allows us to speak to him anyway, safely, intimately, from afar. Our technology, ourselves: For us, at the heart of this revolution, they were increasingly the same.

Philosophy of a Fly

It is the season of falling.
Rust creeps, turns leaves
to marmalade paper and branches, stripped mostly bare by birds,
drop their fat bellied fruit.
That pulpy mound of damson bulbs
heaves with maggots
and, for some,
it is home.
I like to watch the world crawl
long and slow—
pay attention, do all things
with intent: feed, pupate, manifest
and expire. You see death
as stillness, stopping.
Perhaps
it is the lack of a compound eye,
or living always for the next thing,
a mad parade
of ticking clocks and calendars.
But death, too, has a pulse—
the rhythm of a rotting plum
as it bleeds sweetly into the grass
and stains the blades
having ripened
when no one was watching,
least of all you.

Seanín Hughes

Fist at Full Mast

Here you are again
hammering the door, begging ghosts
to let you in—
you, a missile
the room, a swollen chest.

They say *don't go upstairs*. You must listen now. When memory insists,
remember the room before all this.
Think of Beckett, paper-thin; find a form for the chaos.
Wrap it tenderly. Cradle the ache
so your arms aren't empty

and bird-foot through the debris
of his memory—glory glory boys in jerseys,
six beer cans with scarlet ladies,
leather jacket with lunatic fringe.

Then, a fist at full-mast;
at last, a point-score roar for the underdog.
From here, give grief
new language, sister tongue, celebration.
Don't go upstairs. Step back
before all this, against the red brick wall:
small again, beside your brother,
blinking at the sun.

Seanín Hughes

Ditches

Julia Calver

The cause of bleeding is the wound. The wound is given the blood and the blood is real. Real blood makes the love real and corporeal, although concealed. Concealed because the corporeality of the love is the sex, the genitals. And the body is become the sex, love's head being the head of the sex concealed. Now the wound is visible on the body. And this scene which the blood invites is the shape of the tale.

Sex takes on the wounds; the love is sexless. The love is alive, life maintains it, keeps it in the necessities of living, that is, in sustenance and air. Without sex, the love is a love in youth, and by this not in its full shape. The youth gives the love qualities of beauty, what is new, early. This also being apt, pertinent, timely, face up, as a letter. Foreshortened, so that the point of view is very close to the level of the ground. Also lying on the ground are flowers. And being read in the time of year, the time of new flowers, is also the nature of love's face.

A woman—reading the nature of love's face—calls this child to come out. There are several children, playing dead, demonstrating many deaths upon the grass. Waiting to be tested by the one who seeks their identities, this woman who is taking the role of an adult.

The players play their deaths as injuries. And their injuries as the escaping blood. The blood is turning like a cord that as it twists creates a simulation— of continuous motion. In this it is quite like a stream—if that, like it, went unrenewed. Light runs from one end of the cord to the other.

Here the woman is, having the name of a month that is the month in which she is walking. She is walking along the hedge. Sweet consonance of her name with the time of year.

Another woman, taking the name of another month, is one of many. She is wearing a shirt. The face is drawn forward over the breasts, shielding the eyes.

The month who called out, over the players, is also the month who sees in the last crop of the first flowers. In the village these are set along the boundary walls and offered for sale. The cut stems of the flowers sit in water. Jars are lined up along the path beside early produce, including the lettuce with its wilted leaves pared from the white stalk. For the alloted days that are belonging under her name she sees to the health of her animals, the land's maintenance, her own interests on the land. It is during these days that she finds love behind her cottage, at the place where the path opens into the expanse of the field and most particularly in the hollow in the ground, filling with light that is as estranged from a body as a dead body is from its life, being all the more estranged for the hollow being able to hold a body, or two bodies lying close.

The back gate of the cottage opens over a hollow that has collected water. Drops hit the bottom of a metal bucket. Voices from the field travel up and fall towards the ditches. And the music from the marquee fluctuates according to the wind.

Jars are empty of flowers and full of water. My month goes to the village, following the other, on her way back.

My month is climbing back into her ditch. Going with some little flowers. With a face which is of neither sex. With hair curled ambiguously. Without any direct look. A direct look that comes over only mediated. Which mediation is a wound, emotional, psychic that passing, falls to its object. The object is a space between the hollow and her house.

FEATURED POET

Conor Cleary is from Tralee, County Kerry and lives in Belfast. He has recently graduated with an MA in Poetry from Queen's University, Belfast, where he was the recipient of the 2016 Seamus Heaney Centre MA Award. His poetry has previously been published in *Icarus, The Tangerine*, and *Poetry Ireland Review*. He was a participant in the 2017 Poetry Ireland Introductions Series.

to my mother at my age

while the bubble still glistens like a weekend away
and each year of the nineties sits on the calendar
in front of you like a fat promise
and both your parents are alive and around the corner

and in the papers and the magazines and on the weather
the threat of nuclear annihilation has subsided
to the point you can start buying garden furniture
and speaking candidly to your doctor about sex

drive west to the fuchsia and the holiday homes
where on hot late nights you are implored
by friends and strangers alike to sing and sing and sing

because the icecaps are melting
and xtravision despite its robust complexion
will liquidate its stock and eventually cease trading

wild divine

this old god only haunts heaths and hillsides and quaint places

he has been impoverished by cities

he missed his chance to carve out a new niche when he refused grooming

the ordnance survey dealt him a sore blow

his petty revenges range from bog drownings to muddied boots to death
    from exposure

all are more avoidable than he'd like

he's become less deliberate

his outbursts are more frequent and starting to worry his friends who
    keep urging him to talk to someone (which he refuses)

he is dirty from crawling under gorse bushes: keeping account of and
    hoarding their secrets

his spheres of influence are shrinking and rolling away

whatever he's holding down you couldn't call it a job

he refuses to get a car but is always borrowing his sister's

he gorges himself on fistfuls of robins

when you encounter his apparition it doesn't look like he's been eating

Meditations on a Vine; or, I am the Sand Guardian, Guardian of the Sand

I mean, we're all looking for something to buy into. Tell me you're some kind of Guardian, or on a Quest, or that the Kingdom depends on your doing X or Y, and I'll buy it everytime, hook, line and sinker. I have an overactive appetite when it comes to wanting to believe in things. I've wanted to believe in toothpaste and car insurance; I've wanted to believe in most things you see on TV. I've even wanted to believe in the economy and that on average we all more or less get what's coming to us.

And so, when the guy on screen manages to fit so much conviction into so small a phrase, I'm already taking his word for it. That kind of rhetoric is hard to come by, these days. It reminds me of the books I used to read as a teenager, with knights and lords and castles. I would fall asleep almost every night imagining myself surrounded by battlements and impregnable walls.

By the time Poseidon is insulted, I'm picturing an ancient, never-ending feud between the sea and the shore; the Sand Guardian and the God of the Ocean. This is the kind of story I can get my head around. Elemental. Instinctual. Played out over and over again in primary colours. It's huge and it's exaggerated like Lex Luthor vs. Superman or Sauron vs. Frodo or my desire to work hard and succeed vs. my desire to stay in bed all day and masturbate.

It's easy to empathize with someone shouting at the tide and at some point or another, everyone's diction burns away and like a sauce is reduced to a single, viscous *fuck off*.

I'm sure if I wanted, I could want to believe in sand. There's something encouraging about the way a beach will follow you home, inside your shoes and under your fingernails; and I like the idea of something like a god I can pack into a bucket and make castles out of. And no, sandcastles are not impregnable, or even insoluble, and yes, there is a sense in which a sandcastle is the exact opposite of a castle. But I mean, we're all looking for something to buy into, and you can say what you want about sand, but you can't say it's hard to come by.

piña

after Oviedo's sketch of a pineapple

of course there will be botanists
ripe with pride on their knees in front of monarchs
across the whole of this temperate continent
there will be hothouses and pineries
and the sheer graft and inconvenience
of forcing you to flower at these latitudes
you'll find yourself as centrepiece
unsliced uneaten recycled for dinner parties
until you begin to rot from the core
and once in the mind of the nobility
the idea of you has been firmly established
as something prestigious and expensive
you'll be abstracted further still
from your flesh and juices and fashioned
into stone bollards along grand driveways
but for now before any of this
you are a drawing of an armoured thing
risen out of sierras half a globe away
you are as close to mythological
as the modern world can allow for
with potential inside you for hatching dragons

Priced Out: 1

you've been learning how to want to stockpile
like a hoarder like a burning obsession
for newspapers jars of garlic peel old t-shirts
will keep you safe below the rampart

you wake up one day and realise you're overextended
like alexander the great without telling you
has been pushing your borders into india
against the better advice of his generals

your nerves can't handle any more smalltalk
or the year long intervals between award ceremonies
wax wings don't offer the kind of contingencies you require

and the summer sky though pink and turquoise
and the kind of thing you used to lust after like a trophy
is crowded with demigods burning up on reentry

Priced Out: 14

romantic impulses if films teach us anything
rarely go unpunished and so you are amazed
after stealing yourselves into the law building
and daring to push the button for the top floor

to be rewarded with an entire city
and the full clean panoramic of a september morning
its clarity waking you up like a coastline
like salt water in the air on your skin

and you both pick out a portion of belfast
according to greenery architecture mere whim
and like emperors in careless negotiation

swap church spires and bridges back and forth
exchange on credit vast chunks of landscape
wide segments of the bright prodigal river

Cover
Bud Cho-O'Leary

My first day at work placed me behind the bar of a pub nobody knew about. Five flyer girls were charged with turning its fortunes around, but looking at them drinking their vodka and Cokes, having convinced me that a free drink was a perk of their job, I had little faith. A shot of fear ran through me when I saw her standing at the back of the group. They had mobbed me, sensing the blood of a new barman, and, panicked, I had never made sure each one was of age.

'You at the back,' I said, 'what age are you?'

'Old enough to know you can't do your job.'

'Denise, you've some cheek,' one of the others said, jokingly shoving her shoulder.

'Who does he think he is?' she asked, permitting the slightest of smiles to emerge among her friends' laughter.

Her voice was soft, fitting her small frame, but the tone was cutting. Before I knew it, the five glasses were emptied and scattered along the bar. The girls went laughing into the cold afternoon to shove blindingly bright fonts and colours into the hands of disinterested coffee-drinkers and sandwich-eaters. I was left alone with Johnny, the one silent regular.

It was boredom that had led me to take the job. That, and the fact that there had been no application required, no interview, none of that. But after thirty minutes I had reached a level of boredom I had not believed existed. By lunch, I was truly down and getting worried. I knew college was nothing but it had a hold on me. I wanted to go on saying that I was a college student. That morning, when I took the job, I had made sure someone would be around to cover my shift during my lectures but no one had arrived. It was getting late. Denise came back alone, her bravado tamed, holding the spare flyers collected from the others. She stacked the flyers in the closet with an assuredness that made it seem she had been forever part of the pub. Watching her, I still struggled to connect her with the voice that had been so searing. With a swift nod of the head, she let me know I was to leave. I took my coat and jogged to college. In the lecture I worried about going back, about seeing her and what she might say. When I did return, a nod of the head was enough and she left.

My shift started each morning at ten. After restocking the bottles and scattering the stained seats around the stained tables, I stood by the taps of beer until four in the afternoon. Besides Johnny on his stool, I would serve one, maybe two people who wandered in, their faces alive to the bleakness of the place, not knowing the clock was the only important thing to see, its hands in charge of her arrival.

One day the clock made a mistake. She came in, though she was neither handing out flyers nor covering my shift. She sat on the stool drumming her fingers on the counter, as if for a moment she was one of the oblivious wanderers, and said she needed to kill some time. I waited before realising what I was to do.

'I'm not paying for this,' she said as I handed her the vodka and Coke. When I said nothing, she tentatively, not allowing object and self to touch, took a drink. She asked me what my story was—what year I was in at college—what I studied—how I got the job—what was my past bar experience. Her eyes shone grey when I told her I didn't have any experience. She looked steadily at me. I was being instructed to defend myself but instead I went to the back room to get the mop. 'I'm in college too,' I heard her say.

After that, she began to come to the pub regularly just to sit at the bar. She continued to do this even when I began to refuse her free drink. More customers seemed to come in when she started to hang around. The clock was a lot less noisy. Johnny became less sullen. We didn't talk all that much but when we did, we argued. Everything I did would incite her. She would click her tongue and ask how Nudge had had the audacity or the stupidity to hire me. She never seemed to have to go to class. I had never seen her around the campus and at no time had she mentioned assignments. I would always tell her that she looked too young to go to college just to get a rise out of her. It made little sense, since, if she were too young, she should have been in school, but people drop out of school, so she might have done that.

'When did you start working here?' I asked. It was raining outside. She had been waiting for me to open up, something she had never done before, and her hair stuck to her cheeks, making her look even younger than usual.

'Before you did,' she said.

I tried to feel bad about getting the job, or at least sorry she had been overlooked for it, but it wasn't some grand calculation I had made. I had just been in a certain place at a certain time. I gained, while she lost out. She would look at me with her grey eyes, willing me to confess. I wanted to tell her that it was just life and that she should understand. If she really were in college, it might have been her who had been walking to the bus that morning having decided the rain was a good enough reason to give the day a miss. I had not fully realized how much of a loner I was before having to spend the majority of each day in my own head—walking from lecture to lecture, sitting in the library pretending to study, moving quickly while I ate so people would think I was rushing to an appointment. It was all getting too much for me. Nudge had been smoking in the alley speaking loudly on the phone, like a stage performance of a guy managing a pub, shouting about his barman who had up and quit with no notice, and that he would now have to rely on the 'young one' to run the bar for the day shifts.

It was a strange compulsion I had, but not an evil one.

'You can't have some girl run a bar,' I said, braving the rain, all but making him hang up the phone. When he did hang up, not saying bye to whoever had the displeasure of listening to him, there was a look he gave me, his eyes conspiratorial below his hood.

'She has experience. Have you ever worked in a bar?' he asked, not taking the cigarette from his mouth.

'No,' I said. He nodded, appreciating the affirmation of how we, the inexperienced, looked. 'But I'll learn, and I can work whatever hours besides the few I have for lectures.'

'Can you work now?'

'Yeah.'

'Grand job,' he said, looking at the clouds. I followed him into the bar and after ten minutes of showing me around, he left me in charge of a place I had never known existed.

In Denise's absence, there hardly seemed need for a barman at all. Johnny could pour his own and I could cover the loss from the two, maybe three, other customers with my wage. I was able to do my readings and assignments when Denise wasn't there but I could do that a lot better if I studied in the library like a normal person.

'Do you really go to college?' I asked her one morning.

'What are you talking about?'

'You are never in college. You never talk about study or tests or anything. How can you be in college?'

'Just because I'm not a college-head like you.'

'I'm not a college-head,' I said. 'You're the only person I know in college, if you actually go there.'

The nagging question turned to an obsession. She could be talking about anything—reality television, Palestine, serpentwithfeet—and all I would be doing is wondering if she really went to college. And it wasn't just when I was with her: I thought about it in lectures, eating lunch, getting the bus, watching television. I would throw around different explanations for why she would lie about it or how she could go to college when she never seemed to be there. If she were studying Commerce, a far more impressive course than my own, you would think it would take up all her day. I examined all our conversations and every offhand comment she made looking for clues.

On a Wednesday, after back-to-back History and English lectures, I arrived at the pub to find Denise and Johnny talking. It was an unusually sunny day and the room had a silvery cleanness to it and there, amongst the shimmering brass and wood, were the two of them in effortless conversation. Johnny smiled at me. The same smile as the older lads when they asked could they join our game of football. The smile when they asked who, me or a friend, would win in a fight, or when they bought us drink from the off-licence, or when they asked why I still hadn't a girlfriend: gay or a weirdo, or when they scoffed loudly when I said I was going to college.

'What are you two talking about?' I asked.

'I was just telling Johnny about college,' Denise said. 'Nice someone believes me. Are you heading up there when you're finished here?' She threw her zip-up over the bar onto the stool beside Johnny. 'Can I have a pint? I'll go up with you once you're sorted here.'

I couldn't believe her nonchalance. When we left the pub, we walked together as if it was an everyday occurrence.

The college looked unfamiliar at night, with the lights switched on along the path against a crisp stillness. I had no business being there so I kept close to

Denise. I longed for as many people as possible to see us.

'Are you studying, is it?' she asked, stopping outside the doors of the library.

'Thinking of it.'

'Right, me too.' She hesitated. 'God, I hate it in there. Don't you? I mean it's a drag. I just get pissed off the minute I sit down with everyone in there.'

'It's the only reason why I work at the pub.'

'It's so annoying.'

It was as if one of us had been walking the other home after a night out and it was now time to part, except for the fact that we were both supposed to be going into the same building.

'I might go for a tea, if you fancy one?' I said.

She shrugged, so we walked to the cafeteria. Not wanting to walk in silence, yet worried our relationship would always revolve around the pub, I asked what she had been talking about with Johnny.

'Jesus, everything. It got pretty deep,' she laughed. 'He's not a bad guy, you know.'

I saw the silhouette of people through the large window of the old bar and heard whispers in the shadows of the trees by the quad. It reminded me of a camping site I had been to in Italy.

As we walked through the hall of the science building, there were a couple of guys by a dock of lockers talking professors and classes.

'Nerds,' Denise said, grabbing the cuff of my jumper and tugging it down. A trailing finger lightly grazed my hand. She was almost careless in the strangeness of being in the red-tiled corridors so late. I allowed my arm to hang for a moment but her hands were just as soon back in her pockets.

I bought the tea and she found us a table. A group huddled tightly around the table beside us playing some sort of card game.

'When you're in school it's all meant to be here,' I said, nodding to the group as I carefully placed our cups on the table. 'You'll meet other outsiders and you'll discover yourself or some shit but it's worse. At least at school I knew how to pretend to fit in, or I really did fit in.'

She watched the card game, holding her cup with both hands, not saying anything. I hadn't even poured my milk in yet.

'I'm repeating first year,' she said, her eyes on the group. 'But I'm doing even worse this year. I physically can't go here, like.'

'I feel the same,' I said, hesitating. 'Maybe we should help each other. We could have tea together and lunch, and study and all that sort of stuff. We could just hang around, not all the time but as much as we wanted, as much as would be helpful.'

'I don't really have time. I can't get to my lectures for chrissakes.'

As we drank, not knowing what more to say, I noticed her eyes grow watery as she stifled a yawn. When she said she was going home I asked her about the library. She just shrugged and said she'd do it another day. I had it in my mind to go so I went to the third floor, warm from the tea, and opened a book I had taken from a random shelf. I tried to read it but I could hardly focus. I could barely keep myself seated. It felt like my first real college experience. The night could have been film-worthy, but in the end I still didn't even know if she was a student.

Johnny had the same smile the next morning, watching me do my best to look busy. While I was getting him a pint, he spoke up.

'You have a nice night with young Denise?' he asked. 'She's a grand girl, isn't she?'

'It was fine,' I said, thinking that maybe he was leering at me rather than giving me a smile.

'She told me about what she's going through. Tough stuff, real stuff, man. My heart goes out to her.'

His face was firmly set even as he talked about his heart going out to her. I knew he was hoping for a shift in my expression. I gave him his pint and went to the back room not knowing what he was after. Denise had been in that morning with the other flyer girls. I could speak with her when she returned to see if she knew what was up with him.

'You know,' he said, having waited for me to come back. 'Me and Nudge go way back, a long ways back. He tells me everything.'

'That's good.'

'I know how you got the job here.'

'What about it?'

'What about it, eh? Well the moment Denise comes through that door, I'm going to tell her how you got it. What about it? Then, I'm getting you thrown from here and I'll make sure she gets the job.'

'How about you get out,' I said, walking to stand across from him.

'Fuck off,' he laughed. 'What are you going to do?'

'I'm not going to serve you and…'

'You'll call Nudge?'

'Do you think I care about this job? I don't need it at all. I'll quit if you want.'

He took his pint and finished it off in a gulp. He didn't order another but sat back, content with his smile, crossed and uncrossed his arms, looked at his watch. I looked at the clock. She would be back soon. Did he really think she would fall for this act? That she would somehow see him as being different from Nudge, see him as being different from me?

'She's struggling,' I said. 'If I'm a piece of shit or whatever, I can still help her. This is just some job. College actually matters. Don't mess it up for her.'

'You don't care about her, you're looking after yourself.'

'You don't know anything about me.'

'I know enough.'

It was too early for any wanderers to arrive. His relentless smile would chase them away even if any did come in. If I had treated her badly, at least I hadn't been condescending. I had taken advantage of the situation but I didn't believe what I had said to Nudge. I didn't think that way. I began to wash already clean glasses and re-arrange the bottles in the fridge, but in the end I just waited, we both waited, for her to come back.

When she walked through the doors, it was strange to watch her movements—hanging up her coat, putting away the flyers, pouring a glass of water—knowing Johnny was waiting.

'Denise, come here a moment,' he said. I wasn't sure what Johnny's voice had sounded like a day ago but now it could rustle through my own thoughts, threatening me with all these different outcomes.

'What's up?'

'I don't like to be the one to tell you this, but I suppose our talk yesterday made me think I had to say something. It gives me no joy, believe me, but this lad here stole the job from you... Said to Nudge that a woman had no place running a pub.'

As he talked, beyond a small flinch, her face was as if she was being told the day's weather. She was wearing a plaid shirt at least two sizes too big for her, maybe it was a man's shirt, and I watched as she took hold of the cuff and bunched it tightly in her right hand. In her left hand, she still held the glass of water. She sort of nodded to the rhythm of Johnny's speech. He was talking quickly, repeating the same things in new ways to find the right phrase. When he finished, she went on nodding to the silence. After a bit, she turned to me and asked when I next needed coverage.

'Not today anyway,' I said, looking to Johnny. 'I'm not sure about tomorrow but I'll text you.'

'No, don't text me. Either tell me now or I won't be here.'

I went to the cupboard and took out my bag. Crouching down, I searched through the books and copies to find my timetable. She had taken a few steps towards me, standing not on the mats by the beer taps but on the warped, faded wood. She was no longer holding the cuff of her shirt and, as she tilted her head back to take a drink of water, I saw a small scar to the left of her chin that I had not noticed before. She waited for a moment. I couldn't find the miserable timetable and I couldn't remember for the life of me the times of my classes. In the end, she left without a word. I stood up to see the front door creeping closed behind her. I waited for her to come back but by the time I was ready to knock off work, she hadn't come back. I got a last pint for Johnny, got my bag, and walked towards college, hoping I might see her there. It was getting dark. The lights would probably be on when I got there. I thought about her scar and her rigid shoulders. It was pointless looking for her. She wouldn't be around college just as she wouldn't be at the pub the next day. She couldn't care less whether the lights along the path were on or not. It was all the same to her.

Cocoon

You orbit your own sun,
butting your head against
the hot bulb of my kitchen.
You might smash the glass,
light pouring out for you
to swallow whole. But
there is method. You need
a fixed point to guide you
over fern & earth, right?

When a city of insects rises
& makes for the open door
I've left, they'll find you,
behind the cupboard,
lacquered in dust, slapped
by the pale moon-white
of my palm, the fire you tasted
long gone, by then
you'll be someone else entirely.

Simon Costello

Just Like Nicole
Laura Morgan

Isla spends her summer in the polytunnels, breathing dank composty air. At the end of every day she goes home with soil under her nails, her fingers tingling with leaf hair, and every night she thinks about the husband.

The husband has favourite places for smoking. Isla records these in her diary. He'll linger by the farmhouse, tapping his ash in an ancient milk bottle, or he'll wander between the sheds and rolls of netting. She makes a collage from torn bits of Cosmo, glues R–E–A–L next to a felt-tip heart.

Isla imagines driving round with him in his BMW. They park outside the shops and he gives her money for cherry cola. She runs her fingers through her fringe: in the car he strokes her hair while the ones from school look in and see. She takes a hand from the duvet, places her tongue on the wrist, and feels hot breath on her skin.

The other pickers are Polish. Their minibus is parked at the back of The Central where they live in the flat-roofed annex, their jeggings and vests hung between windows like faded bunting. In the early mornings before the tunnel warms up they shiver and mime how cold they feel. When she moves near them to sidestep their trolleys, she feels their foreignness up close.

Isla's often late in the mornings and the wife makes her stay after the others leave. The tunnels are silent then. Echoey. Time goes more slowly with the radio turned off. Isla watches shadows passing the polythene—the gardeners with their spades and hoes. She hears the tunnel ripple. It's only the breeze but she imagines the door flapping shut and turning to find the husband there. He would have a cigarette in his hand. Since they haven't spoken, it's difficult to picture him talking. He's posh, so she gives him a voice like Prince Harry.

'Hi,' the husband-in-her-head says.

'Hi,' Isla says. She often speaks her pretendings out loud—she's tried not to, but words escape in the intensity of the thing. She superimposes him into the space by the fertilizer bags so that she sees both the cloudy polythene and him in his checked shirt and jeans, and then she picks some berries. She doesn't want him to think his being there bothers her. She tries a pout, like Nicole does in her Snapchats. When she looks again he is sucking at his cigarette. He blows the smoke over his shoulder.

'Want one?'

He holds the packet out. She takes one and sits on the raised plant bed, crossing her legs so that the frayed denim of her cut-offs fringes her thigh. She tries to imagine her legs are nice legs. She closes her eyes. They are long and thin and tanned, like Nicole's. At the same moment that the husband sits beside her, stubbing his cigarette, a woman's voice says, 'Finished?' and Isla looks up to see the wife there and the tunnel door ajar.

Fresh air mingles with the staleness of the tunnel.

'Is this all you've managed?'

Isla's cheeks go hot. The husband was about to put his hand on her knee.

The wife stares at the two pitiful crates Isla has been filling since lunch, and Isla tips her tub into the top one. Berries tumble and roll but the mound looks no bigger. Their hands either end of a packing case, the wife helps her load the trolley. Isla's certain that in the awkward squeaks of polystyrene the wife can feel her betrayal. The wife pulls the door wide and waits while Isla wheels the trolley out.

Lying in bed, Isla continues from where she left off. He is sitting beside her. She sees the concrete floor under their feet, the rubber irrigation hoses, the grey tape patching the polythene. She hears his breath deepen. His eyes move slowly over her face. When they kiss, she opens and closes her mouth like a fish. The wet sound brings her back to the bedroom.

On her way to work, she sees him smoking by the porch. Mist hangs over the bay. She thinks he looks bored—probably wishing that he was back in the city, where buildings cut out all the pointless sky. She slows, taking in his loose shirt-cuffs and how his hair sticks up at the front. As he pats it down, she feels its softness in her own palm. Smoke clouds his face. When it clears their eyes meet. Under his gaze her knees lock and each step feels like she is walking through bog. By the time she reaches the tunnels her skin is clammy. She puts the heavy apron round her neck but fumbles with the ties. The others are already there, the radio tuned to a distant station. Isla begins with the same bushes as the night before, waiting for her heartbeats to slow.

She will tell Nicole how the husband had been eyeing her up, that he'd watched her walking all the way to the polytunnel. She won't mention how scared she felt, or how something below her tummy had tingled. She will say instead that he was *gagging for it*. Nicole has told her that all men are.

At noon the wife weighs the raspberries on her big white scales and Isla almost feels sorry for her, knowing that when her eyes meet her husband's—to discuss yields and next week's orders—she feels none of the ecstasy Isla does. Some of the pickers call the wife Mrs Pippa. A Pippa should have fair hair and freckles, but the wife is dark. She wears frosted lip gloss and flicks her eyeliner out at the corners. Nicole is an expert with eyeliner. Isla has watched as she leans into the changing room mirror to reapply it after PE.

The wife nudges Isla's crates, making the scales recalculate. She always pays to the nearest ten grams using the spreadsheet on her laptop.

'Three kilos five-sixty, Isla. For a whole morning?'

Isla looks at the raspberries. They've deepened to crimson since being picked. The colour oozes into a dark aura above the polystyrene, their cores softly gaping.

'This is Nicole,' Mrs Fraser had said, showing the girl to Isla's desk. She had black hair and chipped nails, and didn't smile once the whole of double English. Isla watched her picking the red polish.

'Got them done at Neon.'

It was the only thing she said.

Isla googled it under the desk in French. A place in the city with a hot-pink sign. The window said *SILK WRAPS GELS FILLS*, the photo too dark to see inside.

Later Nicole told Isla other things, like how she'd been dumped on her granny, and about the tattoo on her bum. Isla said no way but when Nicole pulled down her waistband, it was there under the lace thong—a tiny cherub.

In Mrs Fraser's class Nicole refused to read any of the parts from *Streetcar*, but somehow Isla got lumped with Blanche. Every time Stanley came in, Nicole sucked her finger, or made panting noises, until Isla couldn't read for giggling.

'Imagine being called Blanche,' Isla said at break.

'No,' Nicole said, 'I mean, I just couldn't. I mean, your name is everything. It's everything about you.'

Isla wished she was a Dakota or Juno. Maybe a Kirsten. Anything but Isla.

Nicole and Isla made plans to go to the city. Nicole knew a club where the bouncers would let them in.

'What do you drink?' Nicole said in Chemistry.

When Isla said Sex on the Beach, Nicole shrieked, and they looked up to see Mr Taylor scowling. Isla whispered to Nicole that he'd been caught with the blonde teaching assistant in the art cupboard last year. Nicole spent the rest of the afternoon doodling cartoons of him on the desk.

'Why's he holding a baguette?' Isla asked.

Then it was her turn to squeal.

On the last day of term Nicole took Jason Skea behind the wheelie bins and everyone said they did it. Isla knew it was true because Jason is a big lad but in class afterwards he faded into his chair. Later Nicole told Isla that she'd done her mam's boyfriend too and how Jason was a *crap ride*.

Nicole has gone to stay with her mam for the holidays. Isla isn't sure if she's coming back. With the husband showing an interest, it wouldn't be so bad. If the husband groped her boob, or even kissed her, that would do. It's only a fortnight till school starts. Isla will borrow the Fake Bake from the holiday bag on top of her mam's wardrobe. She read in Closer that bronzed skin is more alluring.

Now the Polish women are laughing. They laugh so much one knocks over a stack of seedling pots, and the old one with no bra grabs her chest and rocks. Isla watches the wind drumming the polythene, the change in tunnel light as the sun comes out between clouds. When the wife appears at lunchtime, the tray at Isla's feet has only a thin layer of berries.

The wife shakes her head. 'I'm warning you, Isla…'

'Sorry, Mrs Pippa,' Isla whispers after the wife has gone. She likes how the *p* bursts on her lips like bubblegum.

Isla works away from the others and replays her favourite daydream, the one where the husband comes in for a smoke.

'I saw you that day,' he says.

'I know,' she says.

'What's your name anyway?'

The dream pauses. Isla can't decide.

Juno, and her wild curls. Keira's sexy eyebrows.

But wait. Something's missing.

She rewinds the conversation and begins again.

'Cigarette?'

He holds the lighter for her. When she exhales, he winks and says, 'Get your knickers off,' which is a shock made worse by the foliage shaking and the sunlight suddenly in her eyes.

'What are you at, Isla?' the wife says.

Isla drops the tub. Raspberries scatter.

'That's it,' the wife says. 'Get your things. You're fired.'

Isla turns so the wife can't see her cry. She takes her jacket from the pile under the seedlings shelf. At the front gate, she ducks behind the wall. Her throat stings.

'You all right?'

The voice isn't like Prince Harry's. When she looks up, he's sitting on the dyke, taking cigarettes from his pocket.

She hears herself saying 'fine', feels the grass prickling her legs. *Marlboro*. She notes the red packet. If nothing else, she'll get this detail right in future.

The husband puts a cigarette in his mouth. He's about to stuff them back in his jeans but hesitates.

'Want one?'

'Okay.'

'Who are you then?'

'Nicole,' she says, reaching up to take one. 'Nicole.'

She Became Birds, Poems

Let's talk about something else
said my sister who hangs a star,

underneath her tongue and writes
about love in French stories.

Tragedy is when the neurologist
tested you, and found a lump inside

your brain. Suddenly you were
no longer in the middle of earth—

a girl standing alone on a cliff,
wrapped by darkness.

Waiting for a warmed hand,
like memories opened

by the image of love on
a screen.   There are always

goodbyes—at sunset say goodbye

to hurt   to suffering   to the pain
you caused others and yourself.

And when the night came as a
lonely boat of stars,

you walked into dust.

Ojo Taiye

Memory as a Necessary Pain

this morning, i pluck peonies
from my father's throat & watch it turn
into an old lover's hand upon the water
like a moon that wouldn't heal.

as a child, my country was a roof that's always
collapsing. how it spreads on my mother's
face—a brief dazzle of pink light like
rapture in a stranger's eyes

how memory is a heart that has forgotten
to sing—a bare precis & the isolation that any
alignment of pain can trigger when they are
carved out of grief

what do you do when your body is a pistol
or rifle pulled apart? since most of us bloomed
out of sorrow like swans always bent on pond water
i am afraid of attending a place now green with mold
but still edible for some

after dinner with a friend who dreams of dragons
dancing over a fence. i come home to touch my sister's
sweltering body & i am imagining how one can ride a bullet
toward eternity with a Greek chorus of soul

even now, i open up & shut like a house with only hurricanes
moving through it. reminding me of communion as a child
where we'll stop to mislay our moistures on other's necks

Ojo Taiye

Baby, you ask

Some tea please?   It's no request; you drink too much.
Get these done, baby?   Done   always
        like only a wife can do them—

some days now, years away from Us,   the smell
of   armpits from dry-cleaned shirts weighing   a ton,
hanging from my stick arms, still hit me   and I hear

your questions.   Baby, can we make love?
I've said Okay, sometimes adding Baby without love.
Words wouldn't't come.   How to tell the truth—

Beg you. Order you. Or place a written request
under your coffee mug one day at 5am:
        Let me go, baby, will you?

Once, while attacking the walls, you screamed   What
Do You Want.   Silence can be a tireless stream.

I got the annulment. But   this dull ache sits in the small
of my small back.   From your finger prodding each day
before the birds could sing. You needed coffee or tea.

        You had needs. There was no rest. And

I would've let the river swallow up my life
with you in a country where extremes are natural—
bitter winters and heartrending summers far from home.

But I learnt not to   because it was the river that did it
once upon a time, somewhere in Hong Kong.   Or maybe

it was the shrimp cakes and the cruise. Maybe the lightshow
locked arms with your domineering   and I had no clue.

After everything, baby, I can tell you all I've ever wanted
and couldn't have was lightness   because somehow
I married you. Somehow I said Yes and a river was witness.

Jessu John

The End of the World is a Cul de Sac
Louise Kennedy

The dereliction was almost beautiful, the houses dark against the mauve dawn, pools of buff-coloured water glinting briefly as a passing car took the last bend before town. Number 7 was starting to look like the other units, the lawn stringy with brown weeds. The footpath petered out and Sarah landed hard in a puddle, picking her way over broken masonry and loops of cable until she reached the end of the cul de sac. The noise was coming from the show house. It looked even worse inside than out. Clots of soft dung littered the travertine floor. All the doors had been taken, including the front one, which only seemed to emphasise how small the rooms were. The donkey was in the living room, by the cavity in the chimney breast where the granite fireplace had been. It was plump and skittish, pastilles of dried sleep at the corners of its eyes. Sarah whispered to it, cajoled, pleaded. She tried shooing it, spreading her arms to drive it out to the hallway. It pawed and snattered, and a flume of shit hit the wall behind it. She would have to go and get her neighbour.

She left the estate and started up the steep lane towards Mattie Feeney's house. She had gone there once with Davy, when the old man's wife died. Away from the main road the light was different. It was hard to see. The brambles that coiled back over the dry-stone walls nicked the back of her hands. She walked faster, almost trotting, her wellingtons kicking up small stones and squeaking over the tranche of thick grass that ran the centre of the lane. She was breathing fast when she reached the yard. A light was on in the stables. Someone was mucking out, metal tines scraping the ground. The raking stopped. She didn't hear footsteps until they were very close.

'You're up early,' said a voice behind her. A man's voice, his accent local, from the town.

'I can't see you,' she said and turned quickly.

The speaker was barely thirty, with a clipped beard and hair brushed thickly to one side. The thin electric light made him look drawn.

'Did I scare you?' he said to her hands. She looked at them. They were trembling.

'One of the donkeys got out.' She wasn't used to hearing herself speak and her voice sounded slight, inconsequential.

'Where is it?'

'In the show house.'

'I see,' he said. His eyes were laughing at her.

'Should I go and tell Mattie?'

'He's up in the hospital.'

'Is he alright?'

'He had a stroke three weeks ago.'

'I didn't know. How is he?'

'The speech wasn't affected. He'll be back when they finish the physio.'

He hooked a horsebox onto the back of an old jeep and opened the passenger door. 'You might show me where the donkey is,' he said. She sat beside him. There was a tree-shaped air freshener swinging from the rear-view mirror, but the overwhelming aroma was of dung. At the bottom of the lane he glanced up and down the road, his eyes lingering on her when he looked left.

'Ryan is my name,' he said.

'Sarah.'

'I know,' he said. 'You're the gangster's moll from down the hill.'

'Is that what they call me?'

'I'm after thinking of it now.'

She got out by the entrance and unchained the gate, swinging it wide open to let the jeep in. Ryan pulled in beside a dome of polished granite that had been sandblasted with the words *Hawthorn Close* in a Celtic font that Sarah had thought at the time might tempt fate. Not that she had told Davy so.

Morning had broken. Under the low cloud, the sunflower-yellow paint on the houses made the damp air look noxious. 'I thought the place looked bad from the road,' he said. She followed him to the show house. He side-stepped the shit and stood in the kitchen. There wasn't much left of it. Mould-speckled French Grey paint, dangling wires. Buckled skirting boards and sawn-off pipes. A few days before Davy left a contractor had called to their house and accused him of stripping the place himself, selling the fittings on the sly. Sarah had run the man from the door; now she was inclined to believe him.

Ryan went into the sitting room. He ruffled the donkey's mane. 'Alright, buddy,' he said.

'I didn't know what to do,' said Sarah. 'I think I just frightened him.'

He gave its arse a slap. The animal shimmied and clopped then began to move, colliding with walls and doorframes, reeling back before Ryan got it out the front. He jollied and pushed it across the hardcore, leaning his weight on it to get it into the horsebox. He secured the door and put his hands on his hips. 'Fuck's sake,' he said, the words leaving his mouth like steam.

'I can close the gate after you and walk up.'

'I said I'd drop you home,' he said, getting into the jeep. Sarah understood. He was offering her a lift because he wanted to see the house. Everyone wanted to see the house. Strangers rang the bell on vague pretexts. Selling calendars. Asking for directions. Reaching their necks around to look into the huge hall when Sarah opened the door. Walking around the side for a view of the housing estate her husband had thrown up and abandoned to her.

Ryan waited while she locked the gate. She sat back in the passenger seat and he watched her pull the safety belt across herself. They only had two hundred yards to travel, but it made her feel bolstered, held in place. Her driveway bent up in an arc that mirrored the line of the floating wall at the front. The horsebox swung left and right, and Ryan had to lock hard to park.

She opened the front door. Unopened letters were strewn across the entrance hall. The art was gone, lifted off the walls by the owner of the gallery on a tip-off from the architect. Davy had taken the buffalo hide he had bought when he went to the Super Bowl. It was the only thing he took with him.

'Some spot,' said Ryan.

His voice was still wobbling in the high, empty space as they entered the kitchen. 'Coffee?' she asked.

'Aye, go on.'

She filled the kettle and got out mugs and a jar of instant granules. He moved around the room, taking it in. The dining table was glass and chrome with twelve curved white chairs around it. A globular light fitting was suspended above it, a spiky metal Telstar sort of thing. The kitchen units were at floor level only, high-gloss white with walnut counters. Sarah had had no hand in the décor. Davy had said it was the architect's job.

A vast patio door, bleared with dust, ran the length of the dining table. Ryan tried the handle. 'Pull it right up until it clicks,' said Sarah. He opened the lock and slid it across until it vanished into the wall. The room filled with autumn. The must of leaf mould, the complaints of robins. You could see over Mattie's place and across the glen to the mountain. It was like being outside.

He leaned in the doorframe with his coffee and lit a cigarette. His shoulders were taut, as though he was trying to make himself smaller. The beard both became him and made him unremarkable. He lifted the mug to his mouth and swallowed. He made a face and inclined his head at the Bakelite coffee machine that was plumbed in near the sink. 'How come I got the cheap shite?'

'You can only get the pods online.'

'So get them online.'

'My cards were cancelled.'

He stepped onto the patio and Sarah followed him around to the west side of the house. She stood behind him as he looked down the garden. Terraces of shrubs were growing thickly all the way down to the wire fence, the hard, spherical shape the gardener had once imposed on the box trees blurred with new shoots, the lavender silvery and woody and still flowering. Hawthorn Close was beyond it, lollipop-shaped: twelve semi-detached houses either side of a road that led to five detached houses around the bulb of a cul de sac. From here you could see things you couldn't see from the road. That one of the units had been occupied, that someone had tried to tame a garden and make a home. That the granite dome that read Hawthorn Close had been deposited onto a fairy fort. That beside the dome a tree had been torn down, its roots leaving deep velvety furrows that seemed to bulge when light fell across them.

'Imagine living there,' he said, turning to look at her. Sarah went back into the kitchen.

He followed her in and opened the fridge. It was empty except for dark red nail polish, skimmed milk and a prune yoghurt. He closed it again. 'Do you want to get out of here later? Get a drink or something?'

'I don't know.'

He poured his coffee into the sink and left through the hall. She stood at the front door to see him off.

He opened his window and adjusted his wing mirror. 'I'll come back at seven,' he said. He was looking at her as he drove away.

After he left, she tied her hair up. She swept the floor. She wiped down all the surfaces in the kitchen and washed and dried the dishes. She closed the window and sprayed a section of the glass with green liquid she found in the utility room. She wiped it with newspaper and stood back. It looked worse than before. She sprayed the dining table and began buffing, rubbing newspaper round and round until it disintegrated. She cleaned the sink with bleach and mopped the floor.

She went to the garden with the prune yoghurt and a teaspoon. She sat on a metal deck chair and ate, sucking the spoon clean after each mouthful. A car pulled in by the gate of the estate. The driver got out. He had greased-back red hair and an off the rack suit. He stuck his phone through the railings to take photographs. Before he drove off he made a call, his voice indistinct. He was probably from the bank, or from a firm of solicitors acting for a contractor who was owed money. The reporters had stopped coming, at least until the inquest.

She ran her wedding finger around the inside of the pot and sucked it. Her rings were loose. Her skin tasted of sour milk and chlorine and green apples. At least the place was clean. Maybe she should clean herself up too, in case Ryan came back. She went inside. She had started sleeping in the boot room Davy had built off the kitchen for their sons to use after football training. The arrogance seemed spectacular now; they had never had sons, or daughters. The morning they found the body, Sarah had abandoned the master bedroom and dragged a mattress downstairs. Now she lay every night under the high shallow window with the white blind. There were pale stone slabs on the floor. The modular shelving that ran along one wall was white and empty. It resembled a clinic you might see on television where rich women went to lose weight or go mad.

She shampooed her hair then smeared the contents of a sample sachet of deep conditioner onto the ends, winding it in a coil on the crown of her head. She shaved her legs and underarms. She hesitated then soaped between her legs, dragging the razor from back to front until her pubic hair lay in fuzzy clumps in the plughole. She wrapped herself in a towel and sat on the toilet seat with a magnifying mirror and tweezers, pulling tiny black hairs from her moustache and eyebrows. The tubes and bottles of make-up in the bathroom cabinet were marked to be used within six months. They had gone off, like the prune yoghurt. She used make-up brushes she had bought in Saks on Fifth Avenue—after a boozy lunch, for three hundred and fourteen dollars—to apply liquids and gels and powders. When she was done, her skin was bronzed and dewy, her eyes dark and wide. She blow-dried her hair and wound it around electric rollers. When she was dressed she made a cup of tea and brought it outside. She sat in the metal deckchair again, a pair of knickers on her head to hold the rollers in place, and waited.

*

At seven Ryan rapped a knuckle against the patch in the patio door she had tried to clean. Sarah saw her face reflected in the glass. Her make-up had softened but there was no mistaking the care she had taken. She let him in. He smelled of deodorant and was wearing a soft wool jacket and expensive brogues. Maybe he had taken care too. He pointed at the smudged glass.

'Was it all too much for you?'

'Ha,' she said.

'Are you hungry?'

'Not really.' Her stomach made a hollow fizzle, betraying her.

'Come on. I'll buy you a bit of dinner.'

He had come in a dark convertible with leather seats. 'Very flash,' she said. There was a fur of moss where the soft top met the window.

'You're calling me flash?' he said. Sarah turned to him, smiling. He wasn't smiling back.

She was stricken by her own foolishness. She didn't even know him. Besides, who was she kidding? She couldn't sit opposite a man at a table in this town. She hadn't so much as stood on High Street since Davy left. When the town was asleep she bought milk and cut-price ham in the 24-hour petrol station, with the dwindling bundle of notes she had found in Davy's wardrobe. 'I don't know if this is a good idea,' she said.

'Relax', he said. He had bypassed the town centre and was following signs for Dublin.

'Where are we going?'

'I'm taking you for a spin. I'll have you home before midnight.'

The short stretch of dual carriageway narrowed into a road without verges. They passed white crosses, sometimes alone, sometimes in twos and threes, that marked the sites of fatal crashes. He drove fast, even on hairpin bends where most drivers would have braked, his left hand splayed lightly on the gearstick, fingers flexing and tensing, the rush doing something almost kinetic to him. He turned left at a derelict filling station and drove a couple of miles down a gentle hill. He parked behind a line of cars at a lakeside pub. An extractor fan was belching frying smells into the night. Sarah crossed the road to a narrow jetty that protruded over the lake like a diving board. A band of the water was white with moonlight, small boats rocking and bumping together.

Inside they were seated near a gas fire that had fake embers intended to look like real coal. A young waitress came with menus and listed the specials. Ryan ordered a shandy, and a glass of Prosecco for Sarah. She would have preferred a gin and tonic, but didn't say so.

'How long have you been working for Mattie?' said Sarah.

'He's my grandfather.'

'I didn't know that.' There was a story about one of Mattie's grandchildren, something Davy had told her. She couldn't remember what it was. The waitress put the drinks in front of them, Ryan's first.

He ordered dinner for them both, the most expensive dishes on the menu. Buttered Dublin Bay prawns with garlic chives. Organic fillet steak, well done. Sarah asked the waitress if she could have hers medium-rare.

'Why not?' said Ryan. Maybe he wasn't used to eating in restaurants. Mattie was a bit of a hillbilly, and his grandson probably wasn't much better, with his townie accent and pointy shoes. All the same, who would bring you out for dinner and then choose your food, your drinks? It wasn't that Sarah disliked what he had ordered. Two steaks were carried to the next table and they looked and smelled delicious. But it was odd not to be asked what she wanted.

The waitress brought their starter. They ate in silence, Sarah using her fingers and finishing so fast she was ashamed. Hunger was hard to conceal when there was food in front of you. The main course arrived, two unstable stacks of charred meat, Portobello mushroom, grilled beef tomato and onion rings, served on wooden boards that had to be carried with two hands. The manager carried Ryan's.

'She'll have a nice glass of red with the beef,' he said. Sarah tried to put aside the feeling he had taken charge of her. The food was good, the wine not bad either. It was nice to sit at a table in a restaurant. She'd had worse nights. When their plates were cleared, Sarah leaned back and smiled. Her belly was quiet for the first time in weeks.

'Back in a sec,' she said and picked up her handbag. Ryan reached across and took her free hand. She knew what he had put in her palm before he closed her fingers around it. She crossed the room to the ladies and shut herself into the largest cubicle. She crunched out a line with one of the cancelled cards. He had given her a fifty-euro note too. She rolled it up and leaned over the cistern.

When she came out she looked in the mirror. The light in the bathroom was filtering through a dark red shade and should have been flattering. She had grown thin. Her face was skull-like. There were dark ruts under her eyes and a pair of deep grooves ran from either side of her nose to the corners of her mouth. She put on more concealer and eyeliner and fluffed out her hair. She put her hand on the door to leave. Then she turned quickly and went back into the cubicle. Another bump and she might even enjoy herself.

She sat demurely and smiled at Ryan, nudging his knee gently under the table to pass him the wrap and the banknote.

He spread his hands. 'That's for you,' he said. He called the waitress over and ordered her another glass of red.

'Why thank you,' she said when it arrived. 'Are you not having anything?'

'I'm driving.' He leaned back in his chair and watched her take a drink. 'What's the story with your house?'

'The bank is trying to sell it.'

'How's that going?'

'How do you think?'

'Why did you build the estate so close to your own place?'

'Davy was in trouble. He thought he could turn the development around quickly, generate some cash flow.'

Ryan gave a short laugh. 'He was in trouble alright. What did you think?'

'I thought it would look ugly. That it was a huge risk. But he didn't ask me.'

'But you didn't say anything?'

'I'm the kind of girl men order dinner for,' she said. Connaught's answer to Lauren Bacall or what? Fuck it. She was in the mood for some craic. She took a drink of her wine and waited for him to reply.

'You looked like you were enjoying it,' he said, a flash of something in the way he answered that made her stay quiet. She took another drink and looked around the room. Farmers and solicitors. Overdressed young couples. The usual frumpy lot you'd see in any restaurant down the country on a Friday night. Nosy as well, half of them gawping over and whispering. When Ryan spoke again he had composed himself. 'What about the estate?' he said.

'The receiver will accept a hundred grand for it.'

'Where's your husband?'

'There have been sightings of him in Malaga. Apparently.'

The waitress came with dessert menus. 'I'm full,' said Sarah. Ryan ordered her a crème brulee. When it arrived she tapped at the hard caramel with the back of a teaspoon. It cracked into shards that were shiny like tortoise shell. She pushed the dish away.

Ryan went to the bar to pay. The manager seemed to be apologising to Ryan, spreading her hands as she spoke. She called the young waitress over. The girl was short and Ryan had to bend to speak to her. He whispered in her ear then put something in her hand, closing her fingers around it the way he had earlier with the coke. She leapt up like a cat and kissed his cheek, fleeing to the kitchen. Ryan came back to the table with a carrier bag of clinking bottles.

'What was that about?'

'Ould cunt didn't want me to give the girl a tip. Said the staff did alright with the service charge.'

Sarah stood to put her jacket on. Every single person in the room was looking at her. They recognised her. It was why she didn't leave the house anymore. People remembered her face from the papers. From the photograph of her and Davy the day she won the prize at the Galway Races. Or worse, the one taken the day Eoin and Lizzie moved into Hawthorn Close. Herself and Lizzie. in the centre, laughing, the baby leaning out of Lizzie's arms. Davy and Eoin flanking them, the yellow paint cheery in the sunshine. But was that why they were staring? There was something about Ryan, nothing overt, but it was there all the same, in the deference the manager showed him, the blushes of the waitress, as if she was star-struck. Was it the sight of Sarah and Ryan together that was such a spectacle? She didn't know. All she knew was that she was sick of being stared at by bog trotters. She pulled her collar up and began striding towards the door. She was at the jetty when Ryan came out. He put the bag of bottles in the car and twisted her around to face him.

'What's eating you?' he said.

'They were all looking at us.'

'Why would they be doing that?'

'I don't bloody know.'

'I'd say you've a fair idea.'

'What's that supposed to mean?' she said.

He laughed. 'You're gas,' he said.

She sat in the car and opened the glove compartment. There were CDs in a pouch. She found a compilation of seventies funk and put it on. She did a line off the manual. On the road back to town she moved her shoulders to the music. When they got to the house she asked him in. She took out Murano tumblers for the vodka and filled them with ice. He spelled out her name in coke on the dining table. Up close the glass had tiny scratches, as though it had been scoured. 'You forgot the H,' she said, when it was all gone. 'Sarah ends in a H.'

'Did you ever hear of tidying your room?'

'It isn't my room anymore. I sleep in a room off the kitchen.'

'Do you want to go down there?'

'No.' There was something vestal about the boot room, with its white walls and high window. She didn't want to bring a man in there, especially this man, who was moving around the house as if he owned the place. Still, he was here, and the way he was slinking about with that townie snarl on his beardy mouth wasn't completely repulsive. She took her top off. She lay on the bed so he would have to take her jeans off, wriggle her out of her bra and knickers, tactics she had employed to amuse Davy, especially when he was fucking that bitch of an architect. She hadn't changed the sheets since Davy left. She wondered if they would smell of the woody aftershave she used to buy him but there was just a cold dustiness, like the rest of the house.

Ryan made a circle around her navel with his finger. The skin where he touched her felt like it was peeling off.

'You don't remember me, do you,' he said.

'I don't, to be honest.'

'I was at the door a few times.'

'Are you a contractor?'

He laughed. 'I'm in sales, I suppose,' he said, and suddenly everything seemed clear and bright. She remembered the story about Mattie's grandson. Davy had read it aloud one Sunday from a tabloid they didn't normally buy. 'A kingpin, no less,' he had said as he folded the paper up. 'The wee knacker is a kingpin.'

'Davy owes you the money,' she said. 'I've never bought drugs in my life.'

'That's what I thought. But you're like a Hoover, love.' He turned her over and pushed her face into the mattress. She could smell Davy now.

Afterwards Ryan gave her a Valium. Before it had time to work she told him everything. She had persuaded Lizzie, her sister, to buy Number 7. Davy said if they got one family in the estate would fill up in no time, it had worked with the other developments. He knocked ten grand off the price and threw in geothermal heating that never worked; they had only dug deep enough to disturb a nest of rats.

By the end Sarah was hardly sleeping, Davy beside her with his laptop on, chopping out powder in little Morse-like dashes on the bedside table. Sometimes he watched porn, turning to her for rough, jittery sex that never brought either of them to climax. The sitting room light in Number 7 stayed on through every night, and every night Sarah wanted to knock the door and say how sorry she was. One night the light went out just after three. When dawn gave up the silhouette in the fairy tree she knew it was Eoin, a steadiness about him even in death, in the pendular swing of him. Davy ripped the fairy tree from the ground the day of the funeral. He said the bad luck had already come. Sarah watched him operate the JCB and remembered who they were.

Ryan dressed at seven. He was tender towards her, pulling the sheet up to her chin and leaving a long kiss on her mouth.

'I'll come back later,' he said.

She went into the bathroom. She wiped her arse with the hand towel and put on a dressing gown that was hanging on the back of the door. It was white, made of brushed cotton, deep like velvet. She went down to the kitchen and pulled the patio door across. She lowered herself into the metal chair, letting the dew seep into her robe. Lines had begun to crackle across the yellow plaster of the houses. The roadway appeared sunken, even where there was pavement, the gardens too. Another day was breaking over Hawthorn Close.

vol-au-vent

'a loved body'
un
responsive   *un*
wonted   *un*
permissive

        O negative
        tincture on tiling
        69 x 41 inches

weighs
of a swamp
mahogany piano
        professional movers
        bent their knees for

                knowing
                where it   had been
                where it   had to go
                  the classical   cannon
                  in sheet music   on its lip

                        the two-noted siren-riff off-by-
                        heart   doubles
                                as a rally cry.

a gasp coming at you
           doppler shifts

                to silence.
                to mortify.

                                                    L-O-V-E is shrillest at

                                                                          t

                                                                          h

                                                                          e

                                                                          e

                                                                          x

                                                                          i

                                                                          t

                                                                          :

                                                              past the octave's

                                                                        rem-
                                                                         it.

what are the chances letting air in
makes it easier to lift?
OPEN
a   window   chest   fallboard   rib   oven   district of the throat
brittle case   of the dormant instrument   inflate his lungs with   anthem.

is there truth in: too much water makes a person
inoperable
+
derogates a house?
there go the double   leaf   doors   on   the   wind
—
glass intact as the neighbours' miraculous sleep.
red flare of day firing for the horizon.
the brigade! what are the chances
that it makes no sound? as scavenger
to meat. as one bureaucratic mouth
to another. it is here nor
there? coming nor going?

Caoilinn Hughes

The mean temperature of water

is rising. Every hat cut is a hat passed
      for the warming. See:
butter slip from a hot scone. Lotto
      ticket bearer's freeze-frame smile.
Man's calligraphic morals pissed into snow.
      Once upon a time, so it's said.
Heat transfers through the holy water whet
      of an infant's silken forehead.
What sweats through militant
      antiperspirant. The intravenous drip
of your life for mine.
      In the Liffey, in the Tigris, Euphrates,
in the Rhine. And yes, in the poem,
      in how you read it (cold water
having no simile), getting warm, sleazily
      warmer the second time.

Caoilinn Hughes

Bullets
Darran McCann

You mightn't think to look at it but there's a lot of skill involved in bullets. It's all in the hands, and how you read the road. The technique of getting the bullet to spin just how you want, guiding it round a corner, knowing the exact moment to let go—some people never master it, even after a lifetime. It's not always the biggest men who do it best, and you're better being flexible than strong most of the time. To play you need a twenty-eight-ounce cannonball and a stretch of country road to throw it along, and that's all you need. They only play this game in Armagh and Cork, though they have variations in parts of Germany and the Netherlands. It's a game well-suited to a netherland all right.

JP Flynn walks towards the bridge at the foot of Drumbreda, the meeting point and starting line. Beneath Drumbreda stands a bowler, feet together, facing into the incline, practicing. When the score begins he'll turn around and throw out the road into the countryside, but while he's warming up he can use the hill like a driving range for bullets. It's maybe two hundred yards, all uphill and steeply banked for most of that. The bowler takes off, a jog at first. He gathers speed. Hits a sprint. A whirr of the right arm. The bullet is fired.

It's airborne.

Hits the road with a clack, maybe fifty yards up the hill.

Skips on. Another fifty yards. Seventy. Rolls on further. Finds a new burst from somewhere, fuck the laws of physics. Ninety yards.

Peters.

Dies.

Lingers. Cannot move forward, isn't for rolling back.

But of course it rolls back, as it must. Nature will have its way. The road would have to be a lot rougher and the ball a lot more callused to make evitable the inevitable.

The bullet gathers momentum as it trundles down to the hill to where the bowler, Noel, awaits. He watches its return. JP watches Noel watch it.

Did anybody ever manage to crest the hill?

Noel turns sharply—he's not great when you catch him unawares—but he smiles when he sees his big brother.

Not too many.

Noel wants to throw a bullet clean over Drumbreda. He's out there every day, just hurling that cannonball into that hill. It's not a new thing, he's been at this for a while now.

Are you getting close?

I just need to find another twenty yards.

Those last ones are the hardest.

If I could just find another twenty yards. Another fifteen.

Noel is in polo shirt and jeans and the belly hangs low on him. He has shaved off the beard and probably shouldn't have, because the beard took the worst of the bad look off those evacuated jowls. He looks younger but sadder too, and when he's clean-shaven you can somehow tell he doesn't shave himself. He looks more like a patient than he has for a good while. JP puts a hand to his elbow, a kind of embrace, and Noel just nods, juggling a bullet from left to right, right to left.

You're looking well.

I am like fuck.

JP takes the bullet, has a couple of warm-up throws. Noel shakes his head pityingly.

I wish I didn't have to be in a team with you every year. You're fucken shite.

At least I can keep count of the score, you fucken innumerate.

Just try and keep it on the road, you pen-pushing cunt.

I got something for the boys, says Noel. He has a hold-all with him, and from it he produces five twelve-ounce bullets, one for each of JP's children, all sons.

You know my youngest is only two?

Two's plenty. As long as I mind, I was throwing.

There doesn't be too many scores down the Malone Road, to be honest with you.

You should be pushing them to keep it up. It's their heritage. I'll be very disappointed if they don't play.

Noel loves bullets and so does JP. It brings him back like little else does. Yet this is the only day of the year he throws. They don't play bullets in Belfast, where he lives now, and even if they did, his wife Saoirse wouldn't approve. Saoirse is from Cork and in Cork, she tells him, *bowling* is a lower-class game. It's not exactly polo in Armagh either. Saoirse puts a lot of store by these things. Her father is a Blueshirt judge who likes to boast about how his grandfather was one of the first Guards recruited in West Cork, and Saoirse idolises him. JP thinks if he'd met Saoirse anywhere other than Trinity she wouldn't have given him the time of day.

A really big bullets score can attract hundreds, even thousands of spectators, and some of the most absolutely degenerate gamblers in the country turn up and throw down great bundles of cash on the road when two great bowlers meet. This is not one of those scores. This is a get-together of old friends, a nice walk into the gentle undulations of the County Armagh countryside for men now undeniably in middle age. It's the twenty-third annual Pearse Donnelly Memorial Cup, and it has never struck anyone as strange that there is no actual cup. The players are the members of the old gang, and every year they get together to remember Pearse, the one who's missing. Pearse, who loved bullets.

Pearse played electric guitar and had perfectly ragged hair to the collar and epic mutton-chop sideburns and his Da was on the run. He lost his virginity at the age of fourteen with a nineteen-year-old woman while the rest of them lived with pubescent frustration, always on the verge of tears or murder or both. He was handy with a hurl, handy enough with his fists that he rarely had to use them, and had that reckless abandon that adolescent boys revere. See him? they'd say, he doesn't give a fuck so he doesn't. He was the most glamorous person JP ever met.

One time Pearse was in JP's house listening to his brand new tape of *In Utero* and they got to talking about what Kurt Cobain's problem was anyway, when suddenly Pearse burst out crying about how much he hated his Da, though you could tell he was only saying that, and then he admitted he loved him really and just wished he was around. You must miss your Ma? Pearse asked, and JP said Yeah. What did you call her? Kathleen. JP was pretty sure Pearse never showed that side of himself to anyone else. Looking back he can see Pearse was very lonely and very scared, but at the time he just thought Pearse was unbelievably cool.

The first time they held the Pearse Donnelly Memorial Cup, soon after it happened, they had fifty lads out throwing, but last year there was only seven.

This year it'll be fewer again. First to arrive is Beaker—his real name is Ciaran—home from England. Once upon a time he was a beanpole with bushy hair, long, thin face and permanently shocked expression, and years ago somebody noticed he looked like Beaker from *The Muppets*. He looks different now, all burly and jowly and baldy.

Here comes Tony Soprano.

Been eating the profits, have you?

Beaker works for some big biscuit company over there.

Sure look at the state of youse. Bandy-legged bastard and Uncle fucken Fester.

They embrace.

Monty arrives, wearing sunglasses.

Here comes Bono, says JP.

Monty takes off the glasses. His eyes are red and spidery. It's just as well you have the brains because you sure as hell don't have the looks.

Rough night?

Aye. Tell your Ma to go easy in future.

Monty has this theory that you should always begin a conversation with an insult. Make a terrible first impression and see who sticks around. If they go swooning on the fainting couch, well, it's good to know that about them straight off. Fuck you, move on. JP can see there's a mad logic to the idea.

They all embrace.

Monty got put out of Armagh in the late nineties for selling a few joints. The 'Ra gave him forty-eight hours to leave the country, so he got to keep his knees but left behind a pregnant girlfriend. He has a twenty-year-old son he never sees except when he passes him on the street. Selling a bit of weed doesn't seem such a big deal now, the son must think it's a thin enough excuse.

So who all's coming?

Pigeon has a big surgery.

What the fuck's wrong with that pigeon-chested bastard?

No, he's doing a big surgery.

Oh right. Pigeon is a consultant neurosurgeon in Dublin. Not bad going for a man of forty-one who still breakdances, badly, when he's pissed.

No word of Chunk?

Maybe next year. Chunk is still inside. He got four years when they caught him driving a tanker full of washed diesel across the border.

Monty shouts over to Noel, who's still taking warm-up throws into Drumbreda: All right there Rain Man? Are you getting close?

Noel looks back blankly.

Come on to fuck or we'll start without you.

Noel sprints over in a mild panic.

Will we make it interesting?

Nah. I don't like gambling, says JP.

Sure actuary is nothing but gambling.

What the fuck would you know about actuary?

Well, you get a bow, and an arrow, and…

JP doesn't laugh from one year till the next the way he laughs on the day of the Pearse Donnelly Memorial Cup. He doesn't laugh much at all these days, to be honest, so it's good to come home, back to where he feels seventeen again, where he can be again who he once was.

One day Pearse said: let's go on the mitch down the town. JP was no truant, he actually liked school, but when Pearse said *let's go on the mitch* you went on the mitch. They lingered near the edge of the yard at break-time and waited for the bell to go and the crowds to start confusing the doorways, then slipped away. They went to the Snook, the amusement arcade / snooker hall at the Shambles Corner. Every mother forbade their darling sons from darkening the door of the Snook, it was a place for corner boys, so of course everybody went there, corner boys and altar boys alike. Being forbidden gave it an appeal it didn't have itself because it was a dingy little hole, looked at objectively. Just poker machines and one-armed bandits and a handful of arcade games, and a single, three-quarter size snooker table in the middle that you could never get a game on. That morning there was no one in the place apart from Jakey Schmig McKeown behind the counter, him and his Jimmy Hill chin, so JP and Pearse had the Snook to themselves.

Never seen this place so dead, Pearse said.

Should you children not be in school? said Jakey gruffly.

JP was a little bit afraid of Jakey, but Pearse didn't give a fuck about him.

Free period.

Don't be telling me about your periods.

So that's why this place is so popular. It's that sunny personality of yours.

Fuck up.

Monty pours a measure, downs it. When he fires his head back you can see ugly scarring under his jawline, from the day he was sitting in a parked car when a bomb went off in the Land Rover next to him. He was only an infant and has no memory of it but it scarred him for life. *Monty*—as in Mr Burns. JP lets the whiskey warm him. He enjoys the arms race of put-downs but sometimes he wishes they could talk more. Like, Monty and JP have been best friends all their lives and JP still has no idea whether Monty is happy or sad, or even how he's making a living now. But mainly it's Pearse he wants to talk about, on the day that's in it. He'd love if the other lads shared their memories of him. But apart from a toast, Pearse hardly gets a mention any more.

The others pair up, grumbling as usual that JP gets to team with Noel just because they're brothers. The bullets course runs from the bridge at the foot of Drumbreda out to The Arena. The Arena is gone now, there's only a hole in the ground where the boreen meets the main road, but back in the Nineties an out-of-town nightclub stood there. Even the young bowlers with no memory of the place still say *out to The Arena*. Bullets is like that. Along the road there's a house called the New House which must be there seventy years. There's Connolly's Corner, though nobody remembers any Connollys. There's the Screaming Peacock. The Black Stick. The Foxes' Gap. The Banshee's Bend. To the bowler the present is a thin film on top of a present past.

It's a simple game but below the surface is infinite complexity. Bullets takes skill, poise, strength, subtlety, stamina. The inches count. Beaker takes the first shot: the ball flies off the road after twenty yards. Next up is JP, who fires the bullet sixty yards from the start line before it disappears into the ditch. Not a bad start. Monty throws twenty yards beyond that mark; his smugness disappears when Noel sends the bullet screaming along the road, past Monty's almost before it hits the asphalt. It strikes the kerb just at the bend, bounces on at the perfect angle, keeps going forever.

She's still rollin' boooyyyy! JP cries. Over the years he's been away his true accent and true manner have flattened out, but when he's home they come back to the surface.

Don't be getting too cocky, it's your throw next, Thalidomide arms, says Monty.

It was an atrocious break. Reds splattered everywhere, and immediately Pearse started mopping up.

What are you missing? Anything important?

Nah, JP lied. Just Economics. Ricardo. You?

French. Only took it for A-Level because there's a placement.

When's that?

Over the summer. I'm going out to La Rochelle to see my pen pal. Lovely *Aurélie*.

The relish he packed into his perfect, rolling pronunciation of those delectable syllables.

Orally?

You'd never know, he winked.

JP was so impressed, so excited, he could have humped the billiard table.

That's some muscles you have in your right arm, says Beaker. How come your left arm is weak as water? What sort of training are you doing, that you're only using your right hand?

Bending your Ma over and riding her like a mechanical bull.

Will youse fucken remedials hurry up and take your shots? says Monty.

JP's throw cannons off the kerb, makes a turn around the corner and runs up a little hill for forty or fifty yards till eventually it comes to rest against a telegraph pole.

Not bad, Noel admits.

But the flight of a bullet is never an easy thing to predict. When judging the camber, curves and idiosyncrasies of the road, the laws of physics can sometimes seem more like guidelines. Suggestions. Next turn, JP throws what he thinks is his best shot of the day, and the bullet ricochets crazily off the kerb into a field, startling cattle. Then Monty hurls a terrible shot straight off the road but somehow it lofts high over the hedge, flies clean across the corner of a field and another hedge beyond and rejoins the road around the bend. Even Noel whistles at that one.

Pearse lit up a cigarette. On the jukebox, the drums shifted direction. Who's this, Madness? Pearse asked.

Supergrass.

Who?

Supergrass.

JP said it awkwardly because it was a supergrass that got Pearse's Da sent down. Pearse just crouched over the table and caressed in another red. They're good. Rammed home another black. They sound a bit like Madness.

You look like you'll be here for a while, I'm away for a shite, said JP.

Pearse peered down the thin shaft of the cue. It grazed gently against his chin, then another ball dropped. Don't be too long. There's always the possibility I'll miss. He raised an insouciant eyebrow and smiled. JP smiled back. You couldn't even be jealous of Pearse, he was just in another league altogether.

Three cars, a tractor and two ladies in lycra power-walk past in the time it them to amble out the road, like some happy funeral cortege. Approaching the final corner Noel and JP are well ahead, and JP stands with the bullet in his hand.

Pressure's on Flynn, don't be shittin' the nest.

Noel runs ahead to caddy for him. Not a peep, not a peep! Noel shouts. No clear line around the bend. Bullets has a language of its own. JP isn't a total makeweight here, he has some game—with a flick of the wrist he sends the bullet skidding from left to right and he's round the corner and down the hill, leaving Noel with a straight road before him. Needing a miracle, Monty sends his shot clattering into the wall. Then Noel leaves JP within forty yards of the finish and an easy shot to victory.

No pressure JP. Don't be fillin' the togs.

Armagh men and Corkmen have different styles of throwing. In Armagh they use a wide, under-arm bowling action, but in Cork they *hinch* it, with a sharp windmill motion. This time, just for the craic, JP hinches it. The ball veers for ten yards, bounces straight off the road and lands deep in the ditch.

What the fuck was that? screams Beaker, incredulous.

You think you're a Corkman now?

Just throw the ball right. You'll still be shite but at least you won't make a dick of yourself, says Noel bitterly. Even though they still win handily, Noel is only partially placated.

JP was still in the toilets washing his hands when the shooting started. He knew straight away what it was, he had heard gunfire before. The only window was far too tiny for escape so he threw his back against the door to stop anyone getting in—it was glorified chipboard, if they shot at it he'd be a goner, but it was all he could do to stand there, shuddering at the feral whine of the guns and the exploding of the glass going on out there. The crying out, the laughing, the noise of their hatred, it seemed to last for a long time. Then eventually without reason or prelude it stopped.

A minute passed. Maybe it was ten. In that time something changed in JP. Terror was there of course, but that receded and something unlikely bubbled up instead: calculation. Standing with his back to the flimsy door, close to death, he calculated the probability of the gunmen still being out there waiting against the probability that they'd be gone. We're in a narrow city street, no arterial routes adjacent, escape will be tricky, and it's a small town, the alarm will have gone up. And we're in a nationalist area, it's possible somebody might be nearby who will shoot back at them, and they're thick but they're not that thick, they won't take chances. They're cowards. They didn't come looking for a fight. Not them. They'll be gone. The Snook will be the safest place in the north of Ireland now. It all seemed watertight, when you calculated it out.

They reach the finishing line where The Arena once stood, and Monty pours another cup of the whiskey to toast again. To Pearse. The Arena had been a gigantic nightclub, among the biggest in Ireland and incongruous as some alien spacecraft landed in the rolling hills. All that remains of it now is an acre of hard standing overgrown with moss and grass and brambles. The car park is derelict and weed-infested but still recognisable as the place where they got drunk for the first time, bought drugs for the first time, got a hand-job for the first time, fought with the Blackwatertown boys for the first time. History happened here. Two thousand revellers every Saturday night. It caused a bit of a moral panic, in more innocent times.

D'you remember before the ceasefires there was no drugs?

The 'Ra were the boys knew how to do Prohibition right.

I knew boys got the knees just for having a few joints.

Monty looks down. He almost got the knees but he left Armagh instead. Then suddenly there was drugs everywhere.

There'd be crowds from the Shankill and the Falls beside each other on the dance floor, the sorts that would normally kill each other, all too blissed out to care.

The Prods and the Taigs united by disco biccies. Give me a fucken break.

Some of the worst times came after the ceasefires.

The Orangemen bringing it to the brink over the Drumcree march.

Remember them out blocking the roads?

I remember my Ma stocking up on candles in case the power was cut.

Filling the bath in case the water would be turned off.

When you think of it now.

Billy Wright was on the loose, murdering left right and centre.

He murdered my cousin in Portadown. Well, his gang did, anyway.

Yeah.

Bastard.

Hope he's rotting in hell.

Every night we were going out to the pub my Da used to make me promise to stay well away from the doors, in case they'd come in and shoot the place up.

They did that in loads of places.

Greysteel.

Loughinisland.

Poyntzpass.

The Snook.

JP is standing within yards of the spot in the trees at the bottom of the Arena car park where one wet summer night he lost his virginity. A pretty, slightly scatty girl from Madden, she's a happy memory, and he latches onto her. She was a couple of years older and game as hell, and they'd fooled around before but it still came as a shock when he looped his thumb inside her knicker elastic, gave a speculative little tug, and she nodded her permission. He remembers she had a bag of chips with her, and after, when they rose to fix themselves, the chips had turned to mush. He wonders what ever became of her.

It was only good luck that the Snook was so quiet that morning, normally there'd have been dozens in there. They would have been expecting that, and must've been disappointed to find the place so thinly patronised. What were the odds? Many times in the years to come he would run the calculations, but could never distil a number. They came from Portadown, the killers, their leader was well-known and notorious, JP had seen him in the flesh twice: once in a passing car; and once when he walked in the door of Hogg's pub in Loughgall, and JP and the other Catholics present made a quick exit out the back. A psychotic serial killer with dozens of innocent victims, and he just lands into a country pub like a normal human being, saluted by the regulars. That's what people don't get.

Noel hasn't said much. It's noticeable because Noel was an Arena regular and he threw himself into the scene more than anyone, back in the day. You all right there, kid?

Noel looks up like he's been far away. Sometimes it's hard to remember now, but he was perfectly normal growing up.

What?

Penny for them.

I was just thinking, the Pearse Donnelly Cup—we should get an actual cup.

The rest of the lads shake their heads. They pity him. They shouldn't.

Noel can be a complete nightmare, and when JP thinks about what he has put the family through over the years... well, JP doesn't think about it. He thinks instead: what's the actuarial probability of a connection between the phenomenal amount of drugs Noel ingested over the years, and the fact that he thinks the trees and the bushes are talking to him? That he's out every day throwing bullets at Drumbreda because the hill itself is talking to him? Mocking him. Daring him to keep trying. Actuarially speaking, you'd have to say a link is pretty fucking probable.

Once, JP asked him: what'll you do if you ever get that bullet up the hill?

Noel replied, as if JP was an idiot: Well, then I can top myself.

JP didn't know what to say to that.

It could be worse. One time, Noel nearly drowned because the river told him to jump in. Another time the trees told him to break a bottle over a fella's head, and the fella was a Blackwatertown scumbag and the trees' advice was good advice, but still Noel got sectioned. He's been in and out of hospitals for years. He's home now for a spot of what they call independent living, and throwing the bullet up the hill is about the worst thing he's done lately. As psychotic episodes go, it's not so bad.

The shooters must have destroyed every video game, every fruit machine with all the bells and whistles, because in the Snook there was only an unreal silence. They say that's common after atrocity, an uncanny stillness, like a sick parody of peace. The smell of bad meat and piss and hot tar and burning hair. The smell of massacre. JP felt like he was walking into a film. Jakey was riddled but somehow he wasn't dead—shot twelve times but believe it or not he survived. Eventually he got back on his feet and they rebuilt his face with a much-improved chin, and he got a new nickname: *Teabag,* on account of all the perforations. Years later they put up a memorial plaque and poor old Jakey never even got a mention. That's what you get for living. In the moment itself it didn't look like the probabilities favoured old Jakey, he looked as dead as dead could be. JP left him to it.

Great times.

They were.

Every Saturday night this place would be pumping. Everybody would be off their tits.

Our Summer of Love.

Fucken yellow-pack version anyway.

Shattered glass was strewn and a smoggy deadness hung over the room. Natural light had no way in here, it felt like a place no one had been for a long time. The baize was shredded, bullet holes bored deep into the lead of the snooker table, and blood ran across the floor like spilled Bloody Mary. Stepping in it, the risible thought occurred to JP that his shoes were ruined, he'd never get the stain out. Pearse was lying on this back, half under the table, with his head exploded, and JP fell to his knees to put Pearse into the recovery position because what do you do in a moment like that anyway? Chunks of skull were coming loose and sticking to his sleeves, blood was pouring out of Pearse's limp torso like a stream and JP hadn't the first clue how to stop any of it. Later he would have a hard time remembering any of this. He would remember instead how Pearse's score on the scoreboard was still at nought—he hadn't marked up his score so he must still have been in the balls. Hadn't missed yet. Might have been on for a record break.

They go to the Harps Club; there's a crowd in, and the craic is good. Here JP, did you ever see your Da's cock?

Wha? No.

Starts to undo zip. That gets a good laugh. The others order pints but JP asks for coffee. Why should it be a surprise that they offer him a menu? Had the machine installed ages ago, it's very popular, cappuccino's good, though that's more of a breakfast coffee, isn't it? Changed times.

JP's mother died when he was eleven, and at her funeral he was a sobbing child. Useless. At Pearse's wake JP felt instinctively that his people had a use for him because Pearse was dead but he was alive, and there was hope in that. He poured tea and gathered up mass cards and told everyone who came through the door that Pearse hadn't suffered, whether they asked or not. He gave comfort to Pearse's mother, held her in her raw desolation; helped Pearse's father too by standing out on the road with the men of the estate, telling the RUC and the British army with wordless, sullen hatred to keep their distance while Pearse Donnelly Snr crept back from exile, silent and unseen, to break down over his son's closed casket. You need to be missing something, in order to be useful in a moment like that. JP has been relentlessly useful ever since.

A couple of drinks later, it starts to get messy. Beaker speaks quietly, deadly earnest, he has serious things to talk about, and you can tell he hasn't been drunk in ages because he has that manic look in his eyes. Listen, sitting down and telling my daughters I was leaving, my two beautiful girls, that was the hardest thing I've ever had to do in my life.

You didn't *have* to do it and you *shouldn't* have done it either, you're just a selfish cunt, Monty tells him.

In the month after Pearse died, JP lost two stone. He thought he was living as normal but even Sean, his father, pulled him aside eventually. You're not eating and you're not sleeping, he said, and it was true enough, JP was developing that hollow-cheeked look they have in the Horn of Africa. I'm making a pot of champ, come on, Sean said, and sat him down to two huge plates of buttery mashed potatoes and scallions topped with fried eggs. Later the lads called and JP went out with them to see the Harps against the Ógs at Abbey Park, but instead of going to the match they climbed the wall of the primary school and sat in the playground where they had played as children, and drank a bottle of Buckfast. He rolled home in bad shape that night but Sean turned a blind eye, and when he awoke the next afternoon, Sean fed him a huge Ulster fry. He needed it badly.

Beaker leaves. He tries to make it seem like he's not storming out in a huff, but when JP follows him he finds him standing on the street looking bewildered, like he doesn't know which way is home. Come on, JP says, I'll give you a lift. They drive in silence till they arrive at the house Beaker grew up in, and when Beaker is about to get out JP asks: Will you come back again next year?
Dunno.
It'll be twenty-five years.
I know.
Some year there'll be nobody there, Ciaran.
There was only four of us today. Used to be there'd be dozens.
If we ever don't do it then that'll be it, for good. We'll forget.
Maybe next year somebody will know what to say.
Eventually there'll be nobody left to give a fuck.
Beaker shrugs and gets out, but lingers by the open door a moment.
You still go to mass? he asks.
Mass? Yeah, I still go. Why?
How can you? What with everything that's come out. Brendan Smith. The Magdalene Laundries. The Tuam babies. All that stuff.
JP doesn't think of himself as religious but he doesn't share his generation's

fury towards the Church, and is suspicious of it. He owes the priests a lot – they taught him poetry and history and Thucydides and Xenophon and advanced calculus, gave him an education as good as any millionaire's son. It was only when he got to Trinity that he realised that's not the norm for kids on free school lunches. Now he's a millionaire himself, and it wasn't lefty fucking do-gooders that did that for him, it was hard men in collars who took no shit that did that for him.

You walked out on your wife and kids so you could snort coke and shack up with a young 'un, and *that's* the reason you hate the Church, JP snarls.

Beaker makes to slam the door. I'll tell you the best thing about coming from Armagh, he says: you never get homesick.

Driving back across town JP thinks about Beaker. He knows lots of people like that now, self-serving and rootless, and it's depressing to see it in one of the lads he grew up with. As he's coming down Drumbreda he's thinking: You've lost another friend. And for what? You had to go and get all moralistic, didn't you? I wasn't the one that brought up religion. Yeah, but you have a vicious fucking tongue in your head all the same. What is it with you, that you always have to say it? Why do you always have to be such a fucking *nordie* about everything?

Honestly, this is what it's like in JP's head most of the time.

Suddenly something crashes into the front of the car. Glass smashes. Metal prangs. What the fuck? Somebody's firing.

He screeches. Slaloms. Leaves a giant tilde marked in rubber on the road. Airbag enwombs him.

He climbs out of the car. Steps into the apologetic glow of orange sodium streetlights. Examines himself inside and out—he's shocked but not hurt. He looks back at the car, sitting askew in the road. Perching insolently in the broken glass of the wrecked headlight is a twenty-eight ounce cannonball.

The streetlights taper off halfway down the hill. The bullet came up from the darkness beneath.

Noel emerges breathlessly from below. Jesus, are you all right there?

JP is sitting on the footpath. He lifts his head from his knees, shakes it in his brother's direction. Noel is hugely relieved. Oh thank God, it's only you.

JP can only laugh.

Why do we never talk about Pearse?

What?

Every year we get together and it's supposed to be about him but we never talk about him.

What the fuck is there to say?

I dunno. Something.

Like what?

If we don't share our memories of him with each other, he'll be gone forever.

He *is* gone forever.

But JP persists. Tell me, one thing you remember about Pearse.

He was a sound lad.

Come on Noel.

Noel shrugs. To tell you the truth, I don't really remember that much about him.

What do you mean you don't remember him?

Like, over the years you hear people saying things and you read things and after a while you don't know what's the stuff you actually remember and what's the stuff you just remember being told later.

JP puts his head back into his knees and thinks about his father-in-law, of all people. Not long after his grandfather became one of the first Guards in West Cork, republicans shot him. You know what they told my father about it? he would say. And what my father told me? The same thing everyone from the Civil War told their children about that time. Absolutely nothing! he would declare triumphantly. You lads in the north had three thousand died in twenty-five years, we had four thousand died in as many months, most of them in Kerry and Cork, and none of the families they left behind had any notion about getting justice. They took it all on their own shoulders and they took it to their graves and that's why the generations that came after didn't have to fight the same battles over and over.

Strong people.

People who *decided* to be strong. They offered it up. Not like people now. There was no such thing as *closure* in those days.

And he packed a lot of contempt into that closure.

Only four of us this year. Next year it'll be less.

We can't just forget.

Of course we can forget.

We have to remember.

Remembering is hard.

But forgetting.

Forgetting takes nothing.

Saint Dearbhla's Eyes

Fleeing from Meath to Mayo
her betrothed gave chase,
she turned to face him, ask
what he loved about her,
'your eyes' came in ardent reply
so she plucked them out
each a perfect orb
cool in her hands like beads
and in horror he fled.

She stood there smiling
surprising even herself
relief rushed down her limbs,
she bent over the well,
splashed her face
and those hollow sockets
with scent of mineral and moss,
sight restored in a flash.

She looked at the world
as if for the first time,
she could finally see
how her God was always
on the side of freedom,
how everything glistens,

and how we must risk everything,
trust we were meant
for this, as if telling
the truth for the first time,

as if our hearts
had been plucked out too
and set ablaze
for all the world to see.

Christine Valters Paintner

Kaleidoscope Eye
Serena Lawless

I was wide awake when the Surgeon made an incision in my left eye, inserted forceps, and, with a tiny pop, slid the cataract lens into place. The procedure took less than five minutes. A speculum held my eyelids, so I couldn't blink. The Surgeon stitched up the incision and breezed out of the operating theatre. I couldn't move for several minutes after the surgery. I laid there with a blue sheet covering my face with a hole cut into it for my eye. This was my eighth and final unsuccessful eye surgery.

It had been five years, one month, and twelve days since my first.

Two days earlier, I'd had my seventh procedure on my left eye.

The purpose of this surgery was to put a lens inside my eye: my cataract was removed two years previously, and now a piggy-back lens was being inserted on top of the artificial one. Elderly patients who have cataract operations usually report that when they open their eyes, it's like they can see the world anew, like a fog has been lifted and what was once cloudy is now clear. I knew when I woke up from the general anaesthetic that it hadn't gone well. My world was blurry, with a distinct outline around everything and everyone, my double vision unresolved. I covered my left eye, then my right, and could see that there was no change in my vision. As usual, my left eye had a soft, dreamlike focus.

'The Surgeon wants to see you on Wednesday,' the nurse said when she came to discharge me.

'Wednesday? Can I not go back to work tomorrow?'

'Oh no,' the nurse looked alarmed. 'No, not at all. You can't go back this week, never mind tomorrow. The receptionist will do you up a medical cert.'

*

Once the anaesthetic wore off, I understood why I couldn't go back to work yet. My head felt as heavy as a bowling ball. The area all around my left eye was hot. My face throbbed in time with my pulse. Lying down increased the pressure, but the pain was so intense I could not stay awake for long. That pain: stinging, red-hot, every blink scratching. The heat, like my face was pressed against an oven hob, eye streaming, the thump-thump-thump of my pulse behind my eye. I slept sitting up, propped against pillows, the summer outside my window hidden away by heavy curtains. Still I had to wear sunglasses indoors over my eye shield to protect against any light that bled through the gaps.

Without my sunglasses, I winced even in weak light. I got up close to the mirror, peeled off the eye guard, and inspected my eye. Burst capillaries coloured the white of my eye red, making the green of my iris startling. What was usually an olive green was now emerald. I was used to that happening post-surgery, but what I wasn't expecting to see was a misshapen pupil. My right eye pupil was normal, round; the left a soft-edged square. My vision was so bad that I didn't trust what I was seeing. My brother looked at my eye and confirmed that I wasn't crazy: my pupil was not round. If this had been my first surgery, I would have panicked. There was something like that simmering with the nausea in my stomach, but more than being worried, I was exhausted. Something was wrong, and I was exasperated that the Surgeon wanted to wait until Wednesday, leaving me to worry all day Tuesday with only local anaesthetic drops to soothe pain. The drops hit my eye cold and trailed down my cheek hot.

Everyone in my family wears glasses, but I always had the worst vision of us all. I was so young when I first started wearing glasses—maybe seven years old— that I can't remember what perfect vision was like. At its worst, my prescription was -5 in my right eye, and -7 in the left. Sometimes, my friends would try on my glasses and say, 'Jesus, you're blind!' I would hold up my hand in front of my face, palm touching my nose, and move my hand backward until it started to look blurry. I usually stopped at around six inches' distance.

I don't remember my first optician's appointment, but I had the same optometrist throughout my life. He was a soft-spoken and patient man who never had bad breath, like he was concerned about being close to peoples' faces all day. Appointments with him never started on time and often went over because he loved to talk. Every pair of new glasses gave me the strangest sensation that the pavement was rising to meet me or rushing down into deep hollows on the ground. The reverberations vibrated up my legs with every misstep.

*

On the Wednesday I returned to the hospital, I went alone. I wore my sunglasses and stumbled along hallways, hissing like an animal until I got to the right ward and waited for the Surgeon. I sat with my head bowed, my sunglasses firmly in place, my knuckles pressed above my eyebrow, below my eye, as close as I dared to get. The waiting room was packed, and people sitting near me shifted uneasily; I could see them glance at me in their peripheral vision, a manifestation of their worst fears.

It would be easy for me to hate the Surgeon, but these constant surgeries and my faulty eye are a source of frustration for him, too. When I first met him for a laser surgery consultation, he told me that there was a one in a million chance of it going wrong. I was that one, a smudge on his perfect record. Part of me wanted to apologise to the other patients in the waiting room, to put them at ease—they would be fine, because I was the anomaly. I had sacrificed my eye so that they wouldn't have to.

Hours went by before I was called into a dark room and greeted by the Surgeon. He led me by the elbow, treating me carefully, and guided me to the slit lamp. He took a brief look at my eye and invited another doctor to do the same.

'There's a tiny little gap between your old lens and the new one, so I'll just need to,' he made a flick with his fingers, 'pop that back onto it to relieve the pressure.'

I'm not sure if I said anything. Inside, I was screaming. This would be the eighth procedure on my left eye. Dimly, I was aware of a nurse leading me back through the hospital. I'm sure I smiled and made small talk, but my body hummed with adrenaline. Up ahead, I could see the exit. I winced against the light, but the urge to run was second only to the pain in my eye. I didn't want the surgery. I needed it.

After I signed the *I Will Not Sue* paperwork and handed over my insurance details, I was moved onto the emergency surgery list for that day. I had a few hours to worry about what all this meant. The pressure must've been what was causing the headaches. The eye drops inserted into my eye for Monday's surgery made my pupil too big, so the lens was leaning forward and pushing against the front of my eye instead of sitting on top of the lens. That gap between the two lenses was what was causing all the problems, and based on how everyone was rushing around me, it needed to be fixed. I was given a paper robe and a bed. I thought about what it must have looked like inside of my eye, how a few millimetres could cause so much discomfort. Somewhere down the corridor, a girl was crying persistently from a dark room, wailing that she was in pain, that it hurt. The nurses murmured quiet reassurances, yet she cried still. I pitied her. She did nothing for my confidence.

With every passing surgery, I had grown more anxious. I was never squeamish about my eyes before, but I quivered on the hospital bed as I waited for a gap between surgeries. I had five years of experience to let me know that I was going to experience not just pain, but anxiety.

My first laser surgery brought more excitement than nerves. I had no idea that it would be the beginning of a long, pointless venture, leaving me only marginally better off than I was when I began. The prospect of perfect vision made the idea of pain manageable. Because I didn't know what to expect, this first surgery was okay. The second was uncomfortable. The third was torture.

At my initial consultation with the Surgeon, I knew there was a possibility that I would have to have two surgeries. My vision was weak; my prescription was not ideal for Lasik. The Surgeon put my mind at ease: the cost involved covered any necessary top-up surgeries.

While I was disappointed that it didn't work the first time, I wasn't surprised. I was surprised to learn that I had double vision. My eyesight had been so bad before that I hadn't noticed it. For a long time after surgery, I couldn't drive or read without headaches. I could write, but my words were illegible, a halo around the edges. The second surgery went much the same as the first, but it didn't correct this impairment. As time passed and my double vision didn't improve, I grew accustomed to it, the double vision became a normal but unwelcome part of my life. It only had an impact in the dark. At night, my double vision revealed itself to me through light; split, burst and fragmented, like a kaleidoscope.

The Surgeon arranged to do a third surgery. This was rare; so unusual, in fact, that he did not wish to perform the surgery until two other specialists from the UK could attend. They looked at me, analytical, and whispered among themselves. Didn't I make an interesting specimen? The Surgeon warned me that since I'd had two surgeries, there was no longer enough tissue on my eye to perform a third by Lasik. Modern bilateral Lasik involves creating a flap on the surface of the eye to expose the cornea. The laser goes through the hole created by the flap to go directly to the cornea and correct the vision. The flap is then put back and heals with the use of eye drops. It is relatively painless—pre-op involves a lot of local anaesthetic drops. For a few days after Lasik, it only felt mildly irritating, like grit in the eye.

As there was not enough tissue to create a corneal flap, the Surgeon had to perform laser surgery the old-fashioned way. Prior to Lasik, patients used to get one eye done at a time and return six months later when the eye was healed to have the other one done. The pain was excruciating; I don't know how they ever went back.

A foam cut-out pillow for your head. Straps for your hands. The speculum to hold your eye open. The drops, hitting your eye and giving you the impulse to blink but being unable to. Your other eye covered so you can't see through that, either. Your pupil, blown out so wide that you can't focus on the machine that rolls over to the bed and hovers directly over your head. For a moment, you're blind; the dark presses down on you, panic, then the light, red as hell. You can hear people moving around, ghostly figures cut through the black, but you can't see them, not really. You know they're there when they put something else into your eye, how the skin around your cheek pulls when you try to see, to blink. Not breathing properly, inhaling but barely exhaling. The flickering red light, fizzling, rippling like something underwater, but it is your eye that floats. Nails biting into palms. The smell of burning, telling yourself lies, *that's not you, that smell is not your eye*. Chemical burning, smoke, the wrongness of it.

I knew what to expect, but it was all this and more, because now, there was pain. I could feel the pressure of the laser on my eye, feel where it bore into my cornea, directly on the surface of my eye. I imagined the thin layer at the top of my eye cracking like burnt land, a volcanic eruption. This surgery lasted longer. My chants became desperate. My jaw ached from clenching my teeth. When it was over, I couldn't move. My body was rigid with shock, an exclamation point. A nurse cradled me under my arm and helped me up. Everyone was quiet. The specialists lurked in the background. Through the fog of pain, I wondered what the point of them was. I shuffled to the Surgeon's office and glared at him as best I could from behind my scorched eyes. I don't remember what he said to me. He gave me a full box of local anaesthetic drops. I used every single one.

At one point, I had been taking eye drops for sixteen months. Betagan, Prednisolone Sodium Phosphate, FML Liquifilm, Chloromycetin. The eye drops were anti-inflammatory, or antibiotic, or steroid. Some kept in the fridge, some room temperature. I had to draw up a schedule to make sure I took the right ones at the right time, as time had to be considered between drops, but then some drops were four daily, some eight, some more, some less. I had to plan my life around my eye drop schedule. They made my eyelashes brittle. I couldn't wear makeup to cover up my bruised, delicate skin.

Tilt back your head, rest the heel of your hand against your nose, open your eyes wide. What you don't expect is the taste. When it happened first, I thought there was something wrong with my eye, some acidic fluid leaking from a rupture, but it was the drops. They settle, then slide to the tear duct in the corner. From there, they sink down the nasal passage and to the back of the throat, where they hit the tongue. Cloying, bile-like, reminiscent of acid reflux but warm, thick somehow. The taste lingered and wouldn't wash away.

Glasses are not a cure. At best, they slow down the inevitable. The older I got, the thicker my lenses were. My frames did little to hide their girth. After thinning, my lenses were close to half a centimetre thick, and the bigger the lenses, the more they cost. I got contact lenses when I was around fourteen years old, but I had a few obstacles: one, my high prescription meant that not all brands stocked lenses for me; two, they were expensive; and three, my eyes were a weird shape.

My eyes are shaped more like rugby balls than footballs. They have a sharp edge to them that meant that standard contact lenses wouldn't sit properly on my eye. They swam around with every blink. I could get tighter lenses with high prescriptions, but just like my glasses, they cost more than normal. I rationed my contacts to make them last, cleaning and storing them carefully, only replacing them when they developed jagged edges. They were too expensive to wear all the time, but when I wore them I recognised myself—ah, there you are. With contacts, I was the same as everyone else. I could see, if only for a few hours at a time.

I loved wearing contact lenses, loved the ritual of them. Peeling back the protective film on a new contact and slipping it onto my palm, a crescent moon. Sterile saline solution to clean the lens, rubbing it gently between forefinger and palm before balancing it on the tip of my finger. Examining it to make sure that the edges were not flat but round, that the lens was not inside out. Then, pulling down my eyelid and slipping it into the space between my lid and eye, slow and careful in case I blinked it out. I wasn't afraid to touch my eyes. That was all it took to see. I didn't even mind the itchy dryness of a lens worn for too long. I can't wear contact lenses now. The surgeries flattened my cornea.

Once, when I was using daily disposable lenses, I was removing the lens when it ripped in my eye. The edge of the left-behind lens was sharp and sore, plastic made of glass. I pulled down my eyelid and poured saline solution in my eye. I ran my finger around the white of my eye, pinching to find the tattered remains. When my eye reddened and went dry from prodding, I stopped. Although I couldn't see it in the sink, I assumed I must have blinked it out. It turned up three days later in the corner of my eye when I was washing my face. I don't know where it went, whether it visited the back of my eye.

The recovery time for my third laser surgery was six months, but the first few weeks were agony. The night I went home after surgery, I walked into my house, my entire body braced, muscles coiled tight. I didn't say anything as I walked through the kitchen without stopping, desperate to be alone in my bedroom. All I could do was hiss in breaths through my clenched teeth. Hot tears ran down my cheek, but I wasn't crying. My eye was streaming nonstop like it was broken. It stung whether it was open or closed. There was no relief.

I couldn't sleep. Lying down, I felt like my heart had moved to my skull and was thumping wildly behind my eye, making it throb. The anaesthetic drops gave me relief for less than fifteen minutes at a time. With fistfuls of bed sheets clutched in my hands, I screamed in pain. Eventually, I gave up on the bed and went downstairs in the middle of the night. My brother came in from working the nightshift to find me sitting in the wing-backed chair, my body curled pretzel-like, wearing sunglasses against the dim under-cupboard lighting in the kitchen. In my hand, I clutched a tumbler of whiskey.

'Jesus Christ, what happened to you?'

I curled the blanket around myself tighter and knocked back a few painkillers with a slug from my glass. What happened to me, or what did I do to myself? Over time, my left eyelid began to droop noticeably, a lazy eye.

The Surgeon was busier than ever when I called to see him with a pain in my eye. He was going away for a month; I have a vision of him surrounded by nurses, patients, people hanging from him, wanting a piece of him before he left. He prescribed me eye drops. I wouldn't see him again until he returned.

The pain got worse. There was a small red dot—if my eye was a clock, the dot was two o'clock, just barely visible under my eyelid. The dot grew larger and curled around the curve of my iris, the pain increasing to something like a hot needle, barely a millimetre thick but pinching its way through my cornea. I went back to the surgery and saw another doctor. My chin barely brushed the slit lamp when she pronounced I had conjunctivitis. She promptly began sanitising the equipment and everywhere I had touched, and she was careful not to hand me the prescription.

And still, it got worse. It wasn't just my eye, but my entire body. Days were spent on the couch with a blanket, my eye too sore to look at the TV, or computer, or read, my body too weak to do anything else. My eye was so badly infected that I was regimental in my treatment. I sterilised water by boiling and cooling it before cleaning my eye, and then used bleach to clean anywhere I touched. My hands cracked and dried.

Once again, sleeping was uncomfortable. The pressure vibrated behind my eye when I was lying flat, so I could only sleep lying on my right side, because the area all around my left eye was swollen from the infection. I sterilised water nightly and left it by my bedside to cool so that in the morning, I could clean my eye. Overnight, my eye glued shut. The area was tender to touch, but I stuck to my routine, dabbing cotton wool into the sterile water and disposing of it immediately after. Because I had to sleep on my right side, the infection wept from the left, trickled across the bridge of my nose and spread the infection into the right eye.

When the pain became so intense that it was clear I wasn't getting better, I went to A&E. My eyelid had puffed up, shiny and red, allowing only a slit of my eye to be seen. Every blink scratched my cornea. My eye wept continuously; I dabbed at it under my sunglasses with a tissue and worried about how I would dispose of it without making anyone else sick. I was moved from the waiting room into a room by myself in A&E, where I waited even longer still. The doctor who came to see me was a tall, thin man who didn't look old enough to have earned his grey hair. He was stern, all business. I explained my situation to him and showed him the eye drops I had been taking.

'This is it?'

I nodded.

'You may as well have been taking skittles.'

He was angry, but not directly at me. He prescribed me different eye drops, an oral antibiotic, something for the pain, and an eye cream.

'Since you can't see anyway,' he joked.

The cream was to be put directly onto my eye three times a day, and while it would impair my vision, it was the thing that helped my recovery the most. I was told to report to outpatients after the weekend, and thereafter I went three times a week until I was better. On my last appointment, I was explaining to the outpatients' doctor that I still felt a pain every time I blinked. This doctor had become used to me, and even remembered me a year or more later when I ended up being a patient of his again. It was a little frustrating that this doctor—a young, handsome, kind man—was seeing me at my most disgusting, but the ordeal had stripped me of my dignity. I felt subhuman, hideous. I had one more layer of repulsiveness to reveal to him.

'Let's have a look,' he said.

He pulled his stool closer, so he could examine my eye. Without much warning, he flipped my upper eyelid inside-out.

'Aha. I see the problem.'

He released my eyelid and disappeared out of the room for a moment. When he returned, he had a small package in his hand, from which he removed a sterile tweezers.

'Hold on.' I hitched in a breath. 'What are you going to do with that?'

'There's just a tiny flap of skin on your eyelid from one of the blisters,' he explained. One of? Blisters? 'I just need to pull it off. It won't hurt, I promise.'

'You're going to—no.'

The doctor smiled patiently at me. 'You'll feel much better when I remove it.'

It became very real at that moment, everything I had been through. The pain. The severity of it. I didn't realise there were blisters under my eyelid, but it made sense now. I remember seeing something white in the mirror when I blinked. Still, the idea of this doctor—this handsome doctor—coming at my eye with a tweezers was almost too much for me to handle.

His smile began to waver. The waiting room was full of patients, and I was wasting time.

'I just need a minute,' I said, thinly.

I took a few steadying breaths, and he flipped my eyelid inside out. He instructed me to look down. I began my inner chant, lying to myself again. *This isn't happening. Those tweezers are not going near your eye.* The doctor pulled away the flap. I blinked rapidly, and it didn't hurt.

'There,' he said, smiling again.

He showed me the slip of white skin. It was the size of a fingernail. He handed me a tissue to wipe my eyes. It came away red.

When I finished the antibiotics, it was obvious that my vision had deteriorated. I returned to the Surgeon.

'The last time I heard of that strain of conjunctivitis was in Scotland,' he said after examining my eyes. 'It's a vicious strain. They had to close the entire ward and quarantine the patients who had it. The ophthalmologists who worked there couldn't work again.'

'Why?' I asked, thinking of medical malpractice.

'Because they contracted the infection. It remains dormant in the system, so they couldn't work on people's eyes again. It was too risky.'

The infection wasn't done with me yet. Like those doctors, it remained dormant in my eyes. The infection left scars all over my corneas, tiny scratches that weren't visible without the use of microscopes, but that left lesions deep enough to refract the light that entered my eyes. Once more, I was on eye drops—this time, steroids, for far too long.

Long-term use of steroids is never recommended, but I was on doctor's orders. Between the scars and the drops, I couldn't tell if my vision was improving, but I noticed a soft focus to my vision. The steroids caused a cataract to develop on the lens of my left eye.

I was furious. I thought of my grandmother who was in her eighties before she had cataract surgery. It gave her a new lease of life—she lived to ninety-six—but it was a condition I associated with elderly people, and not without evidence.

The steroids gave me the eye of an old woman. As the infection was still dormant in my eye, I couldn't have cataract surgery until it was no longer there, so I had to continue taking the drops. I was intensely frustrated that after all this time, all the surgeries and the infection and the treatments, that I now had another issue to resolve. When people asked me if I could see yet, I said that I was going to have my eye removed and have a prosthetic put in, like Mad-Eye Moody in the *Harry Potter* series.

After a few months, at one of my check-ups, the Surgeon shocked me by performing a surprise surgery.

'That's healing up nicely,' he said, looking at my eye through the slit lamp. 'We'll just pop you into the other room and do a quick bit of laser to get rid of those scars.'

Once more, I found myself lying on the bed, my head held in a foam pillow, my pupil dilated. My nerves were raw, screaming. At least it was over quickly this time, just a quick zap to get rid of the stubborn scars, but emotionally, I was wrecked. It brought it all back, the terror. I didn't allow myself to think too deeply, to probe this feeling and figure out what it meant. One more surgery, I thought to myself, and it'll all be done, and I'll be able to see, and this will all have been worth it.

I spent a lot of time in the Surgeon's office. As my pupils widened from eye drops, I examined the medical illustration of a cross-section of the eye. I looked at the lens and saw the size of it, tried to imagine what mine would look like, blurred over and cloudy, how clear the new lens would be. I imagined the Surgeon pulling it out of my eye like a slip of silk.

On December 23rd, 2013, I woke up from cataract surgery and still could not see properly. I thought of my grandmother, and how she had known right away that it had worked. Instant results. My vision was microscopically better, but it was far from being fixed. I could almost see, but everything had a soft-focus haze around it, like an inner glow.

Even though I should have known that there would be stitches as there had been an incision, it still came as a surprise to me to learn that I had to have them removed. This was the second time a doctor had come towards my eye with something sharp—while I was awake, anyway—and my breathing became fast and light, panic setting in.

'Just—just wait a second,' I snapped at the Surgeon. I usually tried to treat him with courtesy, but the way he had to do this quickly, to get rid of me to see someone else, it bothered me. I took my time and made him wait.

'Look down for me,' he said when I put my chin on the slit-lens microscope. He pulled on my upper eyelid. I couldn't see him move the tweezers towards my eye, but I felt it when he began to pull the stitches. It wasn't pain, exactly, but an ache, something like nausea but in my eye. My mouth watered like I was going to be sick. I began to panic; he was going to pull my eye out of my head; the white of my eye had grown over the stitches and now he was picking at it. Instinctively, I jerked my head back. The stitches came loose. The Surgeon wasn't pleased that I had moved, but at least the job was done.

Every time I had a surgery, I got my hopes up. I tried to control them, to manage my expectations, but that's not easily done. Hope is not something that a person can exercise any power over. It hurts just the same if you let your hopes rise or not. The disappointment, the dramatic 'why me' is as inescapable as it is pathetic.

When I had a check-up, the Surgeon suggested that he could put a second cataract lens on top of the existing one. The idea exhausted me.

I wished I'd never met him.

A month or so after my cataract surgery, I began to see floaters. Not only clear white lines or dots that swam in and out of focus—these were different. I could see a distinct black shape, a near-constant dot in my vision. I would jerk my head, thinking I saw a wasp, but it was something inside my eye. Cataract surgery demands you to be particularly careful, no heavy work, no bending, and no lifting. While I took care at first, I eventually started lifting things I shouldn't have. Floaters in your vision can be a sign of a detached retina, and untreated can lead to blindness. When I enquired about this with the Surgeon, I was told to come in immediately.

I expected the Surgeon to check my eye through the slit-lens microscope, but instead, he patted the trolley in his office. The Surgeon instructed me to lie on my back, then he leaned over me with a lens roughly the size of a two-euro coin. He placed this lens directly onto my eye and positioned his own eye the other side, only two inches away. The Surgeon moved the lens around my eye. I inhaled sharply and didn't breathe again until he was done. My eye streamed from the pressure. On the other side of the lens, the Surgeon had placed a light. I was blinded by it. All I could feel was pressure, and all I could see was the bright white light. There was no room in my head for thoughts. I was subhuman again; an eye without a body.

I returned to my body in clenched fists, an aching jaw, blood rushing in my ears. The Surgeon told me that there was a tear in my retina, but it wasn't very big, so he would be able to go in and fix it when he did the piggy-back lens. I heard all this from behind a wall of shock. I'd never felt fear surrounding my eyes before I'd started this journey with this the Surgeon, but with every passing surgery, procedure, or examination, I was beginning to grow more and more anxious. I couldn't get out of his office fast enough.

During one of our meetings, the Surgeon once more gave me a surprise surgery —this one minor. I never noticed the upright laser machine in his office before. He led me to a seat and tied a strap around my head, effectively attaching me to the machine. My fingers twitched but I didn't remove the strap. The familiar red dot fizzled menacingly on the other side of the machine, staring me in the eye. It was over in less than two minutes. I didn't notice any difference in my vision. I was coiled tight, all clenched fists and held breaths.

I avoided the Surgeon for a few months, unable to bring myself to tackle the issue of my eye again, but indigence made me return. My vision was beginning to deteriorate already. My right eye was growing weaker to compensate for the left.

'Your cornea is crystal clear,' the Surgeon said, admiring his handiwork.

'Well, I still can't see properly,' I said.

He could spout the clarity of my eye all he liked, but I still felt like I was looking from behind a layer of fog. The Surgeon repeated his suggestion to put a second cataract lens over the first, a piggy-back lens to compensate for the half a step difference in my eye.

'I'm going to put a contact lens in your eye. It's a twenty-four-hour lens so you can leave it in for a few days. If you notice a difference, that'll mean that the piggy-back lens will work. If not, we'll think of something else.'

Luckily, nothing else had to be thought of. The lens worked. It still wasn't perfect, but it was close, and I imagined that having the lens inside my eye would make all the difference.

Sometimes when I am talking to people, I can see their line of vision move to stare at my left eye, a furrow forming in their brow. They look politely confused, a little worried, like they're wondering: should they mention it or not? The two lenses in my left eye have given me a strange novelty that disturbs even me. If the light hits them in a certain way, you can see the silvery discs take up my entire pupil and reflect the light, a cat's eye. I have the flat, deadened eye of a shark. When the light hits my eye, I'm blind; I can almost feel the light bouncing away, like a mirror. The Mad-Eye Moody joke tastes sour now on my tongue now, acidic like eye drops on the back of my throat.

'Do you regret it?'

My initial response was that I regretted it didn't work. I still had faith that one day, I'd have a procedure that would fix my vision and I would be able to see properly for the first time in over twenty years.

For my eighth procedure, the Surgeon operated on my eye with only local anaesthetic, sliced into it while I was wide awake, and at once, I regretted it all. I regretted every moment of the past five years when my eye caused me problems: the anxiety, the infections, the surgeries, the procedures and examinations, the months without makeup to hide the puffy, purplish-red skin, the lazy left eye, the pain and the fear and well-intentioned enquires from everyone wondering if, at last, I could see. The disappointment in delivering bad news. I missed my glasses. I missed my contacts.

I wasn't given a general anaesthetic before my surgery that Wednesday, and everything about it had the feel of a secret emergency. Eye-searing agony had already set in when my father picked me up from the hospital. He was outraged that I needed another surgery. I waited in his car, while he filled my prescription for me, my fist pressed to the area around my eye, grinding my teeth together to chew on the need to scream. I knew what was waiting for me: more eye drops, sleepless nights propped up against pillows, sticky glue from eye-guards on my cheek and forehead that wouldn't come off easily but had to be worn in case I applied any pressure to my eye in my sleep. No makeup. No lifting. No exertion. No reading. And no improvement.

Glasses suited me. I had no issue with contact lenses. My initial motivation was cost: between glasses and contacts, I could spend anywhere in the region of €300 to €500 a year. Laser surgery was a little over €3000, and the results should have lasted the rest of my life. It wasn't just the potential savings or the practicalities; it was an investment in myself. I wanted to open my eyes in the morning and see without fumbling for glasses. I wanted to see without my eyes growing itchy and sore from dry contact lenses. I wanted to see. Every failed procedure compounded my frustration, but I went back, sure that this time something would fall into place.

The last time I saw the Surgeon, in the outpatients' department, I put it to him bluntly:

'At this point, would glasses be an option for me?'

'They would be, yes. We can discuss that if you make an appointment at my office.'

Five years and eight procedures later, I would be back where I started.

After my first cataract surgery, when my eyesight felt like it was weakening again, I decided to go back to my old ophthalmologist. The same receptionist and nurse were there and welcomed me warmly with smiles and enquires into what I was doing now and how my mother was. I took a seat in the office, and he did an eye test with me. My right was nearly perfect, my left quite weak.

'Who did you say you got your laser surgery with?' he asked me, and I told him.

'He's apparently the best,' I said.

'Is he?

I frowned; I could've sworn when I was talking to him about the possibility of my having laser surgery, that he had told me about the Surgeon. But apparently, I misremembered.

'I wish you had come to me before you had your surgery,' he said.

*

There was a trend in photography that was popular a few years ago called Bokeh photography, an out-of-focus effect that used a point of focus and blurred everything else. This worked best when used with lights, or lens flares.

My eyes do it all on their own.

Between my double vision and the remnants of the scars caused by the infection, the light refracts before it hits the back of my eye, splintering it. I don't notice it much during the day, but at night it causes a noticeable distortion. Many people who have laser surgery complain of bright glares from lights, especially at night, but this is different. Streetlights leave long fat streaks in my vision. I notice it most at traffic lights, the filter arrows turning right. I know which light the real arrow is, but to the right of it, above it, below it, off-centre, there are multiple arrows, some bright, some dull, some sharp and some soft. I've tried to count, but they shift and merge. There are at least a dozen lights, probably more, suspended above the traffic. They all point the same direction, at least.

The First Real Time
John Patrick McHugh

The first is efficient, mature: 'Hey xx i have a free house Friday ... Wanna come over ?'

It only took you four drafts.

The second text is written five minutes later, after chewing on the edge of your baby finger, after stomping downstairs and peering into the fridge and cupboards, after retrieving the phone from where you had flung it on the carpeted floor. It is blasé, indifferent, shitting-itself: 'If u want to.'

You press send without looking and immediately a structure bends in the gooey pit of your stomach and you turn off the phone and turn it on again and pace your box room and hate yourself deeply and wait and wait and wait.

Of course, you've kissed others. At discos, or in the front row of the cinema, or while standing on a broken pallet behind Lavelle's; your tipsy right hand ambitiously hiking up inside the zipped tight fleece. At a house party over the Christmas you even managed sex with a red-cheeked college home-comer named Hannah Heron. An exhausting ten minutes spent flexing your calves to stone and thinking how the plastic snowflakes dangling across the fireplace looked more like rotting teeth than glistening snow. When Hannah asked if you could get off her now please, you pretended to come at that exact second of instruction because, you guessed, it would be rude otherwise. It would be bad form otherwise. But Emily, you tell your sticky private self, is different. She is the first girl you've kissed more than once, kissed when it wasn't dark or sweaty-walled or thrumming with noise. Special, you've decided she is special.

It started when an informer let it be known that she—somehow—fancied you. She was a year younger, fresh, and you were aware of her from narrow corridors and assemblies. In reply to the news, you had only shrugged and muttered sounds like, 'whatever', 'yeah?', and 'who?' You then spent the rest of the week strategically clomping past her locker, roundish belly sucked in and chest tensed, in the pretence of checking the football corkboard. You couldn't talk face to face, obviously, so you messaged her online, chatting with shattered punctuation and three-quarters spelling. Eventually, you arranged to meet down the laneway by Keel beach. A Sunday in February, smoky and dry with copper hinted beneath cloud, and you were early, apparently calm, apparently collected, and her arms were crossed as she turned the corner and you said, 'Emily,' and it seemed then you were playing a game to discover who could avoid eye contact the longest. You talked vaguely about school, the Leaving, weekend jobs, school again, all the while marching towards the cover of the playground, where, pressed against the climbing wall, you finally licked the face off one another. Afterward, walking home, your chest echoed dully like evidence, your skin glowed.

Since then you've been meeting her semi-regularly after school in the basketball court. She's not your girlfriend, technically, but for the last five weeks you've been with her. That distinction has been sealed. You know nothing much about her other than that her skin is the colour of streetlamp against wet pavement, and that when she cracks a proper smile a suicide-edged snaggletooth peeks out. You presume this is all you need to know about her, this is how it works. When together, when between kisses, you act as if you're interviewing for a job you don't truly want, securely jailing all mentions of PlayStation games, the music you actually listen to, your tabletop Elven army, your membership of an online forum for divorcees.

Sometimes, alone, you fantasise about putting yourself in physical peril for her safety, of being wounded in front of her (preferably a superficial gash, preferably because of her idiotic mistake), but mostly, alone, you hate the thought of others pairing you together, you hate the thought of admitting you view her as something precious. You're ashamed in case she doesn't measure up in their estimates. You're scared that she isn't good enough, though, you're not exactly sure who she isn't good enough for. You insist these are normal fears. This is normal behaviour.

It isn't till the next morning—a Thursday—that you receive her answer to your invitation: 'maybe.'

Followed quickly by another rumble: 'But ask in person next time!!'

You breathe again. Life can be so very beautiful. Before the first class of the day, Maths with Conroy, you compose a steely reply, 'will do,' and then daring yourself add a ';)'. It feels like a significant weight has been lifted. It feels like a significant weight has been piled onto your shoulders.

At lunchtime, you roost with the lads as normal. By the far far wall, defaced by chalked names, its slim crevices treasured with crisp packets. Cigarettes are shared, tabs of Coke cans tssked, gelled skulls bob, and abuse bleeds over silence. The crew's currency is what you have done versus what you haven't. Alcohol, smoking, petty drugs, and the laddersteps of sex grant privilege. Allow you to escape slagging, nicknames, being pathetic at sports. But that means you have to cash in when presented with an opportunity. That means you must tell them about her and the free house.

Throughout lunch, you loiter in the borders of conversation. Laughing only at the safe jokes, agreeing heartily about who is a wanker and who isn't, and, when possible, siding with Mitch—the leader. As wrappers are tossed down by dandelions, as chat swings to the burden of afternoon French, you feel your stomach tighten, this clench between ribs, and you decide it would be best to stall, to tell them when you hear the bell. Less time, you figure, for interrogation. For mockery. And when the bell eventually sounds—wide and strangely chirpy and too soon to your ears—and the lads crank their shoulders and begin the theatrical process of strolling towards class, you blurt it out. Blunt as a mirror in the morning.

'Yeah, so,' you say, scuffing the ground with a heel drag. 'Yeah, so, she's coming over tomorrow.'

Faint sunlight on your neck.

In the surrounding trees crows squabble and beyond the glazed windows, the dreary screech of chairs hauled out from under desk.

Within the group a moment of headtilts, sniffy nostrils, tetchiness, as the lads turn inward and reflect quietly on this information and on their own wet failures, their own staleness in comparison, a moment thawed only when Mitch pucks you on the arm and winks: 'Fuckin Casanova here! You kept that one under your blanket.'

The rest pile in then. Voices bright and filled with taunts, best wishes, and professional advice. 'Nice one,' 'fair play,' and 'johnny.'

Modestly, you fend off their enquiries. You spit out a dangling web and it lands on your own runner, but you're unfazed. 'Might as well, like,' you say.

The lads whoop. They call Emily names. Cruel names, but you don't correct them. No. Instead you snigger along as triumph knocks heavy in your chest.

When you arrive home that evening, your mother is sat in front of the box. By her feet are three or four stacked mugs. The only light in the room is the intermittent blink of the television.

In the same breath you cry hello, you wonder about dinner.

She says there is risotto on the counter.

You thank her and retrieve a pizza from the freezer.

Over the last three months, you've noticed how the cuffs of your mother's woollen jumpers have become flecked with hardened chips of paint, how her hair, unkempt and long, has started to grey. MammyMayo, a regular on the forum, often says that your general appearance is important, both for immediate healing and, in time, for a new vibrant future.

After setting the oven, you check the fridge and wearily count the three cartons of milk. A glass windchime sings, the curtains aren't pulled closed.

From the doorway, you ask what's on the telly, though you know the answer.

She swivels, smiles at you with squared teeth: 'Judge Judy.' She has every series recorded and watches the episodes nightly in three-hour blocks. 'It's a good one, too,' she says.

'You went to the shop?'

The back of her head nods.

Your fingernail picks absently at the wooden doorframe, the cream paint wrinkled and crunchy, as you fumble with the next question: 'Did you get much work done today?'

'Not today,' she responds cheerfully. 'No, not today.'

The TV gets louder.

'The cases are real,' a voice booms, 'The people are real.'

Rarely now does she venture out to the glasshouse, her studio, disordered with clay and plastic buckets and woven sacks. Rarely now does she seek your approval of her creations, casts of women with bull horns. You understand from the forum that neglecting your work is not a great sign. You're reminded of what Debbie67 says about bad days. Bad days can morph into bad months if you're not careful. You could be experiencing a spell of the sorrys without even realising it. The sorrys, Debbie67 writes, are not an example of positive defiance. The sorrys are, in fact, the opposite of positive defiance.

Hunched on the stairs, you eat the pizza and watch your mother watching the TV. The house is free tomorrow because she is heading to one of her hippie conventions. Where flocks of twig-heads gather in a field to pound on African drums, hum communally, purchase crystals and beeswax soap, and stretch out their glutes. She invited you along last summer. To Clare. Where you munched a veggie dog, had your face painted, flirted badly with a mother of four, smoked a joint that tasted of paraffin, and then spewed up as everyone clapped around a fire. In the car, you pleaded food poisoning. She narrowed her eyes and asked, 'Do you think I'm stupid?'

When she mentioned she mightn't attend this one—it was such short notice, she said, I have nothing planned—you reminded her how much she loved these weekends, how all her friends would be there, that you'd be fine on your own, that she must go. Your intentions only partially selfish. Okay, she said with a convinced tut, okay, okay, okay. She was happy, you were both happy, until a question, an impulse, slipped from your lips: 'Sure, Dad could be around anyway?' Instantly you regretted the question. Her face grew slack like an unmade bed.

'We'll see,' she replied after what felt an age. 'Maybe. We'll see.'

While rinsing the plate, you decide tonight you want to watch TV with her. Keep her company. You want to keep her company. Or maybe you want to quell the itch of doing something without her permission. But what difference does motive make here? She smiles when you perch beside her. 'Howdy partner,' she whispers inexplicably.

During the last case, involving a buck in a fat-collared lime shirt and his former partner, your mother starts to chuckle dryly, grinning. They are disputing over rent and a VCR and she says: 'Please, don't ever end up like them anyway.' You let out a smirk and glance at her and then your phone. She is running her bauble necklace between thumb and forefinger. 'Listen to him,' she says, skitting. 'Judy has him figured. Wait now. She'll eat him in a minute.'

On cue the lime shirted man struggles over the particular date of a particular payment and Judy explodes.

You produce a single, conforming 'Ha.'

'What did I tell you?' your mother says.

You offer another laugh.

'You must think I'm desperate,' she says then, without looking at you. Her voice is uneven and you hold your breath, command yourself to stare directly ahead, only at the screen. Your right hand withers into a fist. You want the TV to blow, the walls to crumble, the roof to buckle.

The credits finally flash, the rose-gold titles staining the carpet to rust, and you hurry to excuse yourself, declaring that you'd better head to bed. It's late. It's a school night. You have study to do.

Your mother nods, pains a smile, and you can see her tongue, bunched as it is between upper and lower teeth. A quirk of hers. 'There, there,' she says.

After hesitating for a moment, you peck her cheek, night, and then go upstairs. You wonder: why can't she be dignified?

In your room, you try to distract yourself by hitting on the PlayStation. Find a reprieve in guns and car-jacking. But thoughts tickle the inside of your head. You recall your mother, drunk at her fortieth, saying she should have flown back to Frankfurt, should have gone back to real art. You recall your father pinching the bulge of his nose as you drove home from Mass at Christmas and the peculiar, tight silence in the car. Were these signs you should have been able to read? Should it have occurred to you earlier? You shut off the PlayStation and walk to the bathroom. There, you turn on the hot tap and drown your face for a minute at a time. Steam ghosts the mirror, your cheeks appear rashy as if nettle-stung, but the water seems to you mild. In bed, you toss about the sheets until you feel numb, drained. You text Emily then, the green of the lit screen softening, soothing. You send messages like 'Xxxx', 'WUA', ':)', and 'hahah.'

Over breakfast, your mother goes through the protocol for the free house, marking each on a separate finger:

Lasagne will be made.

Just-in-case money will be under the fruit bowl.

A spare key will be left by the backdoor.

A phonecall will arrive at half-nine and it will be answered at half-nine.

She concludes with warnings against parties, shadowy gallivanting, and the potential dangers of the hob, using words like 'don't' and 'dare.'

You nod when appropriate, spooning more cornflakes into your gob. Your mind whirring. Already savage. Already horny.

In school, your Friday is focused on avoiding her. At short break, you sag from the group when you reckon she might be over at the shop. During the stroll between French and History you perform an anti-clockwise loop to dodge her leaving English. You can't face facing her. But during the afternoon you clock her figure fifteen feet ahead, braced against a discoloured radiator. You're beside Dicey, plodding towards Miss Nolan's class, a bag slung on one shoulder. You realise immediately there is no alternative backroute, no chance to reverse and hide by your locker until she saunters past.

You have to continue forward.

The hallway is echoes and yells and the rubber-squeak of runner. The two-minute turmoil between classes, the smell of mint gum, lozenges and cloggy, afternoon underarm.

A light blazes in from the window, graphing the floor into squares.

In your head you rapidly prepare greetings, visualise yourself opening your mouth and saying 'Hello, what you at?' Maybe giving her a thumbs-up. A thumbs-up would be cool.

You then glance at her.

Her navy cotton socks stretch below the face of her knees. She is holding a purple folder to her chest. Her hair is loose, clearly straightened. Her converse are untied, the left foot arched just so.

Jesus Christ.

You bite hard the inside of your cheek and, passing her, choke out a scrawny, 'Howya.' No eye contact, of course, but you do flinch a sharp, gentlemanly nod.

'Hey,' she says, smiling without showing teeth. A nearly imperceptible smile.

You pretend not to hear her friend's teasing squeal as you wheel into the classroom, you pretend not to feel your face boil to scarlet as girls in your year gawk at you and then her, and as you lurch down to your desk, you tell an oooing Dicey to shut his fuckin hole quickish.

After school, you hitch a lift with a neighbour, jangle out key from flower pot, sling bag under the stairs, and remove lasagne from the oven.

Despite feeling no hunger, you gouge down a banana.

Glucose.

Upstairs, you model in front of the floor-length sliding mirror, slanting your hips to gain more impressive angles while diligently picking apart your faults: the crusted pimples on your chin, the blackheads pocked on your snout, the unfixable shitness of your hair. You put on a navy T-shirt and then take it off and put on a plain white T-shirt and then take it off and put back on the navy T-shirt. The thought strikes that perhaps this is some elaborate prank, organised by the lads. That it's some sick game. You laugh this off, it's a ridiculous notion, comical, and then, via the spare room, you scan the garden for cameras or bodies cowering in the shrubs. This is normal behaviour.

Your phone vibrates, mooing against the woodgrain desk. For a moment, you freak—she is early, why is she early—but unlocking the phone you discover it's only from your dad. A picture message: a sleeping bag curled beneath a table, alongside a space heater, a chunky cord lead, and the mini-radio you helped pick out last weekend. It reads: 'Cosy with my new radio !'. For six weeks solid, your dad has been camping in his dentistry in Castlebar. At first, he said it was to avoid the morning traffic. But then week nights spilled into the weekend and everyone acted as if nothing had changed.

You reply with a smiley face. There is nothing else to say.

Preparation: You brush your teeth, guzzle your mother's mouthwash, slap your face with your mother's moisturiser, smother yourself in Lynx Africa, and then conclude that now would be the optimum time to trim your pubes. With the vibrating blade, you scud along the curly dark lawn and then skim the fluffy, bally base. When you're done, your groin is gritty with black stitches, full of wayward corkscrews, and your dick isn't ten times larger. You clean some of the noticeable blood, curse your handiwork, and then curse the squiggle patches of hair on your chest, the question marks around each nipple. When you were nine you wanted to shave your newly fuzzy legs. Your father burst into hysterics when you requested a razor. 'You're becoming a man,' he exclaimed with arms akimbo, 'you've nothing to be ashamed of.'

There is something very wrong with you.

You strip posters from your bedroom walls, a staff-wielding Gandalf, the boys walking across Abbey Road. With a shovel-edged hand, you breeze away the creases on your quilt before worrying because said quilt is decorated with teenaged turtles. You hope she won't notice or, better yet, that she won't notice you. You long for her to not even look at you. That perhaps she might shut her eyes throughout and you would guide her and it will happen without effort on your part. That it will run smooth as water along glass and when it's over, neither of you will be able to pinpoint how it exactly happened. But, also, neither of you will be able to pinpoint where it spun wrong. It will just have occurred. You feel like a serial killer thinking this.

You instruct yourself to relax. You change into a maroon jumper. You spray more Lynx.

Your phone goes off again and you lunge for it and then almost fling it against the wall when you glimpse 'dad'. A text this time: 'new radio courtesy of my son !'

Who else is he sending these messages to?

You don't reply and you delete both of his messages with only a smudge of shame, arguing that you need to conserve memory, battery.

In the half hour before she's due to arrive you position the untuned guitar against the radiator in your room, you construct a stable route of conversation in your head, you count and recount the condoms in the drawer. At six, you hear a car, squint at the sulphur flash of headlights through your window. You wait for the text, the rasp on the desk, and pound the stairs when it comes: 'here x'.

Outside, the sky is the colour of damp denim. The dark of oncoming night has already begun to taper the corners of the world but Emily shines clean as she steps from her sister's Toyota. She talks through the passenger window, her posture hunchbacked, her sister glaring in your direction. By the interior light her face is pink, pinkish, and she turns briefly around—are you supposed to wave?—before resuming her discussion with the sister.

You listen to the arid mechanics of your own body, the rattle of your lungs, the stammered breath, the swooning in your chest.

Then Emily glides towards you as if it's simple. The car grudgingly reverses.

She has done it before. With an older boy, she told you after you pushed. Forehead pressed against her bunched knees, she confided in you about being drunk and dumb and not being able to say no. You listened with deliberately timed sighs. When she wept, you patted her shoulder, reassured her it was okay, all okay, despite rank jealousy caking your tongue. 'I wish I hadn't,' she said then, 'I really wish I hadn't. He was a fucking asshole.' Later you will think again about this, about her first time, and fury will flame and you will call her a slut. It was her story and yet you will manage to gouge yourself with it. You will deduce that it ultimately really scalds you more.

At the door, Emily says hey and then eases by you. You forget how to say hello. She peels off her jacket—the fabric whistling free from her arms. She is in her uniform still and you feel wholly unprepared as you lock the door.

She treads behind as you give a tour of the house. She touches things and asks fleeting, incomplete questions like 'When did you…?' 'Is that…?' and 'Who is…?' You answer swiftly, jumping close to the item in question, consciously brushing nearer to her.

In the sitting room, she drifts along the corner table, her finger skimming photo frames. Swirling alive dust motes. You watch her pick up a photograph, tilting it towards her.

She laughs, softly, and shoves it at you.

It's a family portrait: the three of you arranged like unpacked Russian Dolls against a fading backdrop, black to wine to muddy gold. It was taken ten years ago, when you were seven and had the physique of the Michelin Man.

She says, 'Your mom's really pretty.'

You reply after a moment, 'She's a fuckin hippie.' The aggression a surprise to you.

You replace the photograph.

Her nose wrinkles. 'Don't say that,' she says.

'Well,' you shrug, 'it's true.'

She doesn't reply, goes instead to the couch. You join her, contorting your legs so your thighs don't touch. Not yet.

You begin to flick through the channels, stopping at the news—you don't want anything too stimulating. 'This alright?'

She crosses her legs but says nothing. A heat radiates from her. You try to smile normally, sit normally, but your body is fidgeting, fighting, you find a new rickety variation in how you exhale. The mood is unexpectedly formal, dangerous. You recall jokes—bad, sappy jokes—and tell them and in return she only gifts you this pinched-mouth, no-teeth smile. It could be a frown, you suppose, hard to split the difference between them, but you assure yourself, nipping your jumper from your stomach, it was a smile. Not to worry about it, you reason, it had to be a smile. Not to analyse it, it must be a smile.

Nothing is said. A minute, then another, crawls by.

On the TV, Obama is speaking. You point with the remote. 'He's great, isn't he?'

She nods, seems to consider something more, something deeper, but only answers, 'Yep.'

Why is it difficult now?

'Yeah,' you say. 'Obama's sound. He's a sound man.'

She leans forward and rummages in her handbag and then sits back.

You can count how many buttons are undone on her shirt and you do count and suddenly you feel yourself get a horn, a judging heat, and you fold your arms and jut out your chest. *So, Now You're A Man*, the paperback left clandestinely on your pillow for your twelfth birthday, suggests visualising doing the gardening to rid yourself of any pesky, undesired erections. You do this now, you envision clipping the hedges but then she hums and readjusts a leg and you are trampled. You surely can't fuck this up? And yet here you are, fucking it up, dreaming about hedges. You beg yourself now to do something, to act, and start imagining potentially enticing actions—a hand on her thigh; an arm dipped sensually over her shoulder; a proposal to show her your guitar, maybe strum a G chord or two—and you're thinking about all this when she turns, smiles with teeth, and kisses you.

Her tongue is sugary. You store your hands by your side and kiss and kiss and kiss until she pulls away. Everything is amplified; the cushions rustles like woodlice, the TV nags. You feel empty, delightfully empty. With a lifted chin, you motion upstairs. She says something, nods, gathers her bag and then decides to leave it on the floor. In your chest, there is a gasping, squashed excitement. You stand and your hands are shaking so you slot them into your pockets and claw at the inside fabric. You study the ceiling as you lead the way, noting precisely where the paint is wonky, not quite inline.

She sits on the bed, a knee hugged under her chin. You draw the curtains.

From the corner of your eye, you watch as she inspects a spot on her knee, working her thumbnail against it before rubbing the spot with the heel of her hand. You like this. You punch off the lights, deeming darkness, partial invisibility, a valuable ally. On the bed, you cockroach near her, maintaining a forearm's width between you both.

The air feels trapped and impure and somewhere in it there is the fragrance of cinnamon.

Mellow light burns beneath the doorframe.

Her leg drops to the floor, she grabs her upper arms as if cold.

You take long breaths through your nose to shush the thump and throw of your body and then, while thinking about it an incredible amount, you take her hand and face her. It throws you for some reason that she stares back—what did you expect?—and then you lean in and clatter into her front teeth.

You apologise and she apologises and you both reshape, hunching toward one another—you feel her fingers guide your jaw and then feel how her lower lip is chapped. Cautiously, you let your hand cup the hurl-head of her hip. Loving it. You fall sideways together and bump together and the duvet is cumbersome. The air becomes thick like you could pack it in a bag. With assistance, the clip of her bra is unhooked. Her hand, her left hand, lies on your stomach and you will it to go down.

Your finger spiders open the zipper of her skirt and you graze, with the flat of your thumb, the bristles around her slit.

'Go easy,' she whispers.

You open your eyes to make sure this is real and say sorry.

'It's okay,' she says, and then, close to your ear, asks if you have condoms.

You nod. 'Yes.'

'Well,' she says, 'just go easy remember.'

You say sorry again.

You reach for the drawer, grasp a square of cartoon-blue foil. On bended knees, you chuck your jumper and then awkwardly shimmy off your pants. Socks are forgotten. You shrug the condom on and race on top of her once more, kissing her now, moving with her, and, on a sexy spur, you lick her collarbone.

'What are you doing?' She is laughing.

You sputter another apology. Eroticism is live and learn. She grabs you then, bends you, and it starts to be good.

As you work together, your limbs aren't silky, they aren't naturally posed to one other's range, but rather they work like levers. A jerk, a pull. A certain stubbornness of muscle, friction. You feel the tingle of her hot skin, the sweat. Her breath catches. The business is hurried and not slowed or savoured or graceful, it is done as if a timer is beeping somewhere. As if you're both on the verge of being found out.

You roll apart afterwards. No comments are exchanged, no critiques or acknowledgments. You lie as far from one another as possible on a queen-sized bed. Is there ever any pleasure in this? Your body is unfamiliar, gangly as if you have grown.

You stare at the ceiling, the curtains.

There is nothing to say.

She's probably pregnant now, you think.

On the divorcee forum, lynn62 recommends new actives, hobbies, trips. You've got to keep yourself busy. She uses phrases like Positive Thinking, the half-full glass, show the world what they're missing. So you encourage your mother to go to hippie conventions, apply for residencies, you ask questions about art and her fave Bernini. You tell your dad that you want to learn to drive, that you love teeth and dental hygiene. You WhatsApp him possible movie outings years in advance—'New Batman 2020'. He dings an immediate reply, 'I'm on it' as if it were a challenge, as if he were tipped to direct.

Emily begins mapping the birthmarks and moles on your shoulders, on the hairless topmost section of your arm. It feels like she is touching tendon, bone and all. The tantalising sensation of an oncoming storm. Slowly, she engraves her name and then yours and you wish that one moment could last.

It's then the car crunches up the driveway.

She puts a hand to her lips and her voice says things like, 'Who's that?' 'Shit,' and 'Where's my?'

A key is jammed into the lock, the scuttle of letters being fished from the wicker basket. You recognise the weight of the footsteps.

She sweeps up her clothes and for the first time you see her frightened, pissed off—her voice spiky, her gestures accelerated.

'Wait here,' you tell her, lugging on pants. You're the hero.

You pad down the stairs, a hand caressing the banister as a show of nonchalance, and spy him drinking milk straight from the carton in the kitchen. He isn't wearing his glasses. He hasn't shaved the goatee.

'Oh, you're here?' your father says. 'I thought you'd be at a pal's house.'

'Mam's gone to one of her hippie things.' You pause on the threshold to the kitchen. He already knows she is away, you understand that. He scoffs at the word hippie, says it to himself while placing his key on the counter beside the worn, peeling gym bag. There is a delay in your father's movement, a dilemma: should he keep drinking from the carton or pour himself a glass?

'You're home?' you say.

He sort of smiles, folds bridging his mouth. 'Not quite.' He takes a long gulp from the carton, puts it back in the fridge, and snags hold of the gym bag. You should scramble for the handle too, make a scene. Pull a tantrum. Call him a dickhead, a traitor. Scream nonsensically: you're not my real Dad! But you don't react. 'Need to re-supply,' he says. 'But I will be home soon. Once work quietens.'

He lifts the bag. 'Is it just you here?'

Together you pack towels, shampoo, five shirts, three jumpers, Speedos, facial creams, two polos. You carry his shirts on hangers to the car, fold his pants onto the backseat, and neatly stash his shoes in the boot. It takes twenty minutes. You grin at your father's predictable gags and he listens as you describe the High-Elf archer set you've ordered. He acts impressed, regurgitates information he swiped from a manual. 'Increased range,' he says with a raised finger. He has only shown interest in the game because you play it and this, even now, makes you glad.

When everything is packed, he mentions Sunday. 'That new superhero is out, isn't it?' He clicks his fingers. 'The Iron Man.' He climbs into the car and says in a mock, deepening voice, 'Be good for your mother, son.'

You tell him: 'Stall a sec.'

You rush inside and, without thinking, shoddily wrap in tinfoil the lasagne. It is somehow essential, this offering, though you can't decipher why.

'Mam made you this,' you say, you lie. You hand him the still-warm dish through the car window.

'Oh. That was very nice of her.' He places the lasagne in the passenger seat and then has to buckle it in when a sensor starts beeping. You can't decide whose turn it is to speak, and before you can come to a conclusion, he gestures a thumbs-up and closes the window. Neither of you thought to switch on the outside light, the pale-blue solar bulbs which flank the driveway, so in darkness you wave goodbye. He beeps once. For some time you stand there.

Back in the room, she is dressed and insane with questions. Her phone is beside her, alive with texts from friends who always suspected you were a weirdo. 'Who was it?' she says, 'Did you tell them I was here?' You notice she has made the bed and this astonishes you. 'You said no one would be home. For fuck sake, John.' Her face is screwed up and you don't say anything until she shifts close to you, closer to you, and then you clutch her hand and utter words like: 'please,' 'don't,' 'go.'

*

She doesn't and it's only months later, as summer begins, that you fuck it up, that you let her go. You're official by then, girlfriend and boyfriend with an x assigned by her name in your phone. But at some shitshow of a disco you will kiss someone else, tussle with a foreign tongue. And during Emily's break-up speech, you will pretend that you're sad, depressed even, producing moody, music-video faces. On the same day you break up, you will go meet the girl you cheated on her with. And before the end of the summer, you will beg Emily to take you back—the lust for the cheating girl long dust at that stage. You will say you were a fool, a mong, you will plead, you will even cry and it will be no act this time. And Emily will say no, she will take supreme pleasure in saying no, and you will inform your friends that you don't care, she was a dirt anyway, and then egg her house in a drunken stupor of weepy hate and weepy love. No charges will be brought but her older brother will thump open your nose on New Year's Eve. When you ship off to college you will forget her for the most part, her name only cropping up on Facebook when you're drunk and nostalgic. You will message her once, during second year as essay deadlines pile up, asking how's she getting on. She will click on the message and you will tell yourself she only forgot to reply. And years later, when your mam and dad have met other people, when you celebrate two Christmases, when you have scampered off to the States to get lost in a sea of navy suits, you will tell friends the story of your first time during a party. A wine bottle pointed in your direction, you will tell your new friends and the new girl who has the x by her name about that free house, about slanting your guitar in a bid to impress her with artistic flair in the same way you will now stack books by Benjamin and Borges and Woolf in an ordered messy pile in your apartment, about the colliding of front teeth, about your jangling nerves, about it being your first time. The friends will howl, your new girlfriend will feign envy with a pout, and you will spin the bottle and laugh as it points to somebody else. And at that moment, you will believe it was your first time, truly believe that she was your first real time.

STINGING FLY PATRONS

Many thanks to:

Hanora Bagnell
Maria Behan
Trish Byrne
Brian Cliff
Edmond Condon
Evelyn Conlon
Simon Costello
Sheila Crowley
Paul Curley
Kristina K. Deffenbacher
Gerry Dukes
Michael J. Farrell
Ciara Ferguson
Brendan Hackett
James Hanley
Teresa Harte
Christine Dwyer Hickey
Dennis Houlihan
Nuala Jackson
Geoffrey Keating
Jack Keenan
Jerry Kelleher
Jack Kelleher
Conor Kennedy
Joe Lawlor
Irene Rose Ledger
Róisín McDermott
Petra McDonough
Lynn Mc Grane
Jon McGregor
John McInerney
Finbar McLoughlin

Maggie McLoughlin
Ama, Grace & Fraoch MacSweeney
Mary MacSweeney
Paddy & Moira MacSweeney
Anil Malhotra
Gerry Marmion
Ivan Mulcahy
Michael O'Connor
Patrick O'Donoghue
Kieran O'Shea
Lucy Perrem
Maria Pierce
Peter J. Pitkin
George Preble
Mark Richards
Orna Ross
Fiona Ruff
Alf Scott
Ann Seery
Eileen Sheridan
Arthur Shirran
Alfie & Savannah Stephenson
Marie Claire Sweeney
Olive Towey
Debbi Voisey
Ruth Webster
Grahame Williams
The Blue Nib (Poetry Website)
Hotel Doolin
Lilliput Press
Museum of Literature Ireland
Tramp Press

*We'd also like to thank those individuals who have expressed the preference
to remain anonymous.*

By making an annual contribution of 75 euro, patrons provide us
with vital support and encouragement.

BECOME A PATRON ONLINE AT STINGINGFLY.ORG

or send a cheque or postal order to:
The Stinging Fly, PO Box 6016, Dublin 1.

M.W. Bewick's first collection of poetry, *Scarecrow,* was published in 2017. He is the co-founder of independent publishing house Dunlin Press and an organiser at Poetrywivenhoe in Essex, where he lives. Publication credits include *London Grip, The Sentinel Literary Quarterly* and *The Interpreter's House.*

Jo Burns was born in Northern Ireland and lives in Germany. Jo's poetry has been published most recently in *Banshee, Oxford Poetry, Southword* and is forthcoming in *Popshots, The Tangerine* and *Magma.* Her first collection *White Horses* will be published in 2018 by Turas Press.

Julia Calver lives in London. Recent work has been published in *Infundibulum: stories of non-ordinary reality by wome*n, *Makhzin, 3:AM* and *The Arrow Maker.*

Bud Cho-O'Leary is from Cork and lives in New York. A graduate of University College Cork and Trinity College Dublin, he is preparing to start law school in August. This is his first published short story.

Simon Costello is from Offaly and a graduate of Athlone Institute of Technology. Previously published by US poetry magazine *Rattle,* he was both editor's choice and winner of their ekphrastic poetry competition in October 2017. He currently lives in China.

Brian Davey was born in County Sligo and now lives in Dublin. His essays and reviews have appeared in publications such as *Dublin Review of Books, CIRCA Art Magazine* and *Dublin Inquirer*

Naoise Dolan was born in Dublin, where she studied English at Trinity College. She is currently reading for a masters degree in Victorian literature at the University of Oxford and is editing her first novel.

Adrian Duncan is an Irish writer based in Berlin. He is a co-editor of *Paper Visual Art.*

Wendy Erskine lives in Belfast. Her writing appears in the anthology *Female Lines: New Writing by Women from Northern Ireland.* Her debut short story collection, *Sweet Home,* is forthcoming from The Stinging Fly Press in 2018.

Peter Fallon's translations include *The Georgics of Virgil* and *Works and Days* (after Hesiod) as well as poems by Tibullus, Nuala Ní Dhomhnaill, Ailbhe Ní Ghearbhuigh and Caitríona Ní Chléirchín. His most recent collection is *Strong, My Love*. For almost fifty years he has edited and published Gallery Books. He lives in Loughcrew in County Meath where he farmed for many years.

John Harris completed an MPhil in Creative Writing in Trinity College in 2014. His writing has appeared in *Banshee* and the 2015 *Fish Anthology*. His entry for the 2015 Patrick Kavanagh Poetry Award was highly commended.

Patrick Holloway is an Irish writer living and working in Brazil. Last year he took second place in the Raymond Carver Contest and was shortlisted for the Dermot Healy Poetry Prize, Over the Edge New Writer Award and The Bath Short Story Award. His greatest accomplishment is Aurora, his newborn daughter. He is currently writing a novel.

Caoilinn Hughes' debut novel, *Orchid & the Wasp*, is just out (Oneworld, June 2018). Her poetry collection, *Gathering Evidence* (Carcanet, 2014), won the dlr Shine / Strong Award. Her writing has appeared in *Tin House, POETRY, Granta, Best British Poetry, Poetry Ireland Review* and elsewhere.

Seanín Hughes is a poet from County Tyrone with work published or forthcoming in *Banshee, The Blue Nib*, and *A New Ulster*. Seanín is a shortlistee for the Seamus Heaney Award for New Writing, 2018, and recipient of the Poetry Ireland Access Bursary for Cúirt International Literature Festival, 2018.

Rebecca Ivory lives in Dublin. She writes short fiction and works in Public Relations. 'Made in China' is her first short story to be published.

Jessu John is working to complete a first collection of poems. Her poetry is forthcoming in *Abstract Magazine: Contemporary Expressions* and has featured in *Magma* as well as *Ink Sweat And Tears*. She enjoys practising abstract art.

Louise Kennedy's stories have won several prizes and been published in journals including *The Stinging Fly, The Tangerine, Ambit* and *The Lonely Crowd*. She is working on a collection of stories with the assistance of the Arts Council of Northern Ireland.

Wes Lee lives in New Zealand. Her work has appeared in a wide array of publications. She has won a number of awards, including The Over the Edge New Writer of the Year Award in Galway, and The Short Fiction Writing Prize (University of Plymouth Press).

Sophie Mackintosh's fiction has appeared in *Granta* and *TANK*, and she was the winner of the 2016 White Review Short Story Prize. Her debut novel, *The Water Cure*, is published by Hamish Hamilton.

D.S. Maolalai's poetry has appeared internationally in more magazines than he can count. He currently lives in Dublin. His first collection, *Love is Breaking Plates in the Garden*, was published in 2016 by the Encircle Press. He has twice been nominated for the Pushcart Prize.

John McAuliffe's fourth book *The Way In* (Gallery Press) won the Michael Hartnett Award in 2015. His translation of Igor Klikovac's Bosnian poems, *Stockholm Syndrome*, is out in November from Smith Doorstop.

Darran McCann is an author and playwright from Armagh. His debut novel, *After the Lockou*t, was published in 2012. He works in the Seamus Heaney Centre where he Convenes the MA in Creative Writing. He lives in Belfast with his family.

Eamon McGuinness's work has featured in *The Stinging Fly* and *Poetry Ireland Review*. In 2017, he was shortlisted in the RTÉ Francis MacManus short story competition. His debut collection is forthcoming from Salmon Poetry.

John Patrick McHugh is from Galway. His fiction has appeared in *The Stinging Fly, The Tangerine, Winter Papers 2*, and *Granta*.

David McLoghlin is the author of *Waiting for Saint Brendan and Other Poems* (2012) and *Santiago Sketches* (2017), both published by Salmon Poetry. His third collection, *Crash Centre*, is forthcoming from Salmon. He has lived in Brooklyn, NY since 2010.

Laura Morgan's stories are published in the UK, Ireland (*The Moth*), and Vietnam. In 2017, she won the Scottish Book Trust's New Writer Award. She blogs at aremoteview.wordpress.com and is a *Scottish Review of Books'* Emerging Critic.

Nuala Ní Dhomhnaill held the Heimbold Chair in Irish Studies at Villanova University in 2001 and has taught at Boston College and New York University. She has received many scholarships, prizes, and bursaries and has also won numerous international awards for works which have been translated into French, German, Polish, Italian, Norwegian, Estonian, Turkish, Japanese and English.

Fiona O'Connor, a Dubliner, was recently awarded the 2018 Eamon Kelly Bursary from Kerry Arts Office for her play *she had a ticket in mind*, which premiered in London in April. The play was written in support of the Repeal the 8th campaign.

Seosamh Ó Murchú was born in County Wexford. A former editor of *Comhar*, he was a founder member and co-editor of the literary journal, *Oghma*. He has worked with publishers An Gúm since 1986 where he is Senior Editor. *Taisí Tosta* was published by Coiscéim and won the Michael Hartnett Poetry Award in 2017.

Christine Valters Paintner is an American writer living in Galway. Her poems have been published in journals including *The Galway Review, Boyne Berries, Headstuff, Skylight 47, Crannóg,* and *North West Words*. Her first collection, *Dreaming of Stones*, is forthcoming.

Nolan Natasha Pike is a queer and trans writer living in Nova Scotia, Canada. His poems have appeared in *The Puritan, Grain, Event,* and *Plenitude.* Nolan has been short-listed for the Atlantic Writing Competition and long-listed for the CBC Poetry Prize.

Ojo Taiye is a young Nigerian who uses poetry as a handy tool to hide his frustration with society. He loves coffee and can be found on Twitter @Ojo_poems.

Jill Talbot's writing has appeared in *Geist, Rattle, Poetry Is Dead, The Puritan, Matrix, subTerrain, The Tishman Review, The Cardiff Review, PRISM, Southword,* and others. Jill won the PRISM Grouse Grind Lit Prize. Jill lives on Gabriola Island, British Columbia.

Ridwan Tijani was born in Nigeria and now he lives in Indianapolis. His work has appeared in *Cosmonauts Avenue, Lunch Ticket, Brittle Paper, Afreada, Necessary Fiction, Pithead Chapel* and *Mulberry Fork Review.* He is at work on a novel. Twitter account: @RidwanTijani4